T0267498

The Word

The Word

MARY G. THOMPSON

PAGE STREET YA

First published in 2024 by

Page Street Publishing Co.

27 Congress Street, Suite 1511

Salem, MA 01970

www.pagestreetpublishing.com

Distributed by Macmillan, sales in Canada by The Canadian Manda Group.

28   27   26   25   24   1   2   3   4   5

ISBN-13: 979-8890030146

Library of Congress Control Number: 2023945458

Cover and book design by Emma Hardy for Page Street Publishing Co.

Cover illustration © Evangeline Gallagher

Printed and bound in the United States

For My Quarantine Crew:
Madelyn, Kristen, Lenore, Angele.
GOATS!

1

Port Angeles

now

I lie under a single sheet, wide awake. It's hot outside, in the nineties. I'm sweating like a drowned pig.

Thunk, thunk, thunk goes my heartbeat.

I hear them shouting at the door.

Footsteps, yells, voices. My dad, my brother, the cops.

She opens my door and walks into my room, like it's hers. She stands above my bed, looking down at me.

I'm not scared of her, and I don't jump.

I'm the reason the police are here. I'm the reason for all of this.

The officer's wearing a black uniform with short sleeves. She has a gun. She's not worried that I'll go for it. Her hands are folded across her chest, leaving it completely exposed. To her, I'm a victim. She's come to rescue me.

Mr. Doug taught me how to shoot, though. I can hit a dime off a pop can from fifty feet away. I'm a better shot than she is, I bet.

"Are you Alyssa DeAndreis?" As she says it, she kneels down. The gun at her hip moves back in space, farther from me.

If they come, you do what they say, Dad told me. *Don't get yourself hurt.*

"Was," I say. I'm only wearing a thin white nightgown under my sheet. Good thing she's not a man. I'd have to go for the gun then, after he'd seen me this way. Leaving him be after that wouldn't be right.

"What do they call you now?" she asks.

There are footsteps outside. My brother's deep voice races down the hall to meet me. Only the bass comes through, not the words. Still, it's enough. Knowing he's out there gives me strength.

I'm eighteen, Carlo said. *Nothing they can do to me.* Clasped hands with Dad, locked eyes. The connection between two strong men. The kind of bond that can't be broken. Their own little world.

"Where's my dad?"

"Well. Your dad is in custody at this moment. Do you understand why?" She's talking softly, as if she's trying to calm a dog. But I'm not getting angry. I'm not getting all up in her face. I'm keeping sweet. I just want to know the answer: where he is.

"I'm not stupid." I sit up now, let the sheet fall around me. She *is* a woman, after all. Even if she's an outsider. I have to resolve myself to this Trial. This is what we've all prepared for. This is the beginning of my great test. This is how I get home, even if I have to go the long way round.

Is this really happening? This cop is here, but I can't believe it.

They came for me. They actually came.

"Alyssa, your mother has been very worried about you."

"Lisa."

"Okay, Lisa. Can you tell me how old you are?"

"Sixteen."

"What's your mother's name?"

I don't want to say it. I sit up straighter.

"Okay, that's all right. We know that. I just wanted to know if you remember."

"I was seven when we left," I say. I hear the tone of my voice, that contrary tendency boiling up again. I'm not good at holding it back. Never have been and probably never will be, no matter how hard I've tried. But I have to get better at it. Because I need to pretend I'm okay with this.

"Okay." She seems to come to a decision. Light filters through the window. The moon is big outside, and there's a streetlight halfway down the block. She stands up, blocking out part of it. She's a pillar of darkness with light spreading all around her. "I'll give you a couple minutes to get dressed, but then we have to get going. Do you understand why?"

"My mother sent the law to get me back," I say.

"A court granted your mother full custody of you, nine years ago. We've been looking for you ever since. Your father hasn't made it easy. But we can talk about all that later. Right now we just need to make sure you're safe, that you have a few things you need, and then we're going to take you home."

"Yes, ma'am. Can you turn around please?" My heart is racing, but I keep my voice calm. I listen for Carlo's voice, but I don't hear it anymore. I thank God that he is eighteen. Except, he knew I was kidnapped, per the rules of the law. He didn't call the cops to come take me back, like he should have. What if him being eighteen doesn't help him, but hurts him? What if the law thinks he's at fault? He's not really my brother, according to them. Not like Liam, the baby, who must be nine years old now. Carlo's my brother by the Word, but to the law, he's a conspirator. I know all the legal words, all the bad things my dad has done.

The lady cop does turn around for me, so I take off my nightgown. I fold it in squares and place it under my pillow, the way I do every morning. Then I put on one of my long skirts. I have jeans, for those times when Dad says we have to go incognito, when we have to blend in with the Americans. But I don't feel like wearing them. The thought of wearing them repulses me.

They can take me out of this house, but they can't take me away from God. They can't take me away from what I believe, and from my future. Even if I can't tell them what I really want. Even if in my heart, I have to be one person, and to them, be another. So, I pull on a skirt and tuck in a long blouse, which I button up to my neck. I walk over to the little mirror above my dresser so I can put my hair up.

"There's no need to pack up in darkness," the lady cop says. She flips on the light.

I'm facing myself, my pale face and clear lashes, the long, straight hair dyed a dark brown, faithfully touched up every few weeks. But I still have my blue eyes, and a face that hasn't changed much since I was a kid. Dad will think someone spotted me, that I wasn't careful, that I got him caught. But right now, for this minute, he's in handcuffs.

"What's going to happen to my brother?" I ask. I grab my mass of hair and twist it around.

"You mean the boy living here with you? What's his name?" She's still turned away from me.

I don't answer her. It was stupid to ask. Questions just give things away. It's better to watch and listen and find out information from other people. I wrap my bun in an elastic. It doesn't matter how it looks, only that it isn't falling all down my back and worldly sinful. Only that when people see me—these other people of the law, or my late mother—they don't get the wrong impression.

"What am I allowed to pack?" I ask. Surely that question must be safe.

"A few days' clothes," she says. "Your toothbrush and items like that. Someone will come back later and get the rest of your things."

I grab my duffel bag from the closet. It's a big black one with a Nike swoosh on the outside. Dad stole it from a package on someone's porch. That's how we get lots of things. People just let them sit outside their houses. *If God leaves them there for us, why shouldn't we take them?* Dad says. I put my underclothes in the bag, another skirt, another top. Hair elastics. I take a peek back at the lady cop. She's still turned around, all polite. My heartbeat speeds up. *Thunkthunkthunk.* I slide open the top left drawer of my bureau and take out a few pairs of long socks. The little drawstring bag is alone in the drawer now. My hands shake and my vision blurs. This is all happening so fast. I didn't realize they would really come. No one cared about me before. No one's looked for me since I was seven years old. Except my late mother.

What would happen if I left it here, if I just walked out with the cops? I need to know what's going to happen to Dad and Carlo. I can't make a decision without knowing that.

I grab the drawstring bag and throw it in my duffel, inside a pile of socks and underclothes.

Give me strength, I pray. And I don't know what for. For the Trial? For tonight? For the future? None of it seems real right now. Even now doesn't seem real. This is like a dream and a nightmare. Zebulun and Miss Sheila are so far away, they might as well be on the moon with the dead. I feel like I can't get there from here, but I have to believe. I have to try.

I look all around the room. There isn't much for anyone to come back for. A few dresses and skirts in the closet. A couple pairs of jeans. A few T-shirts. A winter coat with the edges fraying and the fake goose down spilling out. A stack of printouts stapled together. I'm about to turn around when I see the necklace on the nightstand. It's a silver chain strung through a little piece of agate, red and yellow and sharp-edged. I quickly hang it around my neck and slip it beneath my blouse.

Home. That's where I'm going. Someday, once the Trial is complete. I believe. I can't stay here, but I can go there. I just have to go through something else first.

"You all ready to go?" The lady cop has turned around.

"Yes."

"It's going to be all right," she says. She's smiling down at me. Everyone, to me, is tall. I'm aware of the pins holding my hemline in place so the bottom of the skirt won't trail on the floor, of the edges of my secondhand blouse rubbing against my thighs. I hold my head up.

"Don't talk to me like a child. I'm not a child."

"All right. I apologize." She holds her hand out for me to pass by her. I do, and I'm aware of her gun again. If I ran, she wouldn't shoot me. But she'd find me again long before I got home. And if I did make it to Zebulun, the people wouldn't even talk to me. I belong to my father until I'm eighteen. I can't go back yet.

I put my hand over the necklace. "Show me the way," I whisper.

"What?"

"Nothing." I walk past the cop and down the hall of what was, for a few years, my house. I walk out the front door and into the driveway, where I find two police cars and three more officers waiting for me. I don't see Carlo anywhere. It's just me and them, and somewhere they're taking me. To someone who, by the Word, is dead.

2

Seattle

age twelve

What I remember most about the day we met Carlo was being cold. It was probably in the fifties, but it was raining, like it always does in Seattle. All fall, all winter, all spring. That spring we were in a spot, as Dad used to say. A spot meaning a bad time, a downturn in our fortunes, a Trial. What he meant was, we were homeless. We had a tent to sleep in that we'd stolen. Dad was in a phase where he was big preaching. This was before we moved to Port Angeles and started living in a house, thanks to Carlo.

We went to the place where they gave out food. I was wearing my long skirt, the only one I had then. My hair was growing out, and you could see a couple inches of blonde on top, so I was wearing an old scarf around my head. Dad hadn't stolen that. I'd just walked up to a lady on the street and asked her for it, and she'd felt sorry for me and handed it over. 'Cause I was twelve, but I looked younger,

I guess. That's one of the advantages of being short, along with it being a disadvantage. People think you're younger and stupider and more vulnerable.

So, I had my skirt and my scarf and my empty belly. Dad's black slacks were streaked with mud from the rain. He was wearing a sign on his back like a turtle shell, held on with elastic bands: SAVE YOUR- SELVES. BOW TO GOD. *Not Jesus, that's blasphemy*, Dad would say. *Jesus was just a man. You don't bow to a man; you bow to God.* Then he would proceed to tell me what God wanted me to do, like clean the bathroom or cook a good meal for the men of the house. God never told him to do anything, I don't think, except to preach and pass on messages to me.

I was aware I was supposed to be doing the cooking, since I was the woman of the household and all, but we didn't have a household anymore, and someone else had already cooked. So, I fell in line behind Dad, looking down at my worn-out, old Converse, hoping no one would notice I was failing at my duties. Point being, if people didn't notice you, maybe God wouldn't either. This wasn't in the Word or anything, it was just my wish. I wanted to fade away into insignificance that day, in the hope that God would no longer be watching me, and therefore I might be able to have a home again. Not a sinful home like the one I had with my late mother—as we called her, since she had died when she left the Word—but just a place that had heat in the winter and a roof.

I was wet and shivering from the rain and having no clothes to change into, and Dad's latest street sermon was ringing in my ears:

Comes a world where there's no rain on the righteous. Comes a world where God creates a sun for each man and each woman, each to his or her own, therefore to warm them. But how shall this perfect, new Eden be created? Not by the mixing of the sexes or the displaying of the flesh! For this form of dress—here he'd pointed at a young woman walking by on the sidewalk—*marks thee out as a whore!*

The woman had picked up her pace and wouldn't look at us.

In the line for food, I slowed down, waiting for others to take their portion, not looking at anyone. My dad was in a deep conversation behind me with a man equally obsessed with the Christian faith, and they were debating the appropriate size of lettering on signs like the one Dad wore on his back—whether more words or fewer would better spread the Gospel—raising their voices over it, scaring people near them. I took the bowl of chili offered to me with a quiet thank-you, head bowed, and I went over to a table on the far side of the room.

Not that I was trying to avoid association with Dad, who was righteous, and who was right about making the letters bigger and carrying a more spacious sign, but simply because I wanted a place for quiet contemplation of all that we had discussed today.

"Hey," a boy said, sitting across from me.

"Good day," I replied, not looking up. My chastity was my armor. A boy couldn't break my resolve without my permission.

"I haven't seen you before."

I shook my head.

"It's okay, he's not looking."

Now I looked up. The boy was older than I was, but not by all that much. He had longish black hair and tan skin. He was smiling at me, and two of his front teeth were chipped. I locked eyes with him in a very immodest way. Because although it was very sinful to look a boy in the eyes, it was also the best way to tell him he'd better not mess with you, or you'd punch him in the face and steal his money.

"Carlo," he said, holding a hand out.

I shook it. I made sure to grip hard. "Lisa."

"That your dad?" He pointed at where my dad and the other street preacher were now laughing together, eating peanut butter sandwiches. Dad's sign was wilting on his back like the wings of a dying bird. His hair was getting longish, too, but it didn't look intentional like Carlo's. It looked like Dad couldn't afford a haircut. People always used to remark on his good looks, but I couldn't see that happening today.

"Yes." I narrowed my eyes. Let him say something.

"What religion are you guys in?" He took a giant spoonful of chili. His brown eyes were big, waiting for my answer, interested.

"It's called the Word."

He took another bite of chili, like he was still waiting for me to talk.

"It's Christian, but we don't believe in Jesus. Not that he's God, I mean. He was just a preacher. And so you shouldn't worship him, because he was a man. You worship God."

"So you're Jewish?"

"No." I sigh. "We believe in the Gospel and miracles. Jesus rose from the dead and everything. But that was because God did it. God can create miracles among men."

"Okay." He kept on eating. Like he was thinking about it.

"And people are supposed to be good, of course, and follow all these rules, so they can go to the heavens—the firmament. And you're still a man there. You don't become like God or anything, but you get to be with God. But only if you're worthy. Otherwise you go to Hell, and there's something called brimstone." *Like my mother has, since her earthly body is only an illusion.* But I didn't say that. It was just what popped into my head every time the brimstone came up. Her face, and then what was truly happening to her spirit as her shell went about her life. What would happen to my spirit if I kept thinking about her.

"Ah, rules. There's always rules." He winked at me. And he was still eating. He was almost done with his bowl.

I took a bite of mine. It was okay. This place was generous with the meat. But when I thought of chili, I thought of my late mother, of the big pot stewing on the stove. Of her standing over it and humming, swishing her long skirt back and forth. There were lots of other things to eat here. I could have had a peanut butter sandwich, or that chicken dish slathered in some white sauce. Why did I have to pick the chili? It only brought me to bad thoughts and a place of sin.

"What religion are you?" I asked.

"My mom was Catholic," he said, shrugging.

Here was an opening to start preaching to him. He had the uncertainty of someone who could be swayed to the Word. Dad liked to point them out to me on the street. *That one's set on her path to Hell.* Or, *That one needs us. You watch.* And then he'd go over to the one he said needed us, and it would be like magic. The person would see his blue eyes and his easy smile and listen to his earnest words, and they'd take his pamphlet. At least, before his hair grew out and he started to smell bad.

I smelled Dad before I heard him speak, and I dipped my head over my chili bowl. I prayed this boy couldn't smell it too, but I knew he could.

"Good evening, son," Dad said. "There room here?" He sat before Carlo could respond, right next to him on the bench. He had a bowl of chili in his hands too. It didn't seem to mean anything to him. He took a dip with his plastic spoon, brought it to his lips as if it was nothing.

"Yes, sir," Carlo said, reading my dad's needs like an open book. "Lisa was just telling me about the Word."

"My Lisa's a good girl," Dad said. He smiled at me in that way that said I had done right. I was always waiting for that smile. He turned back to Carlo. "We may be a little down on our luck, but she never wavers in her faith. She's a real champion."

I kept my head down and ate my chili. I didn't say anything else because the men were talking. It seemed important that I let them be, that they have their own little world to live in. But after a while of them getting to know each other, I did take a peek. Carlo was smiling at me, and my heart skipped a beat. His smile seemed to say, *You guys are cool.* Dad was in a good mood and had been for a whole hour. I knew this moment was important, and I had hope. I thought things might be changing for the better.

3

Seattle

now

It's a two-hour drive into Seattle, where they say my late mother is waiting for me. Of course, they don't say *late mother*. They say *mom*. They act as if she's still alive and well and not condemned by her sin, as if she didn't leave her God-given husband and decide to live as a single woman and a whore. There's no divorce in the eyes of God, but the law says there is, and the law says she has custody of me and Dad is a criminal. The law says he had no right to drive away with me in the night, that I was kidnapped even though I went willingly, even though I waited for the appointed time and crawled out my first-floor window and dropped into the bushes under my own power. He didn't have to force me to do anything, but they don't care about that. He ordered me to keep sweet with them, and I do. Not just because he told me to, but because I know it's the best way to get what I want. I sit in the passenger seat of the car, with the lady social worker driving, and I say nothing.

"You must be nervous about seeing your mom," she says. Her name is Miss Tina. She's a Black lady with hair in a big braid tied around her head. Her voice is soft, as if she's afraid to scare me, as if I'm going to jump and run.

I say nothing.

"You don't have to talk about it," she says, "but it might help."

"I'm a little nervous," I say, because I think it's what she wants to hear. She wants to know about how I'm broken—how I've been terribly hurt and victimized. She wants to feel like she's saving someone and helping, even if she did nothing but drive me around. What if I did talk about it? Nothing would happen. I know that like I know the worms are down and the stars are up. That's why I have to take care of myself.

"Well, that's totally normal. It's a big adjustment."

"I want to see her," I say. "But what if she doesn't want to see me?"

"She's been trying to find you for nine years," Miss Tina says. "There's nothing she wants more than to see you."

"Not me," I say. "Some little seven-year-old kid."

I don't want to think about it, but it comes into my mind anyway: the last time I saw her, the night when I ran away with Dad. I put on my pajamas and got into bed without her telling me. There was no fussing and fighting and begging to stay up. No planting myself in front of the TV and refusing to move. Eight o'clock, and I was all ready to go to sleep. Except I wasn't, really. Except my heart was beating a million times a minute, and there was sweat between my shoulder blades.

Mom came into my room. She was dressed in jeans and an old

T-shirt. Her sneakers were bright white, and her hair was falling loose over her shoulders. It used to be all the way down her back, but she'd cut it recently. She'd gone to a salon and had them do it, and she wore jeans then too.

I shrunk away from her, under the covers. She didn't seem like my mom then. My real mom had butt-long hair and wore a skirt.

"I thought we'd read this one tonight," she said, holding up a book. It had a picture of a little girl on the cover and some animal. Maybe it was a dragon. Maybe it was just a cat. But that didn't matter. It wasn't the Bible. It wasn't a pamphlet from the Word. It wasn't right.

"Okay," I said. I closed my eyes and tried to close my ears. I let the words wash over me, pass through my brain, but I vowed that they would never affect me, these non-Christian words, this blasphemy. I only had to make it another few hours, and then it would be midnight, and then Dad would take me away from here, away from this woman who wasn't my mother anymore but was dead and condemned.

At some point, she stopped reading the book and got up from where she'd been sitting on my bed. She patted my leg. "Goodnight, Alyssa. Love you."

I didn't say anything. I pretended I was asleep.

Now I sit in the car, remembering this, and we've made a turn into the city, and we whoosh down the freeway, and it feels like all the blood in my body has risen to my head, and my head pounds and pulses, and I can't see.

I remember lying awake with my eyes squeezed closed and then opening them every few minutes to look at the clock. The minutes until midnight ticked away so slowly that I could hardly stand it, and then suddenly it was time. Suddenly I was scrambling out of bed and stuffing my feet into my sneakers, and I was fighting with the window, which wouldn't open at first. Fighting with the window and almost crying because I was so close, but I might not be able to make it. I might not be able to get away.

"Here we are," Miss Tina says in her soft voice, her kind eyes looking down at me. We're in a parking lot next to a building. There's a dim streetlight, and that's it. I'm in darkness at some social worker's office, and Dad is in jail, and Carlo is somewhere else. I'm alone. "Your mom is inside," Miss Tina says.

But she isn't. She's come outside, and she's running toward the car.

Miss Tina jumps out and says something, but I don't understand it. I just see my late mother running, her white sneakers pounding on the asphalt, her short-cropped hair flying around her face. She's coming closer and closer, and I'm staring out the window at her, and she's staring down at me, and I take a deep sucking breath. I'm looking into the same eyes I saw in the mirror this morning, the same pale lashes, the same short nose. I can't look away from her eyes, and she can't look away from me, and the seconds tick away as we stare at each other, neither moving a muscle or seeming to blink.

Miss Tina is next to my mother, speaking in her ear, but my mother acts as if she doesn't hear a word of it. The two of us are completely frozen, and Miss Tina is all the life and movement. She moves her arms as she speaks. She looks from me to my mother, from my mother to me.

Miss Tina puts her arm in front of my mother. She nods and says something, and then my mother takes a step back, and Miss Tina opens the passenger side door.

I click off my seat belt. I push the door all the way open and step out into the cooling night. I run my hands over my skirt to make sure it's not too wrinkled. I present my face as a good girl is supposed to, up to my mother, who like everyone else is much taller than me, who I must treat as if she is still alive.

"Alyssa," she says. Her face contorts and tears spill from her eyes, but she doesn't wipe them away. She just lets them roll down her cheeks.

"Mom."

She reaches a hand out as if to hug me, then wipes her eyes on her sleeve, then stops and looks into my eyes again. I don't do anything to stop her. I just return her gaze, and she takes that as a *yes*, as permission, and she wraps her sinful arms around me, and because of her height, my face ends up pressed into her collarbone. My arms end up around her, and her body is warm as if she truly is alive, although I know it's an illusion, and I can't get used to it. I close my eyes and feel the beating of her pulse and the cool breeze on my back.

I remember finally getting the window to open, and pushing it as far to the left as it would go, and pushing the screen away, too, and lifting myself up, and seeing the dark car parked partway down the street just like he said, and getting half my body out the window, and holding myself on my little hands and thinking

Mom.

But I didn't say it. Instead, I pushed myself through and fell into the bush below my window. I got up and looked out at the silent parked car where I knew he was, and then I turned around and looked back up at the house, and I saw the light in the living room, still on, and I knew she was in there. And Liam was in the other room, my baby brother, who was condemned now too because he was conceived in sin.

The lights went on in the car.

I watched the living room window to see if she'd appear in it, to get a glimpse of her one more time. But I didn't see her. And didn't see her. And didn't see her.

Now I pull away from her and take a step back, bumping up against Miss Tina's car.

"Are you all right?" Mom asks. "Are you hurt?"

"Of course I'm all right," I snap. I immediately put my head down. I need to remember to keep sweet.

"You don't have to worry about your dad," she says. She's sniffing, trying to get control of herself. "He can't hurt you anymore. He'll never be able to touch you again. I promise."

I nod, not looking at her. She couldn't protect herself, so there's no way she can protect me. The dead can't do anything.

"Alyssa, we're going to go inside and do some paperwork," Miss Tina says. "And there's a restroom, and you can have a snack."

"And then we'll go to a hotel for the night," Mom says. "Tomorrow, we'll make the drive back to Eugene."

I nod again. All I see is me running toward Dad's car. Me crossing the yard and making it to the sidewalk and to the passenger side, opening that door with my own hand. I hesitated. I waited to try to see her. But she didn't show her face. She wasn't there to stop me, and she hasn't been there for nine years. Now she thinks she can just take me without asking me what I want.

"How's Liam?" I ask. The words come out of me unbidden. I didn't even know I was thinking them.

"Oh, he's wonderful," Mom says. "A really rambunctious, happy kid. Barron and I are married now. Did they tell you that?"

"No," I say. The adulterer, the man who was with my mom even though she was married to my dad. "I thought he left you."

"We worked it out," Mom says.

We're walking toward the silent office building now, side by side. Miss Tina walks in front of us. I could turn and run. But to where?

I won't have to stay with them, I tell myself. I know exactly what's going to happen. Dad will post bail, and he'll find Carlo, and we'll follow the plan. All I have to do is obey my father, which means that for now, I have to go where I'm told and pretend like I'm okay being with Mom. I'll do everything Dad wants, and then I'll be able to go home again. I just have to act like everything's fine.

But as we enter the building and the heavy door falls shut behind me, I suddenly have trouble breathing. I gasp, but no air comes in. I gasp again. Mom wraps her arm around my shoulder and asks if I'm all right, but I keep gasping. My heart is speeding up and my head is pounding, and I can't get any air. I fall to my knees in the hallway of this dim office building, and I think I must be dying. I think I must have been called back to God before I can fulfill my task. I think I must have sinned greatly in my heart. I must have thought about her too much all these past nine years. Maybe it started with the chili, that image I couldn't get out of my head, that I sometimes let play through my mind secretly when I was alone, when no one could possibly know I was thinking it except for God.

I gasp for breath and I remember being stuck in the middle of that window, with my head out and my feet in, and I remember thinking *Mom.*

And I crumple all the way to the floor.

4

Seattle

age twelve

After we met Carlo, our fortunes improved. This is how we went about things:

Dad would set up his sign with the lettering as big as he wanted, saying something like *Know the Word* or *To Live Is to Sin*, and he'd step out into the sidewalk with his packet of pamphlets and start preaching to people. He'd step right next to them, not blocking their way, but not exactly letting them get by, either. He'd speak quietly, asking them if they wanted to listen to him speak the Word and then launching into it anyway. All the time he'd have that wide smile on his face, that smile that made people feel like they mattered, and he'd be giving them that strong gaze with his blue eyes.

So much of life is sin, he'd say in a voice designed not to scare people. *Do you want to learn how to avoid sin?*

The whole technique was Carlo's advice, and Dad took it.

Dad never took advice from anyone before Carlo. But he saw the sense in it, because it all played into the next part.

While Dad was talking to some man or woman in a low, earnest, nonthreatening voice, making them feel like they mattered, Carlo would walk behind them or maybe on the other side and get their wallet or their phone or their credit card—whatever the person had in the pocket of their pants or near the outside of their backpack. Carlo was so quiet and careful that by the time Dad had stuffed a pamphlet into the person's hand, he was long gone. Then, if Carlo had taken a phone and not a wallet, Dad would gesture to me, and I'd step forward holding that hat we used for cash.

Half the time, people who'd just gotten their pocket picked would go ahead and donate too.

But it was all right because stealing from sinners wasn't a sin. It was only a sin to steal from the saved, from the followers of the Word. And we didn't know any of them besides ourselves in Seattle. We'd left them behind and set off on our own, according to Dad, because we were called to bring more people into the faith, and we couldn't do that if we were living isolated among our own. It had nothing to do with Mr. Brandon and the other Elders, or what Dad did.

Anyway, we started getting more money.

We'd walk on the streets during the day, and at night we'd sleep in our little tent that was hidden back in a woodsy area of the park. Usually we'd all three go to the church together to get food, but there was one night when Dad went out by himself to buy us dinner with the day's proceeds, and so for the first time since we'd met, Carlo and I were alone.

I pressed myself against the side of the tent, making sure to keep as far away from him as I could. I was alone with a boy, and I didn't want to give him any cause. Dad was always telling me about how girls gave boys cause and how boys couldn't control themselves. I didn't know why he'd left me alone with a boy. I stared at Carlo like he was some kind of angel. How could anyone without divine powers make Dad do something so rash as to leave me alone in our tent with him?

"You don't have to be afraid of me," he said.

"I'm not afraid of you." I sat with my arms wrapped around my legs. My skirt was dirty, especially on the bottom, where it was lined with mud.

"It's good though, what he teaches," Carlo said. He was sitting with his back against the tent, too, but he had his legs crossed, sitting easy. "You can't be too careful out on the streets."

"It's not about the streets."

He nodded. "Right. It's about being better off waiting to get married, and then when you're married, you'll have someone to take care of you. You won't have to live like this anymore."

I'd tried not to think about marriage and having a normal life ever since we left Zebulun. I just wanted to follow the rules. Obey your father. Don't give a boy cause. Wear modest clothing. Or else. . . .

"But I'm like your brother now. Until you get married, I'll take care of you."

"Don't you have any real sisters?" I wondered where my dad was and when he'd be back. If he thought I was giving Carlo cause, then . . . I pulled my legs closer into my chest.

"No." He rested his chin in his hand. "It was just me."

"What happened to your parents?"

He shrugged. "My mom had me when she was a kid, like my age. So she left me with her mom. But then my dad came and got me."

I froze. I didn't know if I wanted to hear the rest.

"And that wasn't too good." He grinned. "This is a lot better, even if we have to live in a tent. Your dad doesn't use drugs. Doesn't hit you. Gives you food. It's like, you gotta appreciate what you have." There wasn't anything in his smiling face to show what he meant by drugs and hitting. Except that scar that went along his hairline. And the ones on his knuckles. "What about your mom? Where is she?"

I shook my head.

"Oh shit, I'm sorry. You don't have to tell me."

"It's okay." I was getting a picture in my head. The day Dad found out about Barron, the day he found out she was planning to take me and sneak away with him in the night.

"No, no it's not. Listen, Lisa, I'm gonna make you a promise, okay? Let's make a pact." He leaned forward and held out a hand. It was a strong hand, tan from the sun, fingers long and thick and calloused.

"What pact?"

"No talking about the past. 'Cause the bad people from before can't hurt us anymore. I won't let them hurt you, and you won't let them hurt me. Deal?"

"Deal." I grabbed his hand and shook it. He smiled down at me with large brown eyes and brushed some hair out of his face.

I pulled my hand back and sat with crossed legs. Something had softened inside me. The picture was still there, all jumbled together. Me under the bed, her screaming, feet running, the crunch of a fist against a body and me covering my ears, the words *I'm pregnant* coming from somewhere, and then all sorts of bad words, and the sirens, and the lights flashing. It was all there, inside me, but I'd stuffed it deep down. I managed a smile.

Carlo pulled an old pack of cards from his jacket pocket. "Texas Hold'em," he said. He tossed me the bag of dried beans we used for chips.

Dad didn't come back for a long time that night. And when he did, he didn't say anything. It was like I hadn't been alone with a boy at all. That was how I knew it was true, that Carlo really was like my brother, and the bad people from the past couldn't hurt us. I lay awake that night, pressed up against the wall of the tent. Dad was next to me, and Carlo was on the other side of him. Both of them were snoring, making a little symphony.

I closed my eyes and replayed my memories. This was how I did it: I'd take the thing I didn't want to see, and I'd slowly push it out of the way with something else. So the floor of my bedroom became the bottom of the tent. The screaming became Carlo's words. The hand from the police officer who reached under the bed to pull me out became Carlo's hand, reaching toward me to make our pact. Take one thing and replace it with another. Erase it and make it what you want it to be.

5.

Seattle

now

We never do make it to the hotel. I spend the night in a hospital somewhere in Seattle, getting poked and prodded and having fluids pumped into me. A lady doctor wearing pants tells me that I was severely dehydrated. She sits down next to my bed. My late mother isn't anywhere. I wonder if something happened to her. I wonder if my dad posted bail and whether he's found out where I am.

The doctor smiles down at me. It's a fake smile, the kind people put on when they want to give you bad news. Like, *I'm sorry but I'm going to have to ask you to leave.* Or, *This is private property.* Or, *I saw you take that.*

"Has anybody hurt you?" she asks.

That question again. *What happens if I say yes?* I almost ask. I wonder if they'd send me somewhere far away to be with another family, so I wouldn't have to go with my late mother, and I wouldn't have to go back to Dad. That's the third choice for the law, the way out of *parental rights.*

I learned a lot of legal terms back when we were in Zebulun with the Citizens of the Word. Knowing the law is part of the ammunition we need to get by in this world where rules are created by American men.

But I know there's no way out of the choice between Mom and Dad even if I say yes, because the law gave me to Mom, and Mom didn't hurt me the way this lady doctor means. And if I lie, I'll just end up farther from Zebulun than before. Things aren't the way they were all those years ago, when Dad told me to say Mom hurt me. Time and Dad have changed the plan. So I say what I know the lady doctor wants to hear:

"I want to see my mom. And I want to go home."

"I'm going to release you," she says. "You need to drink water, and you're underweight."

My late mother appears in the doorway. "We can stop for breakfast on the way home," she says.

The doctor nods at her with narrowed eyes. This is the part where she could do something, if she thought my mom wasn't feeding me. This is the part where she could make a phone call to someone somewhere who has the power of the law behind them. But I've been through this. This is the part where she does nothing to help me. And so I get out of bed and end up in a diner off the freeway, eating pancakes and drinking all the water I want.

But the doctor didn't know I'd be here. She didn't know my mom wouldn't starve me. It was just easier for her to believe that than to do something. Maybe Miss Tina told her I was safe, but I'll never know because by the time I woke up, Miss Tina was gone. Her job was to take me away from one parent and give me to the other. Now possession of me has been transferred, and her job is done.

I eat fast. You never know when you're going to have a good meal next. Mom watches me carefully, as if she worries that if she takes her eyes off me, I'll disappear. It's weird being looked at by what could be my own face, only older. Before, people used to say we looked like twins born apart. Even when I was only seven years old, it was like my own face was staring back at me sometimes. Now I see lines next to her eyes, a few darker spots on her otherwise creamy skin. Her hair is still blonde, and I don't see any gray in it. Just that it's short, only down to her chin, and it hides the contours of her face. But not the scar on her chin. One side is a little bit different from the other because of how it healed, I guess.

"You look the same," Mom says. She chews her lip. "Even with the hair dye."

I focus on my plate, on scooping the last of my pancakes onto my fork. I don't know what will happen if I say something. Dad might still be in jail. If he's out already, he probably doesn't know where I am. He won't be able to see whether I look at her and hear what I answer. But what if he does know? What if they've let him out, and he's found me?

"I know it isn't going to be easy," Mom says. "You don't have to do anything to try to make me happy, okay? I have so many questions, but I don't want to pressure you. I'm just so glad you're all right."

"Dad would never hurt me." I chew the last bite slowly, let the syrup slide against my gums. I try to remember the last time I had pancakes, but I can't. I used to make eggs, when we had them. When Dad was working at the factory at night, and Carlo and I would wake up before he got back. And we were a brother and sister eating together.

I catch the tear with the back of my wrist before it falls. I blink to chase more away. I don't know when I'll see Carlo again. So many things have to happen and go as planned, and even then, I don't know. Everything will be different.

"I'm glad to hear that," she says. She reaches out a hand and touches my arm. I know she doesn't believe it. I know what she told the judge to get the law to give me to her. She told him about the kicking and the yelling and the hitting. But that was always against her, not me. Then.

I think about the hospital, four months ago. My head spinning, my vision blurred. *Did anyone hurt you?*

I close my eyes and pray on it, on remembering that it's a man's right to punish a woman for her sins. *A son must obey his father, and so must a daughter. The bond between father and son is unbreakable and inviolate, and also the bond between a father and daughter.*

But it's also a man's virtue to show mercy. Just because he had the right to hit me doesn't mean he should have. The way it works is, he might be punished for doing wrong, someday, in the firmament, but I still have to obey here on Earth. But if he wasn't stronger than me, I would have hit him back. If I was bigger, what I said about him not hurting me would be true. You can bet your prize rooster wattles on that.

But I'm not bigger, and I just lied. Because he did hurt me. More than once. But she has no right to know that.

"The Citizens of the Word used to say it's a man's virtue to show mercy," I say. "They talked a lot about peace and living humble on Earth, and sparing the rod to teach the value of merciful justice."

"Did they?" Mom asks. She pulls back her shoulders but not her hand. It's as if she wants to lean back in her seat, get far away from me, but she can't.

"After we left, we went to a town. It was called Zebulun."

Mom nods. "We looked for you there. Barron and I went. The police went. Even the FBI."

"Well, every house has a basement. They have them all filled up with food and guns and water. The police thought it was just a few places, but they all had them. There were so many places to hide there." I set my fork down because all the pancakes are gone. I ate too fast, and my stomach is churning.

Mom is trying to sit up straight again. She's trying to pretend she never leaned back. But I saw it. I saw what she thinks of us. "I'm so sorry you had to go through that," she says.

The waiter comes over and hands Mom the check, and we both get up, because neither of us can sit here. She pays, and I wait for her by the door, and I watch the way she stands in her jeans, one hip to one side, as if she doesn't care whether anybody's looking at her, as if it's okay to just show your ass to anyone who walks in.

I press my hand against my hastily constructed bun, as if it might suddenly have disappeared, as if she could have cut my hair with her mind as I was sitting at the table. When I realize it's still there, I take a deep breath. Because I know that even though I have to go back with her to Eugene, and I have to talk to her and keep sweet and do what she tells me, I'm still me. I still have my chastity and my pride and my God, and nobody can take any of that away from me. Or prevent me from obeying my father *and* protecting myself.

Nobody can hurt me today. Right this minute, I'm safe.

We walk out into the parking lot like a mother and daughter who just had breakfast together at a diner, like a couple of people who regularly eat pancakes. The sky seems very high up and blue, and the parking lot feels small. I look around for anywhere Dad could be hiding, but there are only a couple cars with no one inside them.

"I hope you'll feel comfortable telling me about it someday," Mom says.

"It wasn't bad like you think," I say as I climb into the passenger seat of her car.

I remember being in that basement back in Zebulun, sitting on the bed that folded down from the wall, listening to the men walking around upstairs. The police wanted to take me back then, and I didn't say anything. I pressed my face against Dad's chest as if they could have heard me breathing. Dad glared up at the ceiling, holding that pistol in his right hand, his breathing heavy. And it seemed like the whole world was going to end right then and there, but it didn't.

I could have called out or tried to get away from Dad.

I press my face to the window and search the parking lot and the street as we pull out. He isn't here now, and she is. Everything is opposite. And I don't know whether to call out or be silent, whether to run from her or do what she says. I climbed into a car again, and again, I don't know exactly what I've done.

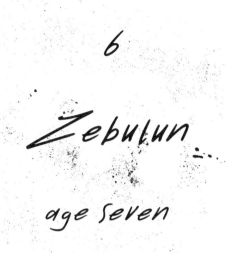

6

Zebulun

age seven

When I was seven, after I climbed out the window and ran to Dad's car, we drove through the night and into the morning. Dad was on edge, always looking behind him. But no one appeared to be following us. We were heading east from Eugene on Highway 126. I'd never been on that road before, never been anywhere but north to Seattle or west to the beach. It was like another world we were driving through, in darkness.

I wanted to ask where we were going, and how long until we got there, but I didn't. I wasn't supposed to speak unless spoken to. That was why Mom was dead. She'd talked back. She'd disobeyed orders given by her husband. I wasn't going to disobey. I was going to be good. I was going to be as silent as I had to be.

It felt like days and days and days that we drove that night, but finally the sun started coming up, and Dad pulled over to the side of the road. I ran over a little hill to pee in the grass, and when I came back, he was changing the license plate on the car.

I didn't ask about that either. All I could think about was that I just peed without washing my hands, and so I got back in the car and tried not to touch anything, and we drove on and on and on.

I was asleep when we finally reached Zebulun. We were already inside the bounds of the town. The first person I saw was Miss Sheila, smiling down on me from outside the passenger side window. She was wearing a white blouse with ruffles and a long skirt, and her hair was done up in a bun so big that you could tell her hair was long and thick.

"Well, you must be Alyssa," she said. Her necklace hung in the air as she leaned toward me, a red-and-yellow rock on a silver chain.

"Yes, ma'am."

"Welcome to our little town," she said. She took my hand and helped me out of the car, and then she led me down a narrow path to a sprawling old house. It had three stories—you could tell from the windows. On top of what must have been a bedroom was one single window, and I knew it was an attic, and I was in love. I'd always wanted to live in a big house. Miss Sheila was familiar, with her outfit and her long hair, like the other Citizens of the Word back in Eugene. Like the way Mom used to look. Miss Sheila looked like the grandmother I'd never had. Stepping into that house was like walking into the home I'd always imagined.

It was just that, when she turned around and smiled at me as she led me in through the door, her face wasn't the right face. She had the face of a stranger.

"What is it, Honey Cakes?" she asked me.

"Is my mom coming?"

She got down on her knees in front of me so she could look at me eye to eye, the way adults do. She had blue eyes like mine, but her lashes were dark. Her hair was dark too, in the places where it wasn't gray. She touched the side of my face to brush a strand of my hair out of the way. "Your mother is dead. Do you understand what that means?"

"She left the church, so we have to pretend," I said.

She laughed. "In the eyes of God, it's not pretending. She's as much dead as if she was gone from this Earth, because her soul has already been damned. She's left her husband, committed adultery, and conceived a child out of wedlock. Now, you can mourn her loss. You can remember how she was in your heart. But you have to remember that she's no longer with us."

I thought about Mom reading me a story before I went to bed. Turning the light out, saying she loved me. How could she be dead and damned and still walking around the house in jeans?

"I know it can be a hard thing, when it's someone so close to you. But listen." She gently touched my chest with one hand. "God loves you. He wants you to protect your immortal soul. He doesn't want you to fall the way she did. And that's why He sent you to us."

I nodded. I knew what my mom did was wrong. I knew it was wrong for her to walk around in jeans, and I knew that somehow my baby brother, Liam, was wrong, that she'd done something terrible to get him. "I thought she'd come here," I said. I knew Dad was taking me somewhere, but I didn't understand that she wasn't coming too.

I thought somehow she would put her long skirt back on and join us. I thought going with Dad was just the first step in all of us being together again, the way it used to be.

"Oh." She ran her hand over my hair. "Honey, no. She's not coming." She pulled me into a hug. "You're safe here with us."

I let her hug me, and I looked over her shoulder at the inside of the big house. I felt the tears welling up, and I pressed my lips together and closed my eyes. I knew that I couldn't cry, that if I did, something terrible would happen. But the tears leaked from my eyes anyway.

"It's all right," Miss Sheila said.

I felt Dad standing behind me. His shadow loomed over us. The shadow head appeared on the floor behind Miss Sheila, wavering through my blurring eyes. The floor was hard. His footsteps were heavy. One step. Two steps.

I pulled back from Miss Sheila. "Can I go up in the attic?" There was water dripping down the left side of my face.

"Sure," she said. She took my hand again. "I'll give you the whole tour."

She did give me a tour, but she left out the basement. It wasn't until a few weeks later that I saw it.

That was when the men came to take me back.

We heard them walking around upstairs. Their steps were heavy, obvious, menacing. Dad's arm was around me, and I squeezed into him.

The steps grew lighter, and then heavier, and then lighter again. Time passed. I shook. Dad barely moved at all.

Finally, the door creaked open.

Dad tensed even more, gripping the gun.

I almost stopped breathing.

"It's all right," Miss Sheila said, poking her head in. Her body was in shadow, lit from behind, high up on the staircase. "They've been gone a while. Our scout down at the junction saw them heading away. So it looks like they're gone for good."

"Praise God," Dad said. He emptied the gun of bullets and locked it in the safe they had down there next to the canned food.

I tried to start breathing normally again.

"Honey Cakes, it's all right," Miss Sheila said. "Nobody's going to come take you away from us."

I looked up at her from the bottom of the stairs, and I knew she was right. Nobody else was going to come for me.

But I also knew my mother had tried to find me. She had sent those men after me to take me back. She couldn't be that mad if she sent them. Even though I ran away, she still wanted me. For only the second time since I'd gotten there, I started crying. Even though Dad was still right there, even though Mr. Doug, Miss Sheila's husband, was standing behind her. I started bawling, and I couldn't stop.

"Stop crying," Dad said.

"Art, tell her she did good," Miss Sheila said. She left the basement door open but walked away. Light from the main house floated down.

Dad put his arm around my shoulder. "Miss Sheila's right, kiddo.

I'm sorry. You did a great job. Real quiet. You've been a champion this whole time." He looked down at me from his great height, and I looked up. I couldn't see much of his face under the big beard he was growing. He was all large blue eyes and patches of pale skin, close-cropped hair revealing a square head. But I could tell he was smiling at me. He squeezed me close to him.

That did get me to stop crying. I hadn't cried until after the men left. Even though I was secretly glad Mom still wanted me, I didn't let her find me. So I didn't sin, really. I was a champion. Dad always said that when he was happy with me. *Champion* or *sport* or *quiet*. These were all good words, and I lived for them.

He kissed me on the head. "Real good girl. Let's get back upstairs now." He gave me a little push between the shoulder blades.

As I walked up the stairs I couldn't help thinking that maybe they were still out there, those men who came for me. Maybe Mom was still out there. But as I came out into the light and Miss Sheila's big kitchen, I knew it wasn't true. The curtains were open, and it was like nothing ever happened. Like no one had ever come at all. Miss Sheila was setting out a big raw chicken on the broiler pan.

"Why don't you get cleaned up a little bit, and then you can help me with the greens?" Miss Sheila smiled at me. Something shifted then, as I looked up at her now-familiar, grandmotherly face. Out through the open curtains, I could see the backyard of her and Mr. Doug's house, its grass tall and unmowed, patches flattened and trod on by the outdoor dogs. And nobody but the dogs and chickens out there.

"Yes, ma'am," I said.

Dad came out of the basement, and I heard the loud thump of the door closing. His footsteps landed hard behind me.

"That chicken looks delicious, Sheila," Dad said from above me. I knew he was giving her his big smile. "Lisa and I appreciate it."

"We're happy to help, Art. You know that." She nodded at me. "Go on and clean up now."

So that's what I did. I changed out of those clothes I'd been hiding out in, and I washed my hands and my face and brushed my teeth for the whole length of the "Happy Birthday" song, and then I came back down to help out Miss Sheila in the kitchen, just like I lived there and this had been my life all along.

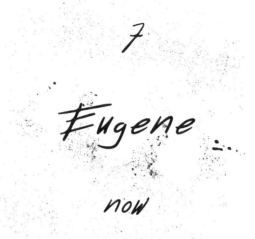

7

Eugene

now

I haven't been back to Eugene since I was seven years old. I know I've ridden in a car on this road before, down I-5 from Seattle, but I don't remember it very clearly. I remember little towns by the road, and cows and horses. I remember the straightness of the road and the feeling that it would go on forever.

Now it feels like it's short. Like God is driving me to my destination, and I'm not ready. I need more time on the road before I can face whatever is going to happen next. Because this time, technically, I'm going back. Mom's told me that she and Barron bought the same house she was renting the day I left, and I can even have my same room. But I don't know Mom or Barron or Liam the way I know Dad and Carlo. I don't know them the way I knew Miss Sheila and Mr. Doug. I don't even know them the way I knew Pastor Garza at the soup kitchen or the way I knew the anonymous people walking past us as Dad shouted the Word. I learned to watch them, to read them, to see where their hands rested and how their shoulders were positioned. I've learned to watch for zippers undone and pockets packed. I know who is going to school and who works in an office and who is just outside because they have nowhere else to go.

I know all these minor things about people, things that explain how much money they have and whether they're missing something big in their lives that the Word can fill. But I don't know what they think of themselves. I don't know who they like and what they watch on TV or what they're sad about today. Because I only observed them. We didn't talk.

The only other person I knew in Port Angeles was Becca, my best friend. My only friend. She won't be surprised to find me gone, but she'll have no idea where I am. How could she, when I told her what she'll think is a huge lie?

"Penny for your thoughts," Mom says. She's just taken the exit off the freeway. I'm looking out the window, trying to find any memories of this place in my brain. But it all looks unfamiliar. Just roads and trees that could be anywhere off I-5.

"My friend, Becca," I reply, still looking out the window. "She'll be worried that I disappeared."

"If you want to call your friend later, you can," Mom says. She purses her lips, opens her mouth as if to say something, thinks better of it. And then says it anyway. "She isn't part of the Word, is she?"

I shake my head.

"Okay. Well. I think it's good for you to keep in touch with your friends."

"My *American* friends." I fold my arms. American is a pejorative for people who aren't part of the Word, which is almost everyone. Citizens of the Word reject citizenship in a country. We live here because there's nowhere else to live, but we don't vote, and we don't join the Army, and we don't send our children to public school. Someday everyone will accept the Word, or the world will end, but until that happens, we keep apart.

"Do you have friends from the Word in Port Angeles?" She looks straight ahead. We're turning onto a city street now. Something is stirring in my memory. A grocery store coming up on the left—I've been there. There's a bike path. We used to ride on it together: Mom on her old beast with the big tires, me with my banana seat and training wheels.

I don't answer that. We went there because no one knew us, and Mom knows that. She knows we were running from the law and from her. So how was I supposed to have the right friends?

I'm glad I did have a friend though. More glad than I'll ever tell anyone.

The day I met Becca, I hadn't spoken to anyone but Carlo or Dad for the entire time we'd been in Port Angeles, which was a few months. I had just turned fourteen. Either Dad or Carlo was always home with me, but they worked different shifts, and Dad slept all morning.

That morning, I went out to the backyard. It was an ugly yard. The grass was overgrown, and the two trees near the back fence were overgrown as well. There was some junk in it that had been there since we moved in: a pair of old car tires, empty plastic storage bins, a pile of wood scraps. But it was the only place I could be outside alone, so I loved it. There was a fence all around the yard, but it was rotting away, and there were a few boards that were missing entirely, and I looked over that way, and there she was. She was standing in the middle of her yard holding a racket and bouncing something on it.

"Hey!" she said.

"Hi." Instinctively, I looked back to the house. But Dad was still sleeping.

"Want to play?" She held her arms open, revealing the racket and something in her left hand.

My heart raced.

"Do you know how to play badminton?"

I shook my head.

"Come on, I'll show you."

I headed toward her. I don't know how fast I was really going, but it felt slow. It felt like every step I took was running a mile. Behind me was our backyard, and the sliding glass doors, and inside, Dad. But he was asleep. He hardly ever woke up before 3:00 p.m., because he didn't even get into bed before 9:00 a.m. That gave me as much as three more hours.

I stepped through the hole in the fence, and it was like I was in another universe. The grass was cut short, the trees were trimmed, and the paint on the outside of the house wasn't peeling. Behind Becca was a short net that I hadn't even noticed before I came through the fence.

Becca handed me a racket. "You go over there, and I hit this to you. You just have to hit it back."

I took the racket and went over to the other side of the net.

"I'm Becca," Becca said.

"Lisa."

She was wearing jean shorts and a T-shirt. Her dark red hair was clipped back so it wouldn't fall in her face, but the rest of it was falling down her shoulders. It was a lot shorter than mine was, though. Mine was all the way down to my butt, although you wouldn't know it because I was wearing a bun. Becca had a pair of sunglasses on her head, and now she pulled them down over her face.

"You have to keep it in the lines." She motioned to the edges of the net. "And try to keep me from hitting it."

"Okay."

She hit the thing at me.

I swung at it and completely missed.

Becca laughed. "You'll get it. Throw it up and hit it over to me."

It took me three tries, but I finally hit it over the net. We went on like that for a while, and I lost track of time. Suddenly I realized how long I'd been gone.

"I have to get back to school," I said, walking around the net.

"On a Saturday?" She tilted her head.

"We only rest on the Sabbath," I said. And winced at my own words. Telling the truth to strangers is stupid. It just gets you weird looks and judgment and pity.

"Oh, it's like some religious homeschool?"

"Yeah." I handed her the racket. "That was fun."

"Let's do it again," she said. "My parents hardly ever play with me."

"You're an only child?"

"Yeah. What about you?"

"I have a brother."

"Right, Dickies Coat Guy." She slipped both rackets under one arm. I stared at her blankly.

"He wears that coat every single day."

"We don't have a lot of coats." *Shut up*, I told myself.

"Lisa!" Dad's voice bellowed through the fence.

I froze. "Bye. I have to go." Without waiting for a response, I walked to the fence and through it, and I was back in my universe. Dad was standing behind the open sliding glass door, arms folded over his chest.

"What are you doing?"

I slipped inside and pulled the door shut behind me. I didn't want Becca to hear whatever he said to me. "She was just out in the yard," I said. "I didn't want to be rude."

"She was just?" He loomed over me. "She was just?"

"I didn't want to be rude," I said. I held still. As still as possible.

"If she's out there, you stay inside."

"Okay. I'm sorry. I wasn't thinking."

He stepped back, satisfied. Usually that was all it took. Pretend to be sorry, hang your head. Say all the things you want to say just to yourself, on the inside. Like, *I should be able to have one friend. I should be able to leave the house. I'm not some moron who's going to die from playing a dumb game in someone's backyard.*

"And be quiet," he said, walking back down the hall. "I don't want to wake up again!"

"Yes, sir."

I vowed to be quieter, to make sure he didn't wake up. And the very next Saturday, she was outside, and I went through the fence, and we played badminton. She told me she lived with her dad and stepmom, and she was in eighth grade. She said they were Catholics and went to church on Sunday, and so I convinced myself that it couldn't be that sinful to hang out with her. Because at least Catholics were also Christians and were known to have better morals than non-Christians, although they were also known to be the hardest to save.

I told her I didn't have a phone, so we made up a way to get in touch with each other. There was a spot in the rotten fence that was perfect for hiding notes, so I'd write a note saying when I thought I could get away, and we'd plan to meet. This went on for a few weeks before she ever asked why I didn't have a phone or why I had to keep our friendship a secret. But one day, I was sitting in front of the computer, listening to Miss Sheila speak, following along in the Gospel, and I suddenly realized that if I got up and walked away from the computer, no one back in Zebulun would realize I was gone. And Becca had said she'd be on a break from American school.

Carefully, quietly, I got up and went through the sliding glass doors, across the yard, and through the fence. She had sliding glass doors too, and they looked in on a family room, and Becca was in there watching TV, just like I thought she would be. So I went in, and we watched daytime TV together. I leaned in, fascinated by the celebrities and the music and the way people looked and spoke on the talk shows.

"You want some chips?" Becca asked.

"Yes, thank you." I couldn't believe my luck, but I hoped it didn't show in my voice.

Becca came back into the family room with a big bowl of tortilla chips and another bowl of salsa. I remembered chips and salsa from when I was little, but I'd never had them since I'd been with Dad. I'd had a bag of chips here and there at the soup kitchen, but that was it. There was never salsa, and there was definitely never this much.

I took a single chip, slid it into the salsa, brought it slowly to my mouth. I couldn't help but smile wide.

"Haven't you ever had chips and salsa before?" Becca asked.

"Yeah, but it's been a long time."

She gave me the side-eye. "So, are you sneaking out right now?"

I licked the salt off my lips.

"You can tell me." She ran her fingers across her lips in a zipping gesture and elaborately pretended to lock her mouth and throw an enormous fake key over her shoulder.

I knew telling strangers the truth was stupid. But if I didn't tell her, she could give me away.

"Yes," I said.

"Why aren't you supposed to see me?"

"I'm not supposed to hang out with people who aren't from the Citizens of the Word. That's our religion. But there aren't any Citizens here." I shrugged.

"Do you have to wear skirts and have your hair like that?"

"Yes."

"Are you guys polygamists? You dress like the people on this reality show who escaped from a polygamist cult."

"No, that's crazy!" I gaped at her. I only knew what the word *polygamist* meant because it was in the Gospel, which said it was a perversion of marriage and steeped in sin.

"I'm sorry! I didn't know!" She held up her hands.

"It's okay." I reached for another chip. That stuff was part of why it was dumb to talk to people who couldn't be saved. They'd just make up mean things to believe about us.

"What else are you not supposed to do?" On TV, someone was singing a song I'd never heard before. Something new and popular. Something from this universe.

"Talk to men. Disobey. Read the wrong books." I ate my chip. I was currently disobeying, but the chips were good. I liked sitting on the couch with Becca listening to American music. Most of all, I liked not being alone in front of that computer, forced to listen and never speak.

"What happens if you do those things?"

"Nothing. You're just not supposed to."

Becca nodded and took a chip herself. She must have known I was lying. She saw me run back through the fence when my dad called me. I always got the sense that she understood things. Maybe it was because she read a lot of books when she wasn't watching talk shows and reality TV. Right then, I realized she had me pegged. But I wasn't going to tell her what could happen to me. I just wanted to sit there and pretend I was a normal kid with a normal friend.

"So we can only talk with the notes?" she asked. "You can't get a phone?"

"We can't afford it," I said. It was better to admit to being poor than to admit that I wasn't allowed to have one because I was a girl. That wasn't normal. And I could tell that even though their house was nicer than ours, they were poor too. After all, we lived on the same street. The TV we were watching was practically as old as the ones in Zebulun, and the couch had seen better days too. Even though the outside was painted, the inside was showing wear. These were the kind of people who didn't want strangers on the street to know how poor they were.

"It's kind of fun. Very cloak-and-dagger."

"Just don't let my dad see you."

"What about your mom? Does she live with you too?"

"My mom's dead."

"Oh, I'm sorry." She shifted in her seat and looked away. "So is mine."

"I'm sorry too."

"She had cancer. Is that what happened to your mom?" She still wasn't really looking at me. Her grief flowed off her in waves I could almost see in the air. She began to curl in on herself.

"Yeah." I sat stiffly. Maybe grief was flowing off me too. I always tried not to think about her, and now I wanted to think about her less than ever. But her voice kept coming through my brain. *I'm pregnant.*

Becca wiped tears out of her eyes.

Without thinking about what I was doing, I reached out and took her hand. She gripped it back. We sat there like that for a few minutes as the TV show changed from a talk show to a soap opera. We were two girls who had both lost our mothers, and that was always there between us, something we had in common, something other people couldn't understand.

Mom breaks the long silence between us by turning on the radio. Country music comes floating out.

"I wasn't thinking," Mom says. "I know the Citizens were never in Port Angeles. The little group in Eugene left too. I think they all went to Zebulun." We're going up a hill now. There are lots of trees. Nice houses. American houses. Places where people who aren't us live.

"We weren't welcome anywhere," I say. There are stories about groups being kicked out of housing, harassed by police, checked in on by child services. No wonder they moved to Zebulun to be by themselves. All that was just part of the reason I couldn't tell Becca a lot of things that were true.

I remember us in her living room, sitting on the floor cross-legged, watching TV. Becca laughed at me for not knowing any of the actors or shows and asked what rock I crawled out from under. I tried to explain the Word without letting the whole truth slip, without being too specific about Zebulun or how we left. Without telling her we'd been homeless and stealing from people and living in a tent. I think about us lying on her bed putting on nail polish, and me stealing her remover so I could take it off once I got back home again.

We're pulling into a driveway.

"This is your house?" I ask. "I don't remember it being this nice."

"We fixed it up. No more puke-green carpets and leaking roof."

I struggle with the door handle, suddenly anxious to get out of the car. My feet land on the driveway, and I definitely don't feel like I'm home again. I only ever lived in this house for a couple months anyway, and then it was a sick yellow color, the paint peeling. Now it's a tasteful gray. There's a new-looking car in the carport. It's just a house that doesn't mean anything to me, and somehow that makes me feel better. I can handle being at just a house. Maybe the people who live here can't hurt me.

The front door opens, and there's a boy standing behind the screen. He stands there staring at me.

Mom waves him forward.

He opens the screen door and steps out. He's wearing a T-shirt and shorts with flip-flops. He comes closer, bounding steps full of energy, even as he examines me with a question in his eyes. He stops a couple feet away.

"You're almost as tall as I am!" I blurt. I put a hand over my mouth and laugh. He's supposed to be a little baby. I knew he would have grown up, but this isn't how I thought about him. I always thought of the baby in the crib. How the night I left, I went into his room and leaned over his crib and whispered that I'd come back for him. But of course, I didn't come back for him, because he wasn't my dad's son, and Dad didn't want him.

"Oh, poppycock," Mom says. "Liam, come stand next to your sister. No, not next to—back-to-back."

"You *are* short," Liam says, standing behind me.

We haven't even been introduced yet. This isn't how I expected it to go. We're already acting normal. We're acting like I'm a part of this family and I never left. As if I know him and he knows me.

"You're a good six inches taller, Alyssa," Mom says. She breaks into a big smile, and then tears are rolling down her face. She keeps smiling though.

"I'm gonna be way taller," Liam says, stepping away. We face each other. He has the same blond hair and blue eyes, the same pale eyelashes. "Did you dye your hair?" he asks.

"Yes, I did," I say. "Don't you like it?" I talk to him like I would have talked to a little boy in Seattle. You can be friendly without becoming an American. You act friendly enough so no one questions you, so no one thinks you're strange, so no one calls the police. You keep what you really think and feel on the inside.

"I guess."

"So, we haven't been introduced. I'm Alyssa." My old name rolls off my tongue like I never changed it. Dad never once called me Alyssa after he decided to make the change. Carlo never once called me Alyssa. Becca would be shocked to learn I'd been lying about my name all this time. But now the law says I'm Alyssa again. I hold out my hand to shake, and Liam takes it. We wave our arms around like noodles more than we actually shake. But he smiles, and I smile.

"I don't remember you," he says. "I was too little."

"That's okay. I remember for both of us. You were tiny, and you barely had any hair."

Liam rubs his hand over his head and looks embarrassed. It's then that I notice the man standing in the doorway. I don't know how long he's been there. As he steps out, I try to figure out if I remember him. He's pretty short for a man, maybe five foot seven, and he's got a belly spreading over his jeans. His hairline is receding. There's something open about his face. Maybe it's the wide nose or the friendly eyes, or the way he squints as he smiles. There's some kind of goodness that comes off him, if I'm any judge. He's the kind of guy who'd put a dollar in the hat just because he feels sorry for you. You know if he takes a pamphlet he won't read it, and you know he probably keeps his wallet inside his jacket so you can't pick it. But he gives that dollar to you without a thought.

That's the way sin hides in men, with a kindness that nevertheless denies God. It was in one of those pamphlets. *And God will place them throughout America to test you, these men who sin with a smile. These men do good works even as they draw you to the ways of the Beast. For it isn't the small actions of men that prove worth in the eyes of God, but a man's heart. And a man's heart will be revealed in his worship and in his choice to separate himself from America and follow the Word.*

Barron comes toward us and stops a few feet away. He's wearing flip-flops too, thick hairy toes poking out over the edges.

"Alyssa, do you remember Barron?" Mom asks.

"A little," I lie. I remember a man, but not this man. If this man had actually walked by me on the street and put money in my hat, I wouldn't have known it was him.

"I sure remember you," he says.

"It's nice to meet you," I say.

"Let's get inside out of the heat," Mom says.

Barron goes around to the trunk and pulls out my bags. There are only a couple of them. I guess the police or Miss Tina or someone did get a few of my other things, because there's a suitcase there that I didn't pack. He also has my duffle bag with the Nike swoosh.

"I can get that," I say, holding out my hand for it. I manage to keep my hand from shaking. I smile as if I don't care at all.

"No, no, I've got it," he says. "You don't need to be carrying anything. That's what stepdads are for." He heads for the house, flip-flops scraping the concrete driveway.

I take a deep breath. He's probably not the kind of man who'd look inside a girl's bag. But he is the kind of man who'd commit adultery, so what guarantees are there?

And *stepdad*. What on earth does that mean for me?

Liam follows his dad inside. His flip-flops don't scrape. Instead, they flop as he bounds away.

"Your bedroom is all set up," Mom says. "I always kept it ready. You can have as much time to decompress as you want." She lifts her arms and leans forward a little as if she's going to go in for the hug. But then she pulls back. It takes a lot of effort for her to do that, and that's good. It takes effort for me to be here, too, for me to act like everything's okay and fine and normal even though I have to do something that is not okay and not fine, and she isn't supposed to be here acting like she's alive. I'm not supposed to be here, but in some ways I am. In some ways, this is the only place I'm supposed to be.

"I'm sure it will be fine," I say. I give Mom the best smile I can muster. I want to go home, and I also want to go inside and prepare myself. And only the second thing is possible. So I do what's possible. I follow the men into the house.

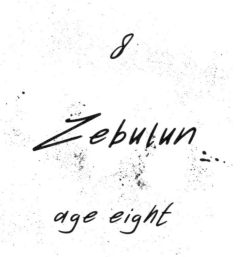

8

Zebulun

age eight

When we first got to Zebulun, Dad said staying with Miss Sheila and Mr. Doug was temporary. We were going to get a house of our own, even better than the house we had back in Eugene before Mom's sin. That house had three big bedrooms and a second floor. But the days went on, and we didn't move. There were empty houses in town owned by Mr. Brandon, who was the head of the church and owned everything, including the house Miss Sheila and Mr. Doug lived in. But you had to earn a house, I heard Mr. Doug say to Dad. You had to work for the Word until Mr. Brandon decided you were ready, and once you were ready, you were awarded Citizenship, and you could stay in one of Mr. Brandon's houses forever.

So Dad worked. Dad was a genius with machines, even Mom used to say. He could fix anything in a house that broke. Washing machines, dishwashers, refrigerators, heaters. They sent him around town fixing things, and he had more work with the Citizens of the Word than he ever had before. I heard him and Mr. Doug talking one night about a year after we got there, when I was being willful again and not staying in bed, wandering around the house like I used to do. I'd make a game of keeping quiet, and I'd walk on my tiptoes. This night, I stood at the top of the staircase and listened to the adults in the living room.

"If I'd have had this much work, I'd have been able to pay the rent," Dad said. A glass clinked against the coffee table.

"God provides," Mr. Doug replied.

The TV whispered in the background. There was a rise and fall to the noise of it, like sports, maybe baseball.

"Can't make an honest living in America. Man knows how to do something useful, but that's no good. You've got to go to their college and read a bunch of nonsense, or you're worth nothing." Dad's voice was quiet but bitter. Like whenever he talked about work or money.

I flattened myself against the wall, holding my breath. If he knew I was here I'd be in trouble.

"We appreciate honest work here, Art. You don't have to worry about America no more."

"Well, we've been here a year. Haven't I proved to Brandon I'm doing my part? Lisa and I need our own place. Need to be able to find a wife."

"Brandon'll come around." Mr. Doug's deep voice was calm. I never heard that man raise his voice in all the years we were there.

"Well, what's the goddamn holdup?" There was that glass clanking again. I imagined Dad picking up his glass, taking a swig, and slamming it down again. Just like he used to do back in Eugene with his liquor, except since alcohol was a sin, he couldn't let Mr. Doug see him drinking it. So he must have been slamming down his glass of juice.

"God rewards patience," Mr. Doug responded.

"I think I've displayed enough patience, Doug. A year? Not getting paid any that whole time either. Gave Brandon my car for the good of the town. Now, that's all right if we get our house. But otherwise, we're expected to live off your charity?"

"Not charity, Art. You're earning your keep. Got a place to live, food to eat, education for Lisa. You got everything you need right here, and more'll be coming. I'd say, pray on that and tomorrow come to the land with a new sight."

"New sight." Dad was suddenly at the bottom of the staircase. He must have moved fast. "Lisa! What the chicken feathers are you doing up?"

I stood there stock-still, shocked.

"You being a nosy little bitch again?" He started coming up the stairs, stomping. His face was hard. That big beard lurched at me in the low light.

I couldn't figure out whether to run or not. I just froze.

"Art." Doug was at the bottom of the stairs. "We don't talk to our women that way here. Women are precious. We protect our women and provide for them. We punish with kindness, not anger." He looked up at me. "Were you listening in on us, sweetie?"

"No, sir, I was just coming down for some juice." The lie popped out of my mouth before I even thought it. I was learning that. How to think one thing and say another and never let it show on your face. How to make sure you always had a reason the men would accept. You do what they say, but you think for yourself. What's inside your mind is yours. And you listen when you can get away with it.

"All right, then, go and get it," Mr. Doug said.

I looked from Mr. Doug to Dad. Dad's face was turning red on top of the beard, but he didn't say anything. So I scampered past him and ran into the kitchen. While I was pouring my orange juice, I kept my ears open for anything else they said, but they must have been whispering. Dad must have been whispering to Doug with his red face. All the time I wondered, what did punish with kindness mean? How could punishment be kind? Didn't punishment mean spanking you on your bottom? Or yelling at you and calling you names? Or making sure you couldn't do something you really wanted, like sing in the school pageant or have ice cream?

It wasn't long before I learned what kindness meant. Instead of *you're a nosy bitch*, they'd say, *God sees everything you do and knows when you commit sin*. Instead of spanking you on your bottom, they'd assign you chores, and you'd have to do them all before you ate dinner, no matter how many of them there were. If you were older, like Miss Sheila, you'd have to do penance, which is kneeling in front of an altar and praying and praying and praying. And there was no talk of taking something you wanted away. You *wanted* to do those chores.

You wanted to do your penance. You wanted God and your husband or your father to love you.

The first time I saw Mr. Doug give Miss Sheila penance, she'd had dinner ready late because she was with a lady down the street who was having a crisis with one of her seven kids. Mr. Doug ate the late dinner, and then he said, quietly, "Forty-five minutes." She cleaned up the kitchen, with me helping, and then she went and knelt in front of that altar. She was so still and quiet it seemed like it was nothing at all, but when it was time to get up, Mr. Doug had to help her. She could barely walk, her knees hurt so bad, and then she went right into the kitchen to do more cleaning.

"Are you okay?" I asked her. Mr. Doug hadn't asked, and I knew that was wrong. I didn't understand how he couldn't have asked her if she was all right.

"I'm fine, Honey Cakes," she said. And she had a smile on her face like it was true. "Just my old bones." We finished up with all the dishes, and never once did she quote any scripture or explain to me why she had to do the penance, and that's how I knew it was wrong. Because when she believed in something, she'd tell you. That's how I learned to read the women in Zebulun. They'd always smile and say they were fine, but I could hear what they didn't say, and that brought us together. We were the Citizens bound together against America, and we were women bound together enduring the tyranny of men. And it was all so that someday we'd be in the presence of God, and there'd be no suffering and no tyranny.

The Gospel of the Citizens of the Word said that once you got to the heavens, all souls were equal. When Mr. Brandon or one of the other Elders got up to speak in church on Sunday, they never read from that part of the Gospel. But Miss Sheila read it to us girls in class. She made sure we knew that we were equal, and it was only on Earth that we had to endure, and that someday we'd be rewarded.

9

Eugene

now

My bedroom could be any bedroom. There used to be a twin bed, but now there's a double. The walls have been painted, and the carpet is so new that it's bright white and even has a faint smell coming off it.

The closet used to have wooden doors that always slid off the rail and got stuck, but now it has the kind that fold, and they slide smoothly as I open them to set my duffel bag on the floor. I kneel down, open it, and fish around until I find the drawstring bag. I open it, peek inside, and close it again. I slip it into the side pocket of the bag, and my heart pounds.

My hands shake as I hang my skirts and fold up the American clothes and put them in the chest of drawers. I try to calm my breathing by focusing on the fine dark wood finish. I'm holding a long-sleeved shirt against my chest, standing there staring at the dresser, when I feel someone in the doorway.

"I did that myself," Barron says. "Not the building, just the finishing."

"Thank you," I say without turning around. "It's very nice."

"We got a new mattress a few months ago. Had an old one in here from way back. Saggy in the middle. This one should be nice and comfortable."

"Thank you," I say again.

"Well, I just wanted to see if you need anything. I'm gonna be starting dinner in a couple minutes. Probably cook up some chili. You don't have a problem with beef, do you?"

"No, sir." Chili. My throat tightens. I don't know what to do, so very slowly, I fold the shirt and set it inside a drawer. If I was trying to act normal, I would have turned to face Barron in the first place, but now it almost seems too late. He's a strange man, so I really shouldn't be around him, not in an intimate setting like this. But Mr. Doug was all right to be around, and he wasn't related. So maybe Barron is okay because he's my stepdad. Except Mom didn't really remarry, since there's no divorce under God.

Chili. I wonder if he's going to make it Mom's way?

"Please call me Barron. I don't like that *sir* stuff. My parents used to make me say that to people, and I hated it."

I turn around. "Okay," I say. "It's kind of weird, the way I was raised. It might take some getting used to."

"Sure. Well, I'll leave you be. Your mom wants to come down here, you know. She's trying to give you space."

"I know."

Barron heads down the hall, footsteps muffled by the carpet.

As I turn back toward the chest of drawers, the window jumps into my sight. There are blinds now, new and white and dust-free. I walk over to the window, separate the blinds with two fingers, and look out. The bush I fell into is still there. The yard hasn't changed much at all. There's a strip of grass that slopes down to the sidewalk.

I let the blinds fall closed, and I sit on the bed for a long time. All of a sudden I'm shivering. And I can't sit here or stay in this room alone. Even though they've changed everything, there are still memories here. It's the same room and the same yard and the same street. I'm trying to catch my breath, and this isn't how it's supposed to go. I'm supposed to be able to keep sweet and act calm. Instead I'm succumbing to the weakness of my own body again, and my memories of the past. *It's not good to dwell on the past*, Miss Sheila used to say. Accept the things you cannot change. *For now*, was always the subtext. Accept things until you can change them.

"Alyssa?"

I let out the loudest scream you've ever heard, and I leap off the bed halfway to the ceiling.

Liam screams back, grasping the doorframe.

"Aaah! Liam." I try to calm my breathing. I try to laugh. It comes out in short bursts.

Liam begins laughing. His face turns red and tears run down his cheeks, he laughs so hard. Seeing him laugh like that makes me laugh too, for real. I collapse on the bed with my cheek to the comforter.

"You scared me half to death," I say.

"I'm sup . . . supposed to tell you . . ." Liam tries to catch his breath, but it takes a minute. "Tell you dinner's ready."

"Okay," I say. I'm coming back to my senses. My face is still pressed against the comforter. It's bright white with black flowers on it. The black lines are thin, leaving the impression of delicate lace. It's cool, and it smells like it's just been washed. Part of me wants to lie here and not go out to dinner. I could just sleep and forget about everything. What if there was nothing I was supposed to do, no plan? What if I could just live?

"Are you okay?" Liam's high voice breaks through my thoughts.

"Yeah." I sit up. I follow Liam down the hall. The house isn't big. It's only one story, a ranch house with three bedrooms, and mine is the farthest one back. Across from mine is Mom and Barron's, and then comes Liam's room, which is across from the bathroom. The carpet is soft beneath my feet, and I have the urge to take off my shoes and run around. And only a minute ago I wanted to sleep, and before that I was laughing, and before that I was terrified of what I have to do. Something is happening to my insides. It's like I feel every type of thing at once, and now I'm dizzy, and I realize I do need food, since I haven't had anything to eat since our big breakfast at the diner, and that was hours and hours and hours ago. Not that I haven't gone longer without eating. I've gone days. One time we went almost a week with nothing but crackers.

Barron is using a ladle to scoop chili into bowls as we approach. The table is already set, and Mom is nowhere to be seen. Is Barron really cooking dinner all by himself?

There's a plate of cut vegetables on the counter, so I pick it up and carry it over to the table. It's a simple meal, not hard to make. But it doesn't feel right to me. I turn back to get salt and pepper, or whatever else we need, and I see Liam getting them out of the cupboard. He also grabs the plate of dinner rolls before I can say anything.

Mom comes in through the front door. She washes her hands, and we all sit down at the table.

"Here you go, Alyssa," Barron says, handing me a bowl of steaming chili. He's serving me first out of everyone. It smells delicious. It's exactly like what I remember. This is Mom's recipe all right. He smiles big, and I know she must have told him how much I liked it.

I take the bowl and try to smile back. We all add grated cheese to our chili, and Mom scoops vegetables onto Barron's plate.

"Would you like to say the prayer, Alyssa?" Barron asks.

Mom shoots him a look. She must think I'm going to say something from the Word, something she thinks is crazy. Something about how women are supposed to cook and be served after their menfolk. But I'm not going to be that stupid. I know what I'm supposed to do.

"Okay." I fold my hands and close my eyes. "I want to thank God for this bounty he's set before us," I say.

There's a squeaking coming from my left. Liam must be squirming in his seat. I remember all those times when Dad would give these long prayers and go on and on when Carlo and I were starving.

"And for reuniting me with my late mother and my brother Liam. Amen."

I open my eyes to find my mom staring ahead past Liam, gripping the napkin in her lap.

"Cheers," Barron says. He doesn't seem to notice what I said. He takes a huge bite of chili. A drop of liquid sticks at the corner of his mouth. I can't help it. I dig in too. It's food. That I didn't have to cook. And it's as good as I remember, thick with meat. It's so much better than the chili at the church in Seattle. So different that there's no comparison—I can't believe I ever compared them. I almost feel sorry for what I said in my prayer. I wasn't supposed to say it. But there's that problem with me. I'm willful. Sometimes I just do things.

Finally, Mom picks up her spoon. Her hands are shaking a bit as she lifts the chili to her lips.

I can tell plain as day that she's alive and not my late mother at all. That's what's always hard for me to reconcile. My eyes tell me one truth and the Word tells me another. The way Miss Sheila explained it, the life of a person who leaves the Word is an illusion, and her body is a shell. That means Mom really isn't sitting here at all but is in Hell, and what's eating chili next to me is like a reflection of a spirit. So I see someone eating, but in reality she's screaming in the eternal fires.

I look around at Barron and Liam. Everyone is quiet as they eat, focusing on their food. Are they really dead, too, and I'm the only living person here? I don't like thinking about this because it's hard to make sense of. The world isn't as it appears. There are a multitude of layers you can't see: everything in the heavens, and Hell, and God himself. And also, we're all just sitting here at the dinner table.

I've eaten the entire bowl of chili, and I'm mopping the dregs up with a roll. I've fallen right in with these people, whether they're alive or not.

I need to talk to Carlo. I need to get my head back on straight. I don't know if they ended up arresting him, and I don't know what happened to Dad, if he made bail or not, or where they both are now. I try to look all around the dining room and kitchen area without anyone seeing that I'm doing it. What I'm looking for is a phone. But I don't see one. They must be the kind of people who only have cell phones. Dad never let me have one, and I barely even know how to make a call. But I have to figure it out. I have to reach Carlo and make sure he's okay, make sure I know where Dad is, make sure I know they've started the plan. As long as Carlo is okay, everything will go right. He's not going to falter, and he's not going to fail. Once I talk to him, I won't either.

10

Seattle

age thirteen

You might think living in a tent is terrible, and you could never get used to it. But if you think that, you might never have lived under a bridge with no tent at all. Dad and I only had to live like that for a few weeks before we managed to get a tent some other people left behind. Well, they didn't so much leave it behind as get dragged away from it, since they got arrested for using drugs. As soon as we saw the cops drag those two women away, we jumped on it. Dad didn't even have to tell me. We moved together like we had it all planned out. If we hadn't gone for that tent, someone else would have grabbed it.

We picked up the ends of the tent and shook it out like it was full of money. What came out was lots of junk, like fast-food wrappings and old tin cans and rotten newspapers all wrinkled up. Also a bunch of needles. Dad said using drugs was a sin, but it wasn't the same kind of sin as adultery or murder or stealing from other Citizens of the Word.

There were tiers of sins, he said. Drugs and drinking were the kind that could be redeemed with penance, same as a man losing his temper and going too far in punishing his wife. Those women who got dragged off to jail by the police could be redeemed if they were to accept the Word.

So that's how we got the tent, and we cleaned it up nice so it didn't smell like those women and their McDonald's anymore. After we met Carlo, it was a bit small, but that was okay. It was still a lot better than having no tent.

But there was one thing I worried about, that kept me awake at night, and after Carlo had been with us for almost a year, it finally happened.

Dad and Carlo and I were downtown doing our preaching. Dad was preaching out loud, and Carlo and I were supporting the ministry financially. Dad had his long hair back in a ponytail, which Carlo said made him look more like a man you could listen to. And it worked. People liked the ponytail better than the tangled hair falling around his face, and he'd trimmed his beard, too, so he looked altogether more clean than he had before. After taking Carlo's advice, he looked almost like the man the ladies in Zebulun used to talk to after church, giggling over their potluck casseroles. This day he was talking to an older woman who'd been walking slowly down the street pushing a granny cart full of groceries. I don't think the woman saw Dad at first. She just stopped for breath right in front of him. She carefully pulled a white handkerchief out of her jacket pocket and wiped her brow.

"Feels like summer already, doesn't it?" she said to no one in particular.

"Yes, ma'am," Dad said. He took a step closer. "Would you like to hear about the Word?"

The old lady waved her hand. "I already believe in Jesus, young man. You're preaching to the choir."

"With respect, ma'am," Dad said, "Jesus was a righteous man, but he was just a man. He isn't someone you believe in, strictly. The commandments and all our prescribed actions come from God himself." He held out a pamphlet to her. We'd been out of the official pamphlets for a while, so this one was a photocopy of a photocopy. The picture on the front of Jesus carrying his cross was breaking apart into black spots.

"And I suppose we know what God thinks because he speaks to you," the old lady said. "That's always how it works. Men say God speaks to them, and somehow he's always telling them they deserve things they want."

"I wouldn't say I hear what I want," Dad said with a laugh. "Far from it."

The woman looked at him sharply. "He tell you not to get a real job?"

Carlo stepped closer to me, stifling a laugh. He was slipping some college student's iPhone into his jacket pocket. The student kept on walking, oblivious, his backpack's zipper pocket hanging open. I'd just scored a twenty from a high school girl I pretended to bump into, and I was feeling that rock in the pit of my stomach. I hated stealing from young people the worst. Stealing from a kid was like stealing from a food cart—you were hurting someone who might not have a lot. Whereas stealing from an adult or a store like Target was okay.

They were what Dad called *deep pockets*. The truth was, I didn't like stealing at all.

"She's got a point, huh?" Carlo said, ribbing me with his elbow.

Just then, a police car slid up next to Dad. Carlo and I moved away instinctively, stepping a little ways down the sidewalk.

"You just try reading it," Dad replied with a grin. "Might like what you see."

The woman took the pamphlet and dropped it into one of her shopping bags. "Fine, fine. Good luck to you." She started moving real slow, pushing that cart like it weighed about a thousand pounds.

Two police officers got out of their car. Both were men. One white, one Black. They were the exact same height and both had shiny bald heads. They were like twins except for their skin color. Both with their guns on their waists and the beginnings of smiles on their faces. This was the part where they started asking questions, and everything came down to how Dad responded. Except he didn't see them yet. He was watching the woman. The farther away she got, the more sour Dad's expression became. His fist crunched around those crappy pamphlets.

The Black officer stepped in front of Dad. "How's it going tonight, sir?"

"It's going just fine, Officer," Dad said. His voice was tight.

The old woman was almost to where Carlo and I were standing. We were off the sidewalk, and she was right in the middle of it.

"Ma'am, can we help you with those groceries?" Carlo asked.

"You stay away from me with your sticky fingers," she said.

Carlo laughed. "Well, you got me pegged."

"You should be in school."

"We got a call a little while ago complaining about a theft of an iPad. You know anything about that?" the Black officer asked.

"Of course not."

"You mind if we search this bag here?" That was the white officer.

"Yes, I do," Dad said.

"You're right, ma'am," Carlo said, falling in step next to the woman. I walked next to him on the grass. We couldn't see Dad anymore, only hear him.

"I said, I don't consent to this search!"

Shuffling sounds. The officers' hands were in Dad's clothes and papers. But we had the iPad. We had all the stolen phones. That was because we were minors, and we wouldn't get in as much trouble for it. And also because if Dad got arrested, they'd take his fingerprints and figure out who he was, and they'd take me back.

This was what we'd worried about for all these years. Right here, it might be happening. I tried to stretch my ears out to listen.

"I want to talk to a lawyer. This is an illegal search! I'm going to sue the Seattle PD until cash comes bleeding out those pig snouts!"

"Well, nothing in here to speak of."

"Of course not." Dad's voice began to calm down. He'd realized he'd lost his temper. He was always telling *us* how to act if the cops came by.

"You better go on now," the old lady said. "No sense in them finding out you have the goods." She looked me right in the eyes. She was pretty short, but that still made her taller than me. "These men don't have your best interests at heart. You know that?"

I stared up at her. Dad was still talking to the cops. The talking was quieter now. The cops were doing their *due diligence*, trying to see if he'd say something to *implicate himself*. My blood was pumping so hard I thought it might burst out of my veins. This could be it. This could be when they took me back.

"They won't send you to school, you learn anyway. Okay?"

"Come on, sis." Carlo put one hand on my back, and we started walking faster. I wanted to look behind us, but I didn't. We kept hearing the voices of Dad and the cops. "Yes, I'm alone," I heard Dad say. "Preaching's a lonely business. Have you been blessed to hear the Word?" The old lady's granny cart scraped against the sidewalk.

You learn anyway. Those words reverberated around my skull. My head pounded.

"It's okay, Lisa," Carlo said, circling his arm around me. "I got you. We'll need to lie low for a while, and I've got an idea."

Anyway. Her eyes had been so sure, and she'd been so strong, even though she was old and frail. That lady stood up to Dad and Carlo and wasn't afraid of any of us.

After we'd been going a while, I did look back. She was still moving forward with that cart, inch by inch. Our eyes met, and she nodded at me, and then I turned back, eyes up at Carlo, hoping his idea was a good one.

Turns out it was a whole plan. Carlo had a friend up in Port Angeles who could get him and Dad work under the table. He said we could go there for a while, and there was even a house we could rent. I almost asked why we never did this before, but I knew. Dad wanted to stay in Seattle and preach. He was trying to get back into the good graces of the Citizens of the Word by doing his penance. Not that there was any penance given. We were just plain banished. But he thought he could repent of his bad behavior and recommit, and they'd take him back. *As long as you're not dead, you can repent*, he'd say.

Now I just hoped that with the police looking at Dad, he'd agree we needed to get away for a while. If he didn't agree, and the cops noticed him again . . . I'd stop my thoughts cold when they went that way. I didn't even want to let the pictures into my mind. What if they found me?

Dad finally showed up at our tent a few hours later. It was easy to tell he was filled with rage, although he kept still rather than shouting and carrying on. He slumped his shoulders and pulled his head into his neck.

"Those goddamn pigs," Dad said. "Accusing me of stealing."

"Pigs," Carlo agreed.

"I have to get out of dodge for a while," Dad said. "Just until they forget about me."

"I might have an idea," Carlo said, as if we hadn't already talked about Port Angeles and come up with a whole plan while Dad was gone.

"Oh yeah?"

"Got a friend who can help us hide out," Carlo said. "Won't be forever, but maybe long enough."

"Hmm." Dad rolled his shoulders back. He didn't like the sound of the word *hide*.

Carlo realized his mistake. "Got a way to make some cash," he said. He put a hand on Dad's back, the way men do. It's like a hug but not a soft kind of hug like women give. It's strong. It says *we're in this together, we'll support each other*, but without saying *you need support*.

"Hmm. Well, that would help."

"We can take our time to think about it," Carlo said, giving Dad another clap on the back. This gave Dad the space to breathe, to be the one to make the decision.

A few days later, we were on a Greyhound bus. We had a row to ourselves, me on the left and Dad and Carlo on the right. Dad sat next to the window, and Carlo was across the aisle from me. He was reading the Gospel of the Citizens of the Word. The Bible has the Gospels according to the disciples, and those were basically true, except they attributed miracles to Jesus rather than to God himself. The Gospel of the Citizens reworked everything to show Jesus's humility and how he subjugated himself before God, never believing he could perform miracles himself. Just like all of us have to subjugate ourselves and have humility.

Carlo held the book close up to his face. The way he held that book gave me a good view of the scars on his knuckles and the dirt under his fingernails. He turned those pages faster than anyone I'd ever seen. Dad leaned over and said something to him, and even though they were right across the aisle, I couldn't hear what it was. Carlo turned a page back, and Dad pointed out a line.

I squirmed in my seat. I was thirsty. But I didn't want to interrupt them to ask Carlo for the bottle of water he had in his backpack. I looked out the window, hoping to distract myself, and watched the rows and rows of evergreens roll by.

I hoped that when we got to Port Angeles, we'd be done stealing. Maybe I'd even be able to do some kind of school. I knew how to read, because I'd known already when I was seven, and Miss Sheila taught me even better with the Bible and the Gospel of the Citizens and some other church works and approved books. But I knew there was more out there. I remembered going to the library with my late mother and looking at the books there, even though we weren't allowed to take them home with us like the other kids did.

You learn anyway.

While I was looking out the window, the world looked big. It seemed like the trees went on forever and if I somehow got out and went walking, I could go on forever too.

"Lisa." Dad's voice intruded on my thinking. "What are you doing?"

"It's pretty," I said.

He glared at me, head leaning toward the seat in front of him so he could get a better view of me. "Listen to your tapes."

I took out my little MP3 player and shoved the headphones in my ears. Mr. Brandon's voice boomed out at me, talking about God and Jesus and lots of stuff that was in the book Carlo was reading. I angled myself ever so slightly toward the window, and my mind drifted. I thought about that old lady and how Carlo had laughed when she called him out.

Another time, Dad was doing his preaching on a different corner, and Carlo and I were doing our thing. This was not too long after we met Carlo, so I was hanging back, watching him work. He was showing me how to pretend to accidentally bump into people and laugh and act like it was all fine. A couple hours went by, and I learned a lot. He got a bunch of stuff off people without any trouble. But then, Carlo was going one way, heading toward this guy coming from the other direction on the sidewalk. The guy might have been seventeen or eighteen, and he had a huge backpack and was wearing headphones. *Distracted and full-up* was what Carlo called them: people with lots of stuff who wouldn't notice a little missing weight. Carlo brushed by the guy, said sorry, laughed, and stepped away. I didn't even see him grab anything, and I was watching close.

"Hey, asshole, give that back!" the guy shouted.

"Give what back?" Carlo asked. He stopped laughing.

"I don't know, but you got something." The guy stepped up to Carlo. He was older, but Carlo was bigger.

Bam. Carlo punched the guy in the face. Suddenly they were off the sidewalk and on the ground. Carlo was on top and punching and punching. The guy was screaming, and a couple people started yelling from the sidewalk, and Carlo jumped off and ambled away, leaving the guy there on the ground. The guy sat up and wiped blood out of his eyes with one sleeve.

I stared at him, and he saw me staring.

"Are you okay?" I asked.

"That piece of shit tried to rob me," he said.

I just kept staring. He seemed to be okay, sitting up and everything.

After a couple minutes, he stood up and walked away, too, hiking his backpack up on his shoulders. I'd never seen anything like that before, and I didn't know what to do. I just stood there in my place off the sidewalk and waited until Carlo came back around.

"Sorry you had to see that, sis," he said. "Couldn't let that shit go."

"What did he do?" I asked.

"Accused me of stealing." Carlo sat down, grabbed a water bottle out of his backpack, and poured some over his right knuckles, which were red and raw.

You did steal. But I didn't say it aloud because Carlo wasn't laughing.

"Worst part is, I didn't get anything off him. Whole thing was a waste." He took a long drink of the water.

I couldn't stop staring at the place where the guy had been sitting, wiping the blood off his face. I felt like I couldn't move at all. I was frozen solid.

Carlo looked up at me. "Hey, sis, I scared you, huh? Don't worry, nothing's gonna happen to me." But that wasn't what I was scared of.

"Hey." Carlo slid into the seat next to me.

I jumped.

"Wow, you're really into those tapes. Brought you some water." He handed me a bottle. I knew he'd never hurt *me*, and I told myself that was what mattered. It was supposed to be us against the world, brother and sister. He had always taken care of me. He would always.

"Thank you." I stopped the audio and took a long drink.

He nudged me with an elbow. "Not too much longer. We're gonna have a nice place to live for a change."

"No more, you know?"

He winked at me. "Right. No more funny business."

I leaned into his shoulder, and he put his arm around me. I closed my eyes and tried to picture our new life. A life with a roof and food and money. But I couldn't see it. All I could feel was the warmth of Carlo's shoulder against my face, and all I could hear was the rattling of the bus as it rolled down the road. Dad never would have brought me water. He would have waited until I begged for it. Ever since we met Carlo, things had been better.

I ignored the twisting in my stomach. I steadied my breathing and tried to focus on the good things: Carlo, not being thirsty, heading somewhere better. No more funny business. But I thought about Miss Sheila. I wondered what she was doing, if she missed me.

"Shh, don't cry." He kissed my forehead.

"I'm sorry," I whispered.

"It's okay, he's asleep."

So I cried, and Carlo let me.

11

Eugene

now

I can't do anything until they go to sleep, so after dinner, I sit with the family in front of the TV. They have a giant one that covers a whole wall. Back in Zebulun, most people had TVs, but nobody had cable, and the kids weren't allowed to watch unless an adult was watching something. After we moved to Port Angeles, I knew better than to watch it. Miss Sheila said most TV was like American books, except even worse, because images corrupted you faster and told better lies.

Of course, I still watched some with Becca. I sucked up those day-time talk shows and soap operas, fifteen or thirty minutes at a time. I watched bits and pieces of Netflix dramas like they were bites of food, chomping down as much as my brain could fit in the short time I had. And when I got home, I'd file what I saw away, bury it as deep as I could.

Mom and Barron just have their giant TV out in the open. Liam is lying on the living room floor watching, and no one seems concerned at all. They're watching some kind of comedy show, and I don't understand the humor. I don't like the rush of images and sound coming at me. It doesn't feel safe the way it did when I was with Becca. This isn't the kind of show she'd watch. I try to sit quietly, but really I'm sitting as rigid as a wooden pole. Mom notices and glances over at me. I can tell she wants to say something, but she's trying not to scare me. Maybe she thinks if she says the wrong thing, I'll run away.

Where am I going to go? I want to scream at her.

I'm never going back to living on the streets. I'm never going without a shower or standing in line for food or stealing ever again. Even being here with my late mother is better than that. Here I can keep to my morals and complete my Trial and have a chance. I just have to be strong enough not to be sucked in by all these American things.

"I'm tired," I say. "Is it all right if I go to bed?"

"You never have to ask permission to go to bed, Alyssa," Mom says. "Here, women don't have to ask to do ordinary things." She tries to make eye contact with me, but I look away. So it's Barron's eyes that I meet. One thing women aren't supposed to do is openly challenge men. If Dad or Mr. Doug looked at me like that, I'd drop my eyes and think my retort. But Citizens of the Word aren't supposed to back down from their morals. We aren't supposed to show weakness in the face of challenge. I look right back at Barron. I try to show him that if he thinks I'm some beaten-down victim of oppression because I choose to follow my beliefs, he's dead wrong.

A long, long time passes. Maybe it's only a few seconds.

Barron looks away. I won.

"I wasn't asking permission because I'm a woman," I say. "I was asking permission because the law requires me to be here and placed me under your control. I have to do what you say or there's some punishment, right?"

"No," Mom says. "This is your home, not a jail. Your dad is the only one who'll be punished."

Yeah right, I think. There's no way anything's really going to happen to him. At least not because of something he did to me.

Liam looks up from the TV. "When he kidnapped you, did he put a bag over your head?"

I laugh.

"That's what happens on TV," Liam says, waving at the giant screen.

"It was a kidnapping by the law, not a kidnapping like that," I say. "I went of my own free will because I wanted to."

Mom stares at me, shock on her face.

"I did," I repeat. "I chose to go."

Mom bursts into tears. She bites her lip and breathes deeply like she's trying to stop. But the tears keep running down her face.

I have to take a deep breath. I have to blink. I have to hold myself back. I can't get started crying too. I don't even know why I *would* cry, because what I said was the truth.

Barron hands Mom a Kleenex.

She wipes her eyes. "Alyssa, it was *not* your fault. I hope you understand that. You were only seven years old. We raised you to believe you had to do whatever he said. It was *my* fault."

I don't know what to say to that. She did teach me to do whatever Dad said. I don't remember her ever saying anything different, even after she left him. But that's not why it was her fault. She should have been there in the window when I turned back. She should have stood up and looked. I was waiting for her to look.

"I should have known he'd pull something like that. I should have realized you were acting strangely that night." She balls the Kleenex up in her fist.

"It's not your fault either, Lynn," Barron says. "I should have been there for you. I never should have let Art scare me away. I was such a coward." He pulls her closer, and there are tears in his eyes too. I never realized Dad did anything to scare Barron, but it doesn't surprise me. I saw for myself how mad he was.

"Everyone thinks it's their fault," Liam says. "But it's not mine because I was only a baby."

I focus on him so I don't have to watch Mom crying. "I bet you don't remember," I say, "but I said goodbye to you. I had it in my head that I'd come back for you."

Mom sucks in a breath.

"I thought you both would be coming to Zebulun with us later. I didn't really understand."

"Oh, honey." Mom wipes her eyes again.

"Was it fun there?" Liam asks.

"No, it was not fun there," Mom says. She manages to give me a sharp look through her tears. But she just promised me no punishment.

"Well, some stuff was fun," I say. "I got to raise chickens and milk cows. We had a big telescope, so I got to look at Saturn. And the moon."

"Please not the stuff about the people on the moon," Mom says.

"What?" Liam sits up.

"According to scripture, those who have died or are spiritual beings with righteousness spend eternity in the firmament, which is the heavens, and—"

"Alyssa, give your mom a break," Barron says.

"Okay." Mom does look like she needs a break, and I don't want her to cry anymore. "Point being, Liam, Zebulun *does* have some fun stuff." I almost tell him that he can come visit when I finally go home, but I'm not sure if he can or not. I'm not sure if he's dead because of how he was born or if he has a chance because he was innocent. I wish I had something to read that would tell me. Except that a lot of things I've read have told me two different things. Like the moon being barren and the moon having people living there.

"I know you wanted to go to bed," Mom says. "Just before you go, will you please let me say this. You are not responsible for going with your dad. You were a child. He's responsible. He kidnapped you. And you just said you didn't realize we wouldn't come with you. You didn't know what you were doing. Please tell me you understand that."

"I do," I say. "Goodnight." I get up and head for my bedroom. I walk there as fast as I can. I can still hear the people talking on the TV, but I don't hear if Mom's crying again. I don't know what to feel. She didn't know I was watching for her. She couldn't have known. And I did know what I was doing, mostly. I chose to climb out that window. He didn't put a bag over my head. And if he had, that would have been his right, because I was his daughter. I didn't say I went of my own free will because I felt guilty; I said it because it was true. But she thinks I feel guilty and that I shouldn't. She thinks it wasn't my fault.

But how can my choice not be my fault? I wonder if there's an age when you're innocent, and then there's an age where suddenly you become responsible, and how old it is. The Gospel of the Citizens doesn't say anything about age, although Miss Sheila did once. Could I have not gone with Dad and not been responsible for that?

I shake my head. I need to talk to the one person who understands, the one person who can put me back on the right track. I need to talk to Carlo. He's the one who's always there for me, no matter what. He's the one who can help me figure out what to do and how to be until my Trial is complete.

I mean to stay awake, but I fall asleep. I dream that I'm lying under that bridge with no tent at all and no blanket, shivering. I smell urine. I wake up shivering. I'm lying on top of the blanket, and the temperature in the house has dropped. I don't really smell urine though. That was all in my head. I was dreaming about Seattle, when I had no bed and not even a tent.

I half climb, half fall off the bed in the dark. The little alarm clock says 3:13 in big red lights.

As quietly as I can, I open the bedroom door and slip out into the hallway. There's some light coming in the living room and kitchen windows. I pad down the hall and into the living room. I kneel next to the coffee table and start picking up magazines, pushing old ones aside. Nothing. I head over to the kitchen. There's a bowl in the sink with a spoon in it. Stuck to the spoon and the inside of the bowl are remnants of little brown nuggets—Grape-Nuts—mixed with yogurt. My mind flashes to being a little kid, to sitting at the table in the morning with Mom. She'd be eating her Grape-Nuts with yogurt, and I'd be eating Corn Flakes. The milk would sit on the table in between us, along with a bowl of sugar. I'd use as much sugar as she'd let me.

I remember this scene as clearly as if it were happening now, and I stare at the bowl for a long time. So Mom still eats Grape-Nuts, just like she did when she was alive. She must have had them after I went to bed. Maybe she was standing here in the dark just a few minutes ago.

I shake off the memories and continue searching the counter, and I see it: a phone plugged into an outlet. I shake it and press the screen, but it won't unlock. There aren't any other phones on the counter. I don't find anything else, even though I spend a half hour looking.

I pad back down the hallway and stop at the first bedroom. Carefully, I turn the knob and push the door open. There's a creak, which makes me cringe, and I peek my head in. Liam is fast asleep, lying on his back in the middle of his bed. His arms are wide open like he's making a snow angel. Next to his left hand is a phone.

I whisper a prayer to myself and tiptoe closer. I reach down and swipe the phone from the bed. Holding my breath, I tiptoe back out. I'm back in the living room before I dare to breathe normally. I whisper one more prayer and touch the screen.

It opens. I almost laugh. *Thank you, thank you, thank you,* I think, looking up.

I dial the number, and it rings. One. Two. Three.

"Hola."

"Carlo?"

"Lisa, is that you?"

"Yes." I'm whispering, and I move farther into the living room. I slide into the corner, as far from where anyone is sleeping as I can get.

"Thank God. Where are you?"

"I'm in Eugene with my mom. I'm fine. They're being nice to me. Where are *you*?"

"They asked me a bunch of questions, but they let me go. So I'm back at our house. Dad is here too. I'd wake him up, but he'll be in big trouble if he talks to you. Part of his release is he can't have any contact."

"I know that. It's okay."

Carlo sighs. "Sis, this is our challenge, right? This is our Trial."

"Yeah." I sit down on the floor. The Gospel of the Citizens of the Word says each Citizen will go through a Trial. You don't get any warning of it, but you know it's there when your time comes. How you pass through your Trial determines your future. If you handle it admirably, you take your place as a full Citizen. After you die, you'll take your place at God's table with Jesus and the disciples and all the other Citizens. But if you fail, you could be cast out. You could be set adrift in America. You could be set to wandering the heavens, not damned but never experiencing paradise. You could end up alone forever.

"We'll be together again soon, Lisa," Carlo says.

"I feel so far away."

"I'm right here. Nobody's gonna separate us."

I cling to Liam's phone and close my eyes. I try to imagine that

88

I'm there, that we're sitting at our old card table together playing five-card stud for beans. Just us and not Dad. It could be like that.

"It's going to be hard for a while."

"I know."

"The law is stacked against Dad. He'll never be treated right in America."

"Of course not."

"I have to get a new phone number. Can I call you here?" he asks. "When the Trial begins?"

"I don't know. It's my . . . Liam's phone. He's only nine."

"Okay. How 'bout this? I'll call and hang up right away. So the call will be in the log. And you call back when you can get the phone."

"Yes. I can do that." Hope surges through me. I *can* do that. I can do this.

"Lisa, you hang in there. You're strong. Dad and I both know you can do your part. It's us who'll struggle, but not you. You never waver."

I think about going over to Becca's, and how Carlo knew but never told on me. That was wavering, for both of us. That was turning our back on the Word by defying our father. What if I started down that path, and now I can't get back on the right one, now when it matters more than ever before? What if my sin can't be undone? What if I wish I could have both: everything at Becca's and going home? What if I'm not sorry I did any of it?

What if it really isn't my fault?

"You still there?" he asks.

"Yes. I'm just scared."

"Fear makes us sharp. Fear helps us choose right. When the Trial begins, your fear will support you."

I nod. The hand that grips the phone is sweating.

"We love you, Lisa. You won't be there for long. You can get through this."

"I love you too."

"Okay, I have to go now. I'll be in touch when I can."

Tell Dad, I almost start to say. But tell Dad what? That I'm sorry? That I sinned? That I'm going to do what he asks of me? None of that is true, and all of it is. My heart races. My hands sweat. "Bye," I choke out.

Carlo ends the call. I think. All I know for sure is that the call ends, and I'm staring down at Liam's phone, glowing in the dim light coming through the window. I set it down on the carpet and pull my knees into my chest.

They let Dad out of jail, I think. Just like I knew they would. Didn't we make a plan assuming just this course of events? Except a plan is different from reality. Doing something is different than preparing for it. A Trial, when it comes, will define your life and everything that comes after. My heart races even faster, and now it's not just my hands that are sweating. The temperature inside the house has dropped with the night, but I feel like it's the middle of the day with the sun beating down on my bare limbs. It feels like the heat from Hell. Maybe this is a preview of what's to come.

I'm afraid, and I don't feel like it makes me sharp. What it does is stop me from moving. I sit there on the living room floor and press my

face into my knees. I want to pray, but my mind won't make appropriate words. Wordlessly, I ask for strength. I ask for a way out or a way
through, and I'm not sure which. I ask for God to protect Carlo. I stop
praying, and I just sit and let the night pass. Everything is happening
the way Dad planned. Every time it seems like he might not get his
way, God turns things back. I'm not supposed to ask questions when
it comes to him.

My attempt to change things just made them worse.

I lean against the edge of the big recliner in the corner and try
to imagine that it's Carlo's shoulder, that we're back on that bus and
none of this has happened yet. I never met Becca, and I didn't know
as much about American things. I never wanted what I couldn't have.
I never read books that said the opposite of the Word.

I curl into a ball on the floor. I imagine that we're just arriving in
Port Angeles, and everything is getting better.

12

Port Angeles

age thirteen

It was nighttime when we moved into the house in Port Angeles. From the outside, it looked like it was going to fall down any second. The roof was sunken. The paint was almost all gone. The windows were boarded over. But if you think I was upset to see that crappy little condemned house, then you've probably never lived in a tent. We'd walked about an hour from the bus stop, and I was exhausted, and I was starving, but when Carlo said, "This is it," and we all saw those boarded-up windows, I began to run.

I opened that front door and ran inside and spun around like I was a princess being gifted with a brand-new castle. My long skirt twirled and got twisted around my ankles, and I tripped on it and almost fell.

"Careful there!" Carlo called out, laughing.

"I bet it's got a shower!" I cried, and I ran down the hallway. Sure enough, that faucet worked. Water came spitting out of the spout, and it was hot too! I knelt by the tub and let the hot water run over my hand.

Carlo turned on the light behind me.

I looked up at him. "I never even thought about the light!" We just looked at each other, big grins on our faces, listening to that water run.

Carlo set my bag down. "Take your time, sis. I'll see if there's any food."

My stomach growled, but nothing was going to get in the way of my shower. As soon as Carlo left, I stripped off those old clothes. It had to have been a few weeks since I'd had a shower. They let us use the one at the church where they had the food handout, but Dad didn't want us using it too much, drawing attention to ourselves. So we used it when things got real bad. By that time, real bad was weeks and weeks.

I washed myself as best I could considering that there was no soap. I let the water get so hot it turned my whole body red. I had to dry myself with my one old towel that hadn't been washed maybe ever, but that was okay. Because I was a lot cleaner than I'd been before. Dad had decided to hold off on preaching for a while and lie low, so we could stop worrying about getting hassled by the law. I could stop worrying for a minute about being taken away.

I stepped out of the bathroom, and I heard Dad and Carlo talking. There I was, eavesdropping again. But it just happened. It wasn't like I planned it.

"They won't check your ID or nothin'," Carlo said. "That's the deal if you work the night shift. I can work during the day. So Lisa won't have to go out and we can be here with her."

Dad muttered something, so quietly I couldn't hear.

"Art, you know you and Lisa are my family now. Ain't no favor."

"I know that, son," Dad said. "Why don't you stop calling me Art? You're my son."

I stepped into the living room in time to see them embracing each other on that old ripped-up couch. The whole room smelled like cat piss. I'd noticed it coming in, but it seemed even stronger now. There was an aura of cigarette smoke, too, floating around everything. It still smelled better than that homeless camp though.

They came out of the embrace with Dad's hand clamped on Carlo's shoulder. Both of them were choked up, looking like they couldn't speak.

"Lisa!" Dad said. "Come on out. Did you hear that?"

"No, sir."

"Well, we just talked about how we feel about each other, how we feel like we're father and son." He pointed at me. "Get the book." His hand was still on Carlo's shoulder. "You know which part I mean, son?"

"Yes, sir," Carlo said. He wiped something from his eye.

I ran for Carlo's bag, which was sitting right inside the door. My hands shook as I pulled out the Gospel of the Citizens of the Word. This was serious. I should have expected it, since we'd all been together for about a year now. But still. *Still.* I brought the book back to where they were sitting. The living room was empty except for that old couch. There was just one lamp on, so the light was low. The house had thick once-white carpet. Even in the dim light, I could see that it was stained with old cigarette juice.

Dad took the book from me and flipped through the back pages until he found the right one. "Are you ready, son?"

"Yes, sir," Carlo said. He stood up and ran his hand through his hair. He still stunk like he hadn't showered in weeks, but something changed about the way he looked right then. There was a transformation. He seemed suddenly older, cleaner, more serious.

"Lisa, you'll have to bear witness," Dad said.

I nodded and took a few steps to the side. I clasped my hands in front of my skirt.

"These are the provisions of the Rite of Adoption. Let those who enter into this covenant hear: This is a solemn covenant that cannot be undone. By these words shall the relationship of parent and child be created, and those who God has joined together, let no earthly authority rend. No man may abandon his son, nor no son disobey his father. As if from birth and unto death, this child and this man will be as if from one blood. You stand and face me." Dad made sure he was standing right in front of Carlo. Carlo stood up straight, facing Dad. Dad was the taller one, but not by much. The light coming through the lampshade tinged his beard orange. Carlo's buzzed head glinted sweat.

"Do you, Carlo Estevez, consent to becoming as a son of my blood?"

Carlo's breath came haltingly. "Yes."

"Do you freely enter into this covenant with no doubts in your heart?"

"Yes."

Dad took a deep breath. He sniffed and blinked his eyes, then turned the page. "I, Arthur DeAndreis, do with these words make you my son."

Carlo put his head in his hands.

"From this day forward, you will be as my blood, and my blood will be your blood. We, together, entreat you, our God, to bind us to this promise we make tonight. We beg you to protect this covenant and allow no breaches, upon penalty of your disfavor. With the connecting of our hands, we hereby complete our covenant and seal our bond." With shaking hands, Dad set the book on the couch. He held out his right hand to Carlo.

Carlo wiped tears away. After a few seconds, he looked up at Dad and held out his hand. Their hands clasped together, and the sound wasn't loud, but I felt the impact. It was as if two cymbals had slammed together, their clash reverberating through the house. They stood there like that for a few long seconds, clasping hands, speaking to each other with their eyes. Dad pulled Carlo in, and they hugged. I'd never seen them hug like that. It wasn't like what they'd been doing on the couch just a few minutes before. I'd never seen two men hug like that at all, and they were both crying too. I'd never seen anything like that in my life.

Nothing had changed, not really. Carlo was already part of our family. But in the eyes of God, everything had changed now. Dad and Carlo owed each other the fealty of father and son. Carlo and I were brother and sister now as surely as if we had the same mother. If I acted out, it would be against both of them, and they were both given power over me. And now, we could never be separated, not in the eyes of God. The family was inviolate, was everything you had and everything you owed.

Carlo will never leave us, I thought. I found myself crying too.

I never realized how much I feared he would, once he realized how hard it was to be part of the Word. I was sure, somewhere deep inside, that he'd run off and leave me alone with Dad again. But now that was never going to happen.

"Lisa, there's some canned food in the cupboards," Dad said. "Go ahead and heat something up for us."

"Yes, sir." I shuffled over to the kitchen to make us a middle-of-the-night dinner. As I was emptying the canned soup into an old pot, I heard them whispering. They must have been speaking about something that was just for men. There were a lot of things like that in the Word. Mysteries only men were supposed to know. And there was nobody more important in the Word than your father.

As I stirred that soup, I thought about the night Carlo told us about how he got those scars on his face and on his knuckles.

We'd been sitting in the tent. It was dark except for the light coming through from the streetlight. It was enough light to see by, with the window flap open. All three of us were playing poker, seven-card draw. Since it wasn't real money, gambling was okay. We'd passed those beans around and around between us. It was Carlo's deal, and his practiced hands dealt out our cards, one to me, one to Dad, one to himself. Maybe it was the angle of the light coming in through the window. Maybe it was the way he was dealing. But something drew the eyes to those scarred knuckles.

"You want to tell us about that fight, son?" Dad asked.

"Not much to tell," Carlo said. He kept on dealing. One to me, one to Dad, one to himself.

"That's all right, you don't want to tell us."

One to me, one to Dad, one to himself. Those knuckles glowed in the light almost like they had a halo. It wasn't lost on Dad, that's for sure.

"Got robbed," Carlo said. "Didn't have the money. My dad grabbed me by the throat, slammed me against the wall." One to me, one to Dad, one to himself. "He got a few punches in, then I fought back." He was done dealing, picked up his cards. "I know what you say about obeying your father."

Suddenly the sound of my late mother screaming leapt into my head, the words *I'm pregnant* singing through the house. I froze, my cards all spread out in my hands.

"Wasn't your fault you got robbed, was it?" Dad asked.

"No, sir. There were three of them."

"A father's punishment has to be just," Dad said.

Dad calling her a whore. The sound of a slap against hard skin.

"He ain't my dad no more," Carlo said.

Dad nodded. Carlo nodded back. Some perfect understanding passed between them.

My hands jittered, and my cards spilled all over the ground. "Sorry," I blurted. "Sorry." I raced to gather all the cards up.

"Lisa?"

I jumped, splattering soup over the side of the pan.

Dad was standing behind me, close. He was peering over my shoulder into the soup.

Why did that memory have to keep coming in? Why couldn't I stop thinking about her? All those times he'd gone off and beaten her, leaving her with bruises all over her face, she'd done something against the Word. As long as I didn't do anything against the Word, I'd be safe. But what he did to my late mother was even worse than Mr. Doug giving Miss Sheila penance. It was his right, but it was dead wrong.

My memories were all jumbled. Carlo and his knuckles. Carlo beating up that guy. My late mother screaming. The smell of cat piss in the kitchen and the smell of human piss back in the tent. I felt like everything was happening at once.

"You lost your voice, girl?"

"No, sir. It's almost hot. I'm sorry." *You could cook your own meal,* I thought. *Or are you too stupid to use a can opener?* Where did those thoughts come from? Out of nowhere, out of my willfulness. But I clung to them. I thought them over and over. *You could cook your own meal. You could.* Just inside my own head and nowhere else.

Dad moved away from me, headed back for the living room.

I scrambled through the cupboards, looking for bowls. There were three of them, and they looked almost clean too. I dished out soup into three portions.

I wanted to go back to dancing through this amazing house, this roof over our heads with hot water and lights in it, but now all those thoughts were running through my head. Something about that ritual had brought them back.

Dad and Carlo came into the kitchen, sat at the unstable old card table that was there. I set the bowls in front of them, and we all sat down. We all folded our hands and closed our eyes.

"We give thanks to God for this bounty he's set before us," Dad said.

"Amen," Carlo and I intoned.

My hand shook as I gripped the spoon. Dad and Carlo were eating normally, calm as anything. No one was angry. No one was yelling. No one was getting ready to punch anybody in the face or drag them by their hair down the hallway while they screamed about the baby in their belly. That was so far from anything that could happen, it was ridiculous to even think about.

I slurped my soup, steadied my hand.

As long as I obeyed and did what was right, I'd be safe. Carlo would protect me. Dad wouldn't hurt me. I just had to pretend to be a good daughter, a good sister, a good woman. I had nothing to be scared of, I reasoned. But what if I couldn't keep it up? I didn't have Miss Sheila and the other women to keep faith with. I was on my own here, being a good woman on the outside and thinking what I wanted inside my head. Even though I didn't like living in a tent, Seattle had been something different. Now that we were in a house again, all the expectations were falling right back into place.

"This is a good night for us," Dad said. A smile spread wide across his face. "I've gained a son, and I have my beautiful daughter."

I looked down at my soup bowl modestly.

"I'm going to get in touch with Doug," Dad said. "Lisa needs to get back into Sheila's class. It's not good for her to be here idle."

"How's she going to do that from here?" Carlo asked.

"Sheila did some lessons by computer for families who lived elsewhere. She can do that for Lisa. It's the least she could do for our good girl."

"What do you think, Lisa?" Carlo asked.

"It's a good idea," I said. I hadn't had a chance to think about what I was going to do. I couldn't have imagined Dad would send me to regular school. That would have been too much to hope for. Some memories of my old elementary school burst in, along with some memories of Miss Sheila. And still my late mother screaming. "May I be excused?" I asked. "I can wash these up tomorrow. I'm really tired."

"Go on, then," Dad said.

I got up from the table and shuffled across the living room floor. I grabbed my sleeping bag from our pile of things and dragged it into one of the bedrooms. I lay down, but all those memories at once ran around like mice scurrying through my brain cells. All these things that had happened—and the smell of the cat piss—kept me awake.

13

Eugene

now

I can't get back to sleep, so after tossing and turning for a few hours, I get up early and start cooking breakfast for the family. It's something for me to do, and I have to keep busy. It won't stop my brain from racing, but maybe it will stop all my memories from flashing around and mixing together and turning to soup.

I'm thinking about what to make. Eggs, maybe, if they have them, or pancakes, or peanut butter sandwiches. I know sandwiches aren't strictly a breakfast food, but a lot of times they were what we had. *Maybe Liam would like them*, I think. But when I open the refrigerator door, the whole idea spins away. My jaw drops.

They have eggs—two dozen of them. Chicken breasts wrapped in plastic. A drawer full of lunch meat. Bacon *and* sausage. A bag of apples. Mini oranges. Broccoli, asparagus, carrots. Yogurt, milk, cheese. I close the refrigerator and open the pantry cupboard.

Canned soups, yes, but also bread, cereal, oatmeal, jam, peanut butter, crackers, chips, pretzels. Fruit snacks and chocolate chips. Canned tuna fish and canned salmon. Flour, oil, and sugar that I could make pancakes with, but also pre-packaged pancake and waffle mix. There's so much food in this house that we could all eat for weeks.

I'm holding the pancake mix in both hands, staring at the largess in the cupboard, when Mom comes into the kitchen. She's wearing a fluffy dark blue bathrobe and slippers with silly bunny heads.

"You like that one?" Mom asks.

I look down at the package. "I don't know." It's not the cheapest brand they sell, so I've never had a package of it in my hands before. My stomach rumbles. And I ate an entire bowl of chili just last night.

Mom takes the package from me and shakes it. "Doesn't seem like there's enough for all of us. You want to help me make some from scratch?" She returns the package to the cupboard and starts pulling out ingredients.

"Okay."

"You know how to make bacon?"

"Yes, ma'am." I take the package of bacon out of the refrigerator.

Mom winces, but she doesn't correct me. She starts putting things together, not even looking at any recipe. I dig into the cupboard next to the stove and find a pan.

"Did you have trouble sleeping?" she asks. "If that bed's not comfortable, we can get you a new one. I had the twin in there for a long time waiting for you, and then I thought you'd want a bigger one, so

I took a full bed that my friend was giving away, but the mattress was kind of crappy, so—"

"The bed is fine," I say. "It's just a little weird being back." I open the package of bacon, begin placing the pieces in the pan.

"I don't want to push you," Mom says. "I just want you to know that your dad probably didn't tell you the truth about a lot of things. I need you to know that right now, in case you think you want to go back to him. In case he told you I'm some kind of monster."

"He didn't say that." I keep stuffing the meat into the pan, piece after piece.

"I know how it is," she says. Her back is to me, and I'm glad for that. I don't want to see her eyes. I don't want to see if she's crying again. "I know he told you I was dead and you'd go to Hell, too, if you stayed with me." Her spoon clatters against the bowl as she stirs the mix.

I can't tell her she's right, because it would hurt her too much. She's stirring that mix like it's the cause of all her problems.

"I'm grateful for the roof over my head," I say. "And all this food." That's something true, at least. You've got to find a way to say something true. That's how you connect with people, how you get by.

"There's a social worker coming today," Mom says. "He's going to check in on us, see if we need anything. We need to get you an assessment to see what grade you should be in for the school year."

"I have a school. Miss Sheila teaches it. All I need is a computer."

"Sheila of Sheila and Doug?"

"Yeah. We lived with them."

"She was one of the good ones. Really welcomed me. She was part of why I thought, this group isn't so bad. They were all about family, community, working hard and being self-sufficient."

"But." I turn on the stove. Almost immediately, the bacon begins to sizzle.

Mom reaches below the counter and pulls out a plug-in pancake griddle. She sets it on the counter. I'll bet that pancake batter is as smooth as milk. She stirred it too much. "But they wanted me to obey my husband and stay with him no matter what he did. And he beat me, and they knew it. That's what family really meant—letting the man do whatever he wants."

"That's not true." I open a drawer looking for something to flip the bacon with. "They say you can't hurt a woman. They say you punish with kindness, not anger."

"Oh sure, they say that. And then what happens when you want to leave? You get a lecture on obeying your husband. You're supposed to forgive him. Even if you're bruised and bleeding."

"You committed adultery," I say. I try to flip the bacon but end up folding it over. I try again. Again, it flops in the pan all folded up. This is ridiculous. I know how to cook bacon.

"You think that was the first time he hit me?"

I don't say anything. I know it wasn't. And I know it was wrong for him to hit her. But she did something wrong too. She can't deny that. She's acting like everything she did was right, and like Miss Sheila and Mr. Doug wanted him to hit her, which they didn't. They're my grandparents. They were there for me when she wasn't.

"You think adultery is the worst thing there is? Barron was my way to get away from your dad. He saved my life."

Barron clears his throat. "I'm sorry. I smelled bacon."

I try to flip the bacon again, and now it's all wrapped up in a ball.

"Let me get that," he says, taking the spatula from my hand. "Why don't you see if the paper's out there?"

I stomp away from the kitchen and fling open the front door. Sure enough, there's a newspaper all rolled up on the steps. I sit down next to it. The door is still open a crack, so I can hear what they're saying, my mom and the man she committed adultery with.

"She's fucking brainwashed," my mom says.

"It's been one day," Barron replies. "She needs time to adjust."

"He took my daughter and sent me back a subservient Barbie-bot. She cooks and cleans and probably doesn't even know how to read." There's a loud clank, as if she's slammed something against the counter. "And she's so *sure* she's right. That's the worst part. She thinks he was right to beat the shit out of me."

"I know how to read," I say, storming back in. I slam the door behind me. "I went to school."

"How old is the Earth, then, according to Sheila?" Mom says.

"Six thousand years."

Mom turns to Barron, who's flipping pancakes, and rolls her eyes.

"I know that because I read a book about it," I say. "Because I'm not stupid like you think I am." I also read part of a book that said a whole different thing, that talked about the big bang and billions of years and evolution and all that stuff. But that book came from Becca's house, where I never went, and so what I read there, I didn't read.

There are things that happened and things that didn't happen.

"You're not going back to that woman's school," Mom says. "You're going to real school even if you have to start in second grade where you left off."

I storm through the kitchen and throw the paper down on the dining room table. I don't know where to go from here, so I just stand facing away from them. I think about Miss Sheila's school, and the library, and the books at Becca's house, and reading, and algebra. All the things I *did* read and *didn't*.

It's all in my brain whether it's supposed to be there or not. I know all of it. Just like I know she didn't deserve to get beat up no matter what she did, and I didn't deserve it either. But also, we did. I wasn't supposed to go next door.

"Maybe we can just have breakfast now and work out the school situation later," Barron says. Hesitantly, he sets the plate of bacon down next to me. It smells good, mouthwatering. I'm as hungry as if I didn't eat at all yesterday. Carefully, I sit down in the nearest chair. I try to stop my hands from shaking. I want to throw something or scream. I want to yell that I don't know if the Earth is six thousand years old or billions. Why can't both things be true, just like a man can't hit a woman, and yet he can? Like my mother is dead but also alive, walking over to the table with a plate of pancakes.

"I'm sorry, Alyssa," she says, sitting down. "I lost my temper. I was frustrated, and it was wrong of me." Her eyes are wet, and she doesn't sound like she's really sorry, but somehow, that makes it better.

Because I'm not sorry either. I never asked to be here. Here is just where I have to stop on my way home.

"Liam, breakfast!" Barron calls down the hallway.

I pick up two pancakes and set them on my plate. Then I take two strips of bacon, and then a third, because we made plenty for all of us. My stomach is all tied up in knots, but that won't prevent me from eating. I don't know if anything will ever stop me from being hungry.

Liam comes hopping out. He's wearing the same bunny slippers as Mom, only smaller, and pajamas with little Boston terriers on them. He sits down next to me, picks up a piece of bacon, and shoves it right in his mouth.

"Half your terriers are upside down," I say.

"They're inverted," he says.

"Oh really, *inverted*, what does that mean?" I ask.

"It means UPSIDE DOWN!" he yells, taking a stack of three pancakes.

Mom laughs and wipes a tear from her eye.

"Well, I like them that way," I say. I pick up the bottle of syrup, Real Maple Syrup, the bottle says, and dribble some of it over my pancakes. In our house, syrup, even the fake kind, was like gold. There was never enough of it. We were always out. I set the bottle down, and then I cut through the pancakes with my fork.

"Mom said when I'm twelve we can get a dog."

"I said, we'll see when you're twelve," Mom says.

I take a bite. It's amazing. I never knew what real maple syrup tasted like.

Loud music starts playing. I almost choke on the bite, I jump so high out of my seat.

"Hello?" Mom is holding a phone. Where did that come from? She must have had it in the pocket of her robe. "Yes, 10:00 a.m. will be fine. Is there anything we need to do? Okay, we'll be here. Thank you." Mom hangs up. "That was the social worker," she says. "He'll be coming at ten."

"Why?" Liam asks.

"To make sure Mom's not torturing me," I say.

"To help Alyssa get settled," Mom says at the same time.

I look up at the clock. It's 8:10 a.m. now. I do some calculations in my head. I try to figure out where Dad and Carlo will be when I'm talking to this social worker. I take a bite of bacon, and I try to enjoy it. I won't be here long in this place with all these cupboards full of food. This can't be my real life. I can't think about the books at Becca's house. It's like there are two whole different universes, and I have to pick one of them to be true. But I can't pick because I'm living in both. I'm here, and I'm back in Port Angeles, and also I'm home in Zebulun with Miss Sheila, and she's the one I cooked with, not Mom.

And I'm back in the hospital, four months ago, lying in that bed with my head spinning. Carlo's voice, a male doctor speaking low, *concussion*. A woman: *Did anyone hurt you?*

"Yes," I said.

"Can you tell me what happened?"

"No," I said.

She stared at me.

"I don't remember."

I never found out what Dad told them. There are lots of ways kids can get hurt. Lots of accidents that can happen. The men decided which lie they would tell, but any lie you tell to Americans is all right.

I'm sitting at the table finishing my breakfast, thinking about lying and telling the truth, and which truth to tell and which to believe. It's all too many things at once, and so I have to focus on the moment. My eyes are drawn to Liam, who's now playing with a small piece of pancake, pushing it around his plate in the pool of syrup.

"Vroom vroom!" he says.

I grab a piece of pancake from my plate and smoosh it into his syrup, rushing for his pancake. "Vroom vroom!"

"Vroom, I got you!" He smashes his finger-pancake against mine.

"Oh no, you got me!" I drop my finger like it's hurt. I wriggle it around like it's dying.

Liam laughs.

I scoop up my piece of pancake with my resurrected finger and slip it into my mouth.

"Do you want some coffee, Alyssa?" Barron asks, standing.

"No, sir. Thank you."

Liam gets up from the table, picks up his plate, runs to the sink, and begins rinsing it off.

"He's a great kid," I say.

Mom smiles. "Yeah, he is." She takes a long drink of milk. I notice that they're all drinking milk except for me. I never wanted to drink it since we left Zebulun and the cows. I get up to grab myself some water. The scent of bacon is still strong, permeating everything. Now Barron's coffee is bubbling into the pot.

Liam's footsteps pound the carpet as he runs down the hall.

My head is feeling clear again. It took a little while after the concussion. It was hard to concentrate at first. Now, as I take a sip of water, I focus on what's coming next: the social worker, some kind of test, acting normal. Waiting and watching. I think about milk: the kind they drink and the kind straight from the cow. How one is better than the other, and you'd never know unless you tried both.

14
Port Angeles
age fourteen

I started slipping over to Becca's house while Dad was sleeping or away. He did sleep heavily, so I might have had several hours, but I never felt safe enough for that. I'd go for a few minutes, a half hour, a little more. We'd play a game of badminton, and then I'd run back. Or we'd watch a half hour of TV. Or we'd hang out in her room.

Becca had books in her room, and I'd look at them, and I knew I wasn't supposed to read them. But I also wasn't supposed to even be there. One day, I picked up one of the books. It was a novel, and there was a picture on the cover of a girl with a sword. I'd never seen anything like it before. I opened it, and the words swam. I knew I wasn't supposed to look, and so I couldn't. It was like when you read in a dream, when nothing makes sense.

"You can borrow it," Becca said. She was lying on her bed, head propped on one hand.

I shook my head.

"Have you been to the library?"

"I'm not allowed to read books."

She stared at me. "Like, any books?"

American books, I thought. But I didn't say that. She wouldn't have understood. "Non-religious books."

She sat up. "You can read them here."

I stared at the book cover. It was something different. Something that didn't come in a badly photocopied packet. Something that wasn't about God and all the things I couldn't do.

"We could go to the library, and whatever you get, I can keep it for you."

"I can't be gone very long."

"It's only a fifteen-minute walk. You've really never been there?"

"When I was a little kid," I said. *In Eugene.* But I didn't say that part. I couldn't tell her too much. Not that she'd figure out who I was. But still.

I knew if Dad found out I'd be in huge trouble, but I couldn't help it. My school was so boring, I was desperate for something, anything else, to enter my brain. We only had this ancient iMac that Carlo brought home from who knows where. It was so old that you couldn't even play video. So I never actually saw Miss Sheila or the other girls. I just heard their voices. Also, even though I was allowed to be in the class, I wasn't allowed to speak because we were banished. And Miss Sheila never spoke to me. All I could do was listen to her and read those stacks of approved printouts.

So the next week, when Dad was sleeping and Carlo was at work, I met Becca outside our houses, and we started to walk.

We got a block away, and I looked behind me. Our house was silent. Dad was still asleep. But he could wake up any minute and find me not just next door, but gone. If he found out about this, it would be so much worse. So I worked on my story in my head, what you have to say in case the men ask, the lie you always have to be ready with.

We were all out of eggs, and I knew you'd want eggs for your breakfast, so I went for a walk to the 7-Eleven.

It was true that we were out of eggs, and there was a 7-Eleven only a few blocks out of our way. I could actually get the eggs on the way back, and then it would be true. Except that if he didn't wake up, and there was no need for an excuse, then I'd have to explain how I got the eggs. And it was a good excuse as far as hiding the other truth about the library, but it was still wrong of me to go out by myself. I couldn't risk actually getting the eggs unless I knew he was going to wake up.

But Dad slept like a log. He wouldn't wake up. He wouldn't.

But he did once.

"Lisa, it'll be okay," Becca said. "It's the library."

She didn't understand, not really. She probably thought it was just some stupid rule. But the rule wasn't stupid. It wasn't even Dad's rule, or a rule some other man made up. It was in the Gospel of the Citizens of the Word. *Thou shalt purify thy mind by expelling the detritus of the outside world.* The way Miss Sheila put it, reading American books fills your mind with lies. But even back then, I knew that *every-thing* American wasn't a lie. I knew there was more out there. I kept hearing that old lady in my head.

You learn anyway.

There just had to be more out there than what Miss Sheila wanted me to read. Because everything ever known and everything God wanted for us couldn't be in those stacks of papers, or inside that run-down little house. I felt drawn toward that library and everything that was inside it.

The building was made of brick, just one story, and it had glass doors like any ordinary business, and when you looked through the glass you saw a room full of bookshelves.

Becca pushed open the door, and we walked inside. It was just like that, like walking into any other building. And there was a lady sitting behind a desk. As we walked in, she looked up at us. "Can I help you girls?"

"My friend needs a library card," Becca said.

Blood rushed to my head. "No, I don't."

Becca looked back at me, and our eyes met. *No no no no*, my eyes said.

The lady behind the desk smiled. She was looking me up and down at the same time, taking in my long skirt, my full-coverage blouse, how everything was secondhand. How my hair was in a long braid down my back. "You don't need a library card to read books here," she said. "The library is open to everyone."

"Thank you, ma'am," I managed to get out. I almost ran past her desk, trying to get away from her eyes.

Becca found me in the children's room. I was staring at a row of books on display.

"I'm sorry," she said. "I wasn't thinking."

"It's okay," I said. I picked one up. It was thick and heavy in my hands. The picture on the front was glossy: the outline of a girl standing inside a gate on a background of green. There was the sense that the girl was somewhere both magical and sinister. The last time I went to a library was with my late mother. But I was too little to read this kind of book then. I knew how to read the picture books, or at least some of them. And what about now? What if all I *could* read were the church printouts?

Becca stood next to me quietly. Her shoulder-length red hair was in a ponytail, and she was wearing shorts and a plain gray T-shirt. Sweat beaded around her hairline from walking outside in the sun. I think that was when she understood how serious I was about all the things I told her I couldn't do.

I opened the book I held in my hand and stared at the words. "She finished the tale about the emperor and another about magic galoshes that made wishes come true," I read. The words came out of my mouth slowly. But they came out. I was understanding them. "What are galoshes?"

"They're like rain boots," Becca said.

"I wasn't sure if I could read it."

Becca was quiet. She looked like maybe she was about to cry.

"But I can," I said. I almost laughed. Maybe I'd only been reading those printouts, but I wasn't stupid. I could do this.

"The YA stuff is over here," Becca said. "Like that one you had at my house."

She headed for another section, and as I followed her, I realized that we were too old for the books I'd been looking at, that we were supposed to read other books. But I held on to the book I had in my hand. It seemed right for me. But the seconds and minutes were ticking by. My dad could wake up at any minute and find me gone.

"Time to go?" Becca asked.

"I'm sorry."

"It's okay," she said. She sped for the desk, and I breathed a sigh of relief. She really understood now. Becca gave the lady her books to check out. "Let's get this one too," she said, taking the book out of my hand.

The lady took the book and looked up at me. "*The Aviary*. Good choice."

I looked down at my feet.

She slid the book across the counter, and I turned away. I didn't say another word until we were outside. Becca had put all the books in her backpack by then.

"I need to get eggs on the way back," I said.

"Do you need money?"

I couldn't look at her. They were poor, too, but we were poorer. Our house was so bad, nobody was supposed to be living there. "No, I took it from our cash drawer."

"Okay. Come over any time to read." She looked sad for me as she turned and headed for her house and I headed for the store.

I hated that. My blood boiled as I went to the store and as I walked back home. Why couldn't I decide if I wanted to read books? Wasn't I smart enough to know whether something was going to corrupt me or not?

When I got home, there was a package on the porch, and I recognized it at once. The perfect cursive on the address was Miss Sheila's, and it was shaped like a stack of papers.

I unlocked the door and slipped inside, carrying the plastic bag with two dozen eggs in one hand and the package under one arm. I set the eggs down carefully and closed the door, holding my breath. The living room was silent. There was no sign of movement, no sign that Dad had been in the kitchen. I wondered if I could have stayed a few minutes longer, if I could have tried to read the book.

You learn anyway. That old lady's eyes drilled into my mind.

I put the eggs away in the refrigerator and opened the package. Sure enough, it was the stuff for my school. Some of the other kids doing her classes from other places had told her about email and how you could send things by computer, but Miss Sheila was old, and she didn't go in for that newfangled nonsense. She had no problem talking on the computer, but you were supposed to read the Word the way God intended: off badly printed photocopies of photocopies.

I opened up one of the packets. There was a story inside it. The title was *The Righteous Child and the Angel of Obedience.* There was a photocopy of a picture of a girl. Her face was so mottled by the repeated photocopying that I couldn't tell much about her.

Just that she had long hair like mine, and her eyes were cast down. I thought about that girl on the book cover, the dark outline with her back to me. I wondered where that girl was going. I didn't wonder about this girl at all.

"Lisa, what are you doing?" Dad came walking down the hall toward me. He was wearing his khaki work pants and no shirt, so I could see his white belly falling over the waistband and the blob of hair on his chest. He had a tattoo on one side that went around to his back. It was of two angels in a swordfight, or something. He always kept it covered in Zebulun because you're not supposed to modify your body. That's why women weren't even supposed to cut their hair. The hair part was different for men, of course.

"I'm looking at the stuff Miss Sheila sent," I said.

"You went outside?"

"It was just to the door." As soon as I said it, I realized my mistake. How was I going to explain the eggs? "I also went out to get eggs," I said quickly.

"We don't need any fucking eggs," he said. He went to the refrigerator, looked in, then looked back at me.

I cast my eyes down.

"What are you doing now? You go get the eggs and you aren't even cooking them?"

I threw the photocopies down on the table and went to get the pan out.

He stood right behind me. "Do you know how stupid you are, Lisa? You know what could have happened to you? You know what kind of people are out there?"

I didn't say anything. I cracked an egg into the pan, watched the yolk break and run.

"Your brother and I, we're just trying to keep you safe. There are men out there who can't wait to get their hands on a good girl like you."

I cracked another egg.

"You understand me?"

"Yes, sir."

"Yes, sir," he mimicked. "You say *yes, sir*, but then you do it anyway. How are we going to feel when you come back murdered, or even worse, God forbid, raped and spoiled?"

"I didn't . . . " I clamped my mouth shut and cracked another egg.

"You didn't what?"

"Nothing."

"No, please, what did you want to say?" He leaned over me, his breath in my ear.

"I didn't see any rapists," I said.

"You think they announce themselves?" He stood up straighter, and at least he was yelling over my head and not in my ear. "You think those men, they walk up to you and announce, I'm going to rape you, little girl? No! That man behind the counter at the store, he's thinking it. He's watching you. He knows where you live! You think he doesn't know where all his customers come from? You went to his store, and now he knows! Now he's going to watch for you. Now he's over there thinking, next time she comes, I'm going to be ready."

I started scrambling the eggs.

"Soon as Carlo gets back, I'm gonna have to make a trip over there," he said. His voice was quieter now. It was like he was done talking to me and more talking to himself. "I'm going to have to let him know what will happen if he does anything to my daughter. 'And the punishment for these crimes shall be death: adultery, lust, incest, murder, abandoning thy mother and father, blasphemy, robbery, deception. No man shall suffer such a criminal to live.'"

"I didn't even talk to him," I said. I scooped the eggs onto two plates, making sure to give more to him.

He took the plate. As he turned toward the table, he lifted his free hand in the air as if he was still talking to himself, even though no words came out. The angels on his back danced.

I stood there by the stove and ate my eggs. I thought about the man at the convenience store. He was a short white man, maybe five foot five, and overweight, with beady eyes that lit up when he smiled.

"That be all?" the man had said.

I'd said nothing in return.

"Well, have a great day." He'd smiled again as he passed the bag to me. That man didn't deserve whatever Dad would do to him. I vowed then and there to do better. There was no way I'd go to the store by myself and put him in harm's way. There was also no way I was ever going back to the library. But Becca had that book for me. Maybe she could get more books. But I'd still have to be over there at her house to read them. What would he do to her? I ran through the list of crimes in my head. What if her keeping it secret that I went over there was *deception*? What if he thought she was guilty?

I told myself he wouldn't hurt her. She wasn't part of the Word, so she was already damned. If he found out, his punishment would fall on me. If Dad thought I broke the law, he'd take the law into his own hands. I knew he would, because that was why we were here and not in Zebulun.

There wasn't anything Dad wouldn't do.

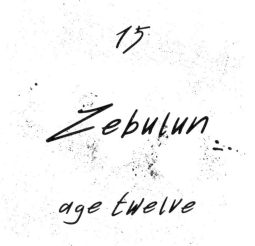

15
Zebulun
age twelve

I was in the back cleaning up after the chickens when Miss Sheila came out, wiping her hands on her apron.

"We've got to go to church," she said.

The chickens were all walking around clucking. It was like they felt something in the air.

I put the old broom down and followed Miss Sheila inside. I knew better than to ask why. When you were summoned to church, you just went, whether you were a kid like me or a woman like Miss Sheila or even a man like Mr. Doug. If it was during the day like this, that meant something important had happened, and everybody had to witness.

I got cleaned up really quick, and Miss Sheila and I went over to the church together. Everyone had a place in church depending on your status. Miss Sheila went to sit with the other married women close to the front on the left side. Mr. Doug was up there with the men in front on the right. Unmarried women, like about fifteen and up, were behind the married women. And behind them were the girls who were too young to be married, like me, but weren't little enough to sit with their moms.

I sat in the girls' row next to my friend Jean. Jean was my age, and she was in the school with me. We spent a lot of our free time together, mostly watching Jean's three little sisters. Or rather, letting her three little sisters do whatever they wanted as long as it didn't kill them. Neither one of us showed too much interest in playing mommy. Jean always said she wanted to be an Elder, but that was stupid because only men could be Elders.

"I bet it's Mr. Arthur," Jean said. "He's not here."

"What do you mean?" I asked. I craned my neck to look for my dad up front with the men, but he wasn't there.

"This is a tribunal," Jean said. "See how the Elders are sitting up front?" She meant Mr. Brandon and the two men on either side of him, sitting behind a table. That wasn't how church normally went. Normally one of them would stand behind a podium and preach. One at a time.

I'd been to a few tribunals before. You had to do something really terrible to get sent to tribunal, and you could get punished bad. You could end up being declared dead.

"It's not my dad," I said. And right then, Dad came walking out with two of the older men on either side of him. He wasn't in handcuffs or anything, but he might as well have been. He certainly couldn't have walked away. He could have turned to look for me, but he didn't. He stood facing those three men: Mr. Brandon and the other two Elders. They were all big white men with graying hair, tan skin, and muscles like they worked all day. Their muscles were covered by a layer of fat that showed they ate all night.

Everyone ate in Zebulun though. That's what you have to understand. Where else in America does everybody eat? Not in Seattle, that's for sure. Not in Port Angeles. Not in Eugene. If my dad had died that day instead of being sent to tribunal for what he did, Miss Sheila and Mr. Doug would have taken care of me, and I wouldn't have gone hungry a day in my life.

"Arthur DeAndreis, you are accused of the killing of a Citizen of the Word, Daniel Stevenson, contrary to the Charter of Zebulun. What do you say to these charges?"

The congregation took in a collective breath. I froze solid. Jean gasped audibly and reached for my hand. I didn't take it though. I felt like I was out of my body, as if I'd suddenly been transported to the ceiling. My head swam. I didn't even see Dad as he talked, but I heard every word.

"You know as well as I do that I did right," Dad said to Mr. Brandon. "I showed you everything." He waved a hand at the other two. "You must've seen it all by now. I was down in the basement fixing that old water heater. The damn thing was done. But I was scraping around down there trying to see if I could find a solution anyway because God knows they cost a lot to replace. I just wanted to save the Citizens the money it would cost, and that's my job around here, and I've done it well. You got any complaints about me?"

"No, sir," Mr. Brandon said.

"'Cept the murder," Jean whispered.

Whoosh. Suddenly I was in my body again, my heart beating in my ears. "Shut up," I whisper-yelled back.

A lady turned to look at us from a few rows up, her eyes narrowed like she was about to chastise. Then she must have realized who she was looking at: Mr. Arthur's daughter. She whipped around again to face the front.

"For those who weren't there," Dad continued, his voice rising. "What I found was, Daniel had a set of loose bricks, and in there were stacks of hundred-dollar bills! He was hiding all that cash from you. From all of us. Now, we all know that's robbery. It's right there in the book. 'He who accepts payment for himself alone, or removes resources from the community, or fails to report resources owned according to law, shall be guilty of robbery. And the penalty for robbery is death.'"

"Arthur—" one of the Elders began.

"Now it's my turn," Dad said, stepping forward and holding his hand up like he was preaching. "I get to tell my side of the story. I didn't, like, turn around and shoot him or nothin'. I turned around and said, 'Daniel, what the fuck is this?' That's when he took a swing at me. And that's when I beat the shit out of him. And he wasn't dead yet when I left, and I went right upstairs to call you."

"When you called, you said, 'I exacted the penalty for robbery,'" Mr. Brandon said.

"That's right," Dad said. "That's true."

"Now, you might've punched him once, he swung at you. But what you did, and him being the age he was, it was more than what's acceptable, you understand that?"

"Not per the book it ain't," Dad said.

"You see, we have procedures," Mr. Brandon said. "Like this one. That's in the Charter. A council of Elders has to verify the charge, and there have to be two witnesses, and we have to make the decision." He spread his arms wide to indicate himself and the other two. "And now we need to make a decision about you. You took the law into your own hands. Now, there's no doubt Daniel was hoarding that cash. We have it, and for finding it, we owe you thanks. But you can't go around exacting justice without our say." Mr. Brandon's voice was calm, but that didn't mean anything. I didn't know what the penalty was for going around Mr. Brandon, but it wasn't good. Mr. Brandon could say it was hanging, and nobody in that room would have objected. I didn't have to wait long for an answer though. Those three men were on the same page. Looking back on it, I'm sure they'd already decided what they were going to do to us before we all walked into the church. Dad had gone against them, and I guess we were lucky they *didn't* hang him.

"I move that Arthur DeAndreis will be expelled from Zebulun," Mr. Brandon said. "He shall take his personal possessions and his daughter and be gone by dark."

"Agreed," said the other two men at once, like robots.

"Agreed," the whole congregation said at once.

I almost leapt into the air. I should have known it was coming, since I'd been to those other tribunals. But it seemed so fast. It seemed like the others had been slower, had witnesses. I tried to remember how it was supposed to be.

Had anyone ever not said *agreed?* I hadn't, but no one had been paying attention to what I said.

"Maybe we can write to each other," Jean said to me as she stood up. Everyone around me was standing up.

"I . . ." I stood there with my mouth open.

"I will," she said. "I promise." Then she slid into the line of people leaving the church, and all I saw was her back. Her long, uneven braid flopped as she walked, head down.

I wanted to call after her, but I didn't. And then she was through the door.

Everyone else was leaving too. Some folks looked at me as they passed, sympathy in their eyes. They knew *I* didn't kill anyone. But I didn't see any outrage over Dad killing that old man either. Mr. Daniel was like a hundred years old. Or maybe seventy. It was hard to tell with old people how old they were exactly. I remembered him coming by our house a few times to have lunch with Mr. Doug, like the men did. They'd come from wherever they were working to one of their houses, and the women would fix them lunch. That old man had a raspy laugh and a hacking cough. I'd hand him his cup of coffee and he'd say, "Thankee kindly, little miss." I didn't like the way he said it, truth be told. I didn't like being called *little miss.* But had my dad really killed him?

How could someone I'd just seen a few weeks ago be dead?

I'd never thought someone could die because Dad punched them.

Hurt, yes. Hurt, a lot. My mind swam. I sat in that church like a zombie. Did he kill that old man? Did he?

He never told me the story, but I heard him telling Carlo about it, later, after we were living in the house. It was another time they thought I was in bed, another time I was committing a sin. Because I couldn't stay in bed at night; I still can't. And since I can't stay in bed, I learned how to be quiet when I'm awake, how to pretend I'm lying down asleep when actually I'm walking down a hallway. This is what Dad said to Carlo that night. At least, this is the part I'll never forget:

"And then suddenly the Spirit came over me. He came inside me and filled me up. He gave strength to my arms, made my fists hard as iron. I knew what I was supposed to do. I knew it was up to me to provide justice. Brandon said I did it in anger. He said I lost control of myself. But I had more control than ever in my life. I took Daniel by the neck with this hand. You see, it's my left hand. I'm right-handed. But the Spirit gave me the strength and guided my left hand to do the work. I held him against the wall, against those bricks that he was using to hide the money. And with my right hand, I smashed his face. It crunched like it was made of candy cane. Bled like tomato juice. Pull back, punch. I ain't never punched like that before. There was no anger, just knowledge that this was what I was supposed to do."

I couldn't see them from where I stood in the hallway.

"He did wrong," Carlo said.

"Yes, he did, son. And when God calls you to uphold the scripture, you'll know. You'll feel it with the certainty of an angel. And you have to be ready. When the time comes to kill a man for the sake of God, you can't balk. You have to be prepared to let the Spirit fill you."

"Yes, sir," Carlo said. I didn't hear any hesitation in his voice.

"Good man," Dad said. I imagined Dad clamping his hand on Carlo's shoulder, or maybe them embracing. They stopped talking then. I heard the noise of the TV. We didn't watch anything but sports on the actual television, so they must have been watching a video. It was probably one of Mr. Brandon's, the ones he sent to Citizens of the Word all over. Even though Dad technically wasn't a Citizen anymore, they still let him buy the DVDs.

I pressed myself against the wall of the hallway, willing myself to become light as air. The penalty for the sin of eavesdropping wasn't death. It was an in-between crime, the kind God hadn't thought to put in the book, the kind your father or husband or brother decided how to punish, with kindness of course.

I slipped as carefully as I could back into my room.

Yes, sir, I heard Carlo say. Over and over, it was like he was right there, saying it in my ear. I didn't sleep a wink for the rest of the night, or for at least a week after.

Miss Sheila was the one who came over to me that day in the church while I was sitting there like a zombie. Everyone else had filed out. Even Dad had left the church without me. He'd gone out the door he'd come in. When I saw her coming toward me, I burst into tears.

She sat down next to me on the bench. "Do you understand what just happened?" she asked.

"We have to leave," I said.

She nodded. A piece of hair had fallen from her perfect bun. Her eyes were wet.

A few long seconds went by, and I thought of something. Hope rose a little bit in my chest. "Can I stay with you?" I asked.

She didn't answer.

"I didn't do anything. It was my dad. He did it." I heard my voice rising. The tears were falling hard now. My chest began heaving. "I never killed anyone."

Miss Sheila put her arm around me and pulled me close. "I know, Honey Cakes. But you belong with your dad."

"I don't! I don't want to leave!"

She just kept on hugging me, and I cried into her blouse until I was done crying. Because you can't cry forever, even if you want to. Finally, we both stood up and walked slowly back to her house. She helped me pack up what few things I had, and we both cried. She tried to pretend she wasn't crying. She'd sniff and turn away from me, and pinch her eyes shut as if she could hold the tears back. I rubbed my eyes on my sleeve and left the Kleenex untouched. Through the window, I could see that night was falling. We were supposed to be gone by dark. Even though *I* hadn't done anything.

When we had everything packed up, Miss Sheila wiped her eyes, and then she unclasped the necklace from around her neck. It was the one she always wore, the agate on a silver chain. She held it out to me.

"My grandmother gave me this," she said. "My grandfather gave it to her. I want you to have it to remember us by."

I had to gasp and gasp to keep the tears back. My hands were shaking so badly that Miss Sheila had to put it around my neck for me.

"Thank you," I whispered.

Miss Sheila nodded, picked up my duffle bag, and led the way downstairs. Dad and Mr. Doug were already down there. Dad had a suitcase and a trash bag.

"You got her ready?" Dad asked Sheila. He didn't even look at me.

"She's ready," Miss Sheila said.

I looked down at my feet.

"We're gonna be fine," Dad said. He said it like it was directed to me, but he was looking over my head, past Miss Sheila, through the kitchen. "Say goodbye to Mr. Doug."

"Goodbye," I said.

Mr. Doug grabbed me and pulled me into a hug. I was so surprised that I almost leapt back. Mr. Doug had never hugged me before. But after a second, I hugged him back.

"Be good," Mr. Doug said as we pulled apart.

"Yes, sir."

Next Miss Sheila hugged me. She kissed my cheek, and while she was doing it, she slipped something into my coat pocket. "You'll be going with God," she said. She put a finger to my heart. "And we'll be here."

I nodded and turned away from her and ran out the door that Dad was in the middle of opening. I was carrying my backpack, and it slammed against my leg as I ran all the way out to the street. I felt like I might burst from holding back my tears, as if I might barf them up onto my feet.

Dad came up next to me. "We're gonna be okay, Lisa," he said. "Just you and me, we're a good team. You're my champion, right?"

I nodded. I worried that if I said something, those tears would come out.

He put his arm around my shoulder. "We don't need this town. Never did. We have God right with us on this street. Don't need any of them."

"Yes, sir."

"All that work I did—this is how they repay me? Had to stay with Doug and Sheila and never get our own place. I gave them my car like I was supposed to, everything I owned, but Mr. Daniel? You should've seen those bills all stacked up behind that wall." Dad whistled. "Robbery, that's what it was."

"Yes, sir."

He gave my shoulder a last squeeze and hiked his pack up on his back. "Let's keep the pace up. We've got a bus to catch." Dad went quiet, and I knew better than to say anything else until he spoke again.

After a while, we stopped to drink water and eat some crackers that Miss Sheila must have packed for us. And then we went on.

It wasn't until we were on the bus to Seattle and Dad was asleep, head lolling against the window, that I reached into my pocket to see what Miss Sheila had slipped in there. It was a letter, all folded up into a tiny square, written in Miss Sheila's precise, ornate hand.

Dearest Lisa,

You will always have a home here. A child who is righteous and obeys her father will sit at the table. Be patient and kind and rewards will come. We love you.

It was signed *Sheila and Doug*, even though obviously only Miss Sheila had written it. I sat there staring at the letter and wondered why, if I had a home there, I had to leave. Of course, I knew the answer. I belonged to my father. Until I was eighteen, I had to go with him. But after that? *Sit at the table* was what happened after you died, when you went into the firmament with Jesus and the disciples and all the other righteous people. But *rewards will come*—maybe that meant that if I was good, I could go back there and have a life someday. Maybe when I was an adult, I could find a Citizen to marry and not have to worry about anything ever again. I folded the note back up and stuffed it into a tiny pocket on the inside of my backpack. That was when I started crying again, softly, so I wouldn't wake Dad up. When I dozed off, I dreamed of those chickens. I dreamed I was feeding them and saying goodbye.

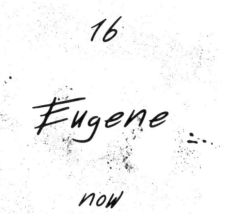

16

Eugene

now

Nobody has to tell me that we're all supposed to shower and fix our hair and wear our best clothes for the appointment with the social worker. You're supposed to tell them that nobody hurt you, and then they go away again. I already know it won't be Miss Tina who shows up here in Eugene. Miss Tina was the Seattle lady, and all she had to do was take me from Dad and give me to Mom. It was just like that time Dad decided to sell the patio furniture that was at the back of our house that no one ever used. Dad posted a picture of it on the internet, and some guy came over and gave him money, and Dad handed over the furniture to him. Dad didn't own the furniture, so it wasn't his right to sell it, but he did it anyway. And now some guy with a big old handlebar mustache has that furniture.

Patio furniture can't get up and walk away. It can't prevent people from sitting on it.

I sit on the couch in Mom and Barron's living room thinking about that. How I'm just like furniture, and the social worker's job is to decide whether I'm supposed to stay in this house or whether they should take me and give me to somebody else. I know that's what Mom's afraid of, that this person will take me and give me to some other family. I also know that won't happen. Carlo had lots of injuries before he finally ran away. I had a concussion.

This person's real job is to enforce the law and make sure I stay here, because it's Mom who owns me now, along with the couch I'm sitting on.

I read this book at Becca's house. Well, I read part of it. I only had a few minutes at a time. It wasn't a library book; it was a book that Becca's father had. It said the universe wasn't created by God at all, that there are all these natural forces at work that caused everything that exists to spring from nothing. I didn't understand it all, that's for sure, but there was one line that I copied down into my notebook, right below what Miss Sheila was teaching me about the Garden of Eden and the Tree of Knowledge. *The universe is the way it is whether we like it or not.* Every time I got a new notebook, I wrote that line down again.

But Eve had a choice whether to eat that apple. She wanted knowledge, and she took it, and it changed everything.

No one created the universe, and God did. A woman is no better than a piece of sagging old patio furniture, and a woman has the power to remake the world. The social worker is here to help me, and they don't give two feathers off a chicken's ass.

The social worker is a white guy with thin chin whiskers. He's wearing a business suit, but the legs are a little bit too short. Either it's a secondhand suit or he doesn't know how long the legs are supposed to be. I'd guess he's barely over twenty years old.

"Hi, I'm Forest," he says, holding out his hand to Mom.

I decide I'm going to pretend like I don't know what he's here for, like I think he's really here to help me.

"You must be Alyssa," he says, holding out his hand to me.

I take it and shake. I make eye contact.

We all sit down. Mr. Forest looks around the room as if he's just being casual, as if he's not looking for cat feces and roaches.

"How are you settling in, Alyssa?" he asks me.

"Everything is just fine," I say. I smile. I sit cross-legged on the couch like Becca would do. She never worried about how she sat, about whether she was showing anything to men.

Mr. Forest asks me a few more questions about how things are, and I tell him that I'm getting enough to eat and I have a nice bedroom. I don't tell him how surprised I was to see the food, or about the window I once crawled out of. He makes small talk with Mom, trying to get a read on whether she's stressed out. Finally, he gets to the point. "Has your father tried to contact you at all?"

"Nope." I shake my head.

Mom squints at me. I realize I went too far with trying to act like Becca. But Mr. Forest doesn't get it.

"Okay, well, if he does, it's important that you tell somebody, okay?"

"Oh yeah. I don't want to talk to him anyway."

"Okay. Okay, that's good to hear."

I smile blankly. It's good to hear that I don't want to talk to my own father? It's good that the law won't even let him call me? Actually, him not calling me I get. Me not being able to call him if I decide to is what's wrong.

Mr. Forest and Mom talk about when I'm going to go down to the high school and have an assessment to find out what grade I should be in.

"Ten a.m. tomorrow," Mom says. "We've got it."

"Tomorrow!" I blurt.

"School starts in a couple weeks. Might as well get it over with."

"Oh. Okay."

"Don't stress too much about it," Mr. Forest says. "It's just a placement test. You can't fail it." He gives me a nod as he leaves. He slinks as he walks, uncomfortable in his suit.

I look at the clock. It's 10:45 a.m. "Is there anything else I need to do today? I don't feel good."

Mom shakes her head. "If you want to read, you can pick anything." She waves at a bookshelf along the living room wall. Becca's dad had an entire room full of books, like a mini library. But there are a lot here. It will take me a long time to read these. I grab something without looking at it and head to my room. I open the book and stare at the words. They swim in front of my eyes. I look up at the alarm clock with its red numbers. I've been here before, in this bed, waiting.

The door to my bedroom opens and Liam slips in.

I look up, trying to focus.

"Alyssa," he whispers, tiptoeing over to me. His movements are exaggerated, and I realize he must be playing some kind of game. I try to focus on him, on what it's like to be a kid, on what it was like hanging out with Jean's sisters.

"What?" I whisper back, forcing a smile.

"I got a weird call. I think it's for you." He holds up his phone.

"For me?" Heart pounding, I take the phone from him and look at the screen. It's a Washington number. "Who do you think it is?"

"I think it's someone from the cult," he whispers. He's almost jumping on his tiptoes. "Someone who wants to kidnap you back."

"Sounds dangerous," I say. I'm committing the number to memory.

"Mom says they are," Liam whispers. "She says they have washed brains and want the world to end."

"Nobody wants the world to end," I say, repeating the number to myself. "It's just going to end someday. Some people say it will happen soon, other people say in billions of years."

"I like billions better."

"Me too. And the phrase is brainwashed, not washed brains."

"Are you brainwashed?" he asks. It's a real question. Funny, it's not a question the cops asked me. Miss Tina didn't ask, and neither did Mr. Forest. They all just assumed I am. Liam is the first person who cares what I actually have to say.

"No," I say. "Brainwashed is when you believe things just because that's what people told you. I think for myself."

"So you *don't* think the world is ending?"

"Someday," I say. "That's all I know."

"Phew." Liam sits on the bed next to me, bouncing.

"You know what?" I say. "I think this is actually my friend from Port Angeles. Mom said it was okay if I call her. Do you mind if I use your phone?"

"It's not the cult?" He sounds disappointed.

"I don't think so."

"Okay." His face brightens. "Will you tell me if they try to get you? I can stop them. I'm learning karate!" He jumps up from the bed and leaps around, doing what look like actual karate moves.

"I'm impressed. I'll bet you *can* protect me."

"Yee-haw!" Liam does a couple more kicks, which take him to the door, and then he becomes quiet and slips out like a ninja.

I want to laugh, but I'm still holding the phone in my hand. He *is* my brother, and even if he's a silly kid, he *does* want to protect me. But what he wants to protect me from is my other brother, and we're not a cult. People call religions cults because they're small, and because the people in them aren't brainwashed by American society. The only difference between mainstream Christianity and the Citizens of the Word is that mainstream Christians have power in the world, and they told everybody Jesus was a god over and over and over again until people forgot to even question it. We're not like that. We question.

I touch the unfamiliar Washington number.

"Hola."

"It's me."

"Lisa? Are you good?"

"Yes, everything's fine." I want to tell him everything that's happened, about the social worker and the food and the placement test, but I know there probably isn't time. And what I have to say isn't important right now.

"The Trial has begun," he says.

I close my eyes.

"So we follow the plan. To the letter."

I don't say anything.

"You understand, Lisa?"

"Yes," I reply.

"Don't be afraid, sis. We'll be together again soon. We just have to have faith."

"I know."

"Man, it's not good without you." He sighs. I hear in that sigh that there's more he wants to say. Maybe Dad's standing there. I can imagine what he's been acting like, with me taken. All he ever wanted was for me to be with him, for me never to be out of his sight. When I got married someday, I would have been living down the street from him in Zebulun. Me and my kids would still see him every single day of our lives. That's how he wanted things to go.

"They have so much food here," I say. I realize I'm whispering. I'm leaning over my legs, hiding the phone from view, even though there's nobody else in this room. "Carlo, it's like a whole grocery store. They have everything you could ever want."

"That's your birthright," Carlo says. "You go ahead and eat that food. You need to be strong."

"I wasn't asking for your permission," I whisper. "I'm just telling you. They're not even rich for around here. There are lots of bigger houses."

"It's your food," Carlo says. "You eat it."

"I can't talk long," I say.

"You know the signal." His voice is calm. Whatever was in it a second ago, whatever issues he's having with Dad, he's not going to talk about it with me. It's man stuff. "So we won't talk again. Until we can be together." He pauses and sighs again. "I wish I could give you a hug right now. Just be sure you're really okay."

"Me too." I hear footsteps in the hallway. "I have to go. I'll be waiting."

"Okay. I love you."

"I love you too." I hang up the phone just as Mom opens the bedroom door.

I sit up straighter. "You said I could call my friend," I say.

"Of course. How about after your test tomorrow we stop by the phone store? You can't be a high school student without a phone."

"Really?" I can't keep the suspicion out of my voice.

"Honey, you're sixteen years old. You can have your own phone."

I set Liam's phone on the bed.

Mom sits down on the opposite side of the bed from me but twists my way. "You know that Liam is nine? Did you really think he can have one but you can't?"

I don't know what to say to that. I assumed I couldn't have a phone. It never for a minute occurred to me that she would buy me one. "What do I have to do?" I ask finally.

"What do you mean?"

"I mean, is it if I go to that school? Or if I do my chores?"

"Alyssa, everyone has a phone. So you get a phone. That's it." Her voice is sharp as she says *that's it*. I realize what the real deal is. I have to pretend like I'm not brainwashed and like I'm a normal person. I have to act like I'm a boy, and besides that, like I always have been. Maybe like I'm the person I would have been if I hadn't climbed out my window that night, if I'd stayed with her. What will make it seem like I'm that person? Materialism. Wanting to dress like one of them.

"Can I get some clothes too?" I ask.

Her face lights up. "Sure. We can do that."

"I don't know if I want jeans," I say quickly. "Just, something more normal."

"Nobody's going to force you to wear jeans," she says. But her face is still shining like I just told her I had a million dollars in my duffel bag.

"I'm not cutting my hair though." I can wear American clothes for a few weeks if I'm trying to prove I'm not brainwashed, but the hair would be too much. Hair takes a long time to grow back.

"You have beautiful hair," Mom says. "I wouldn't cut it if I were you either."

I take my braid in my hand. I don't think it's beautiful; it's just my hair. You wouldn't cut off any other part of your body, like your foot or your fingers.

"It could use a trim, though," she says. "Just to even up the ends. You could wear it down more often."

"I'll think about it." She's still smiling like we're suddenly rich, and I don't want to get her hopes up too high. I don't want her to look at me and feel like I'm the daughter she always dreamed of. I don't want to keep talking to her, with her being dead.

"I'll let you get back to your book," she says. "I just wanted to check in." She has a spring in her step as she leaves the room. It's kind of like Liam's bouncing, but an older version, the happiness old people try to hide. Because happiness is something you're supposed to tamp down, something wild and terrifying.

She's left Liam's phone sitting there next to me on the bed. I could call anyone. I could pick it up and literally dial any number. She just left me with it. But I only know two phone numbers: Carlo's new number and 911. Actually, I realize there's a third number I know. I could really call Becca. I could tell her that I'm okay. And then what, that I'm with the mother I said was dead? I pick up the phone and let it sit in my hand. I want to talk to her so badly. I want to tell her everything. The last thing she said to me was a question I never answered.

I put the phone down. When my Trial is over and I'm in Zebulun, then I can call her. Then I can explain all the things about the Word I never told her before, and all the things about me. Then, I'll know how it all turns out.

17
Zebulun / Seattle / Port Angeles
ages seven to sixteen

When I was little, I thought all I had to do to become a Citizen and sit at the table was to keep quiet and good and sweet. I thought that as long as I behaved and didn't talk back and obeyed my father, my life would be good. But it turns out that as you get older, God asks more of you.

When I was seven and Dad and I were hiding down in Miss Sheila and Mr. Doug's basement, Dad told me what I had to do if the cops found us.

"If they come down here, you keep sweet," Dad said to me.

I nodded. I was listening to the footsteps above us. They came through the floor clear as day. We could tell right where those men were.

"They ask you any questions, you tell them you want to be with me. That's it. Just tell them you want your daddy. Okay?"

"Yes, sir."

"You don't say nothing about your mother."

I nodded. If I said anything about wanting her to come live with us too, something bad would happen. But if I said nothing, then there was a chance. Being quiet and good and sweet led to good things happening.

But the cops never came down and found us that day, so they never asked me any questions. Being quiet and good and sweet had worked to keep us safe, but it hadn't brought Mom back. That meant I had to be quieter and sweeter. So I worked harder at it. I was as quiet and sweet as I could make myself, even after I realized Mom wasn't coming. But after we got banished, I learned that being quiet wasn't enough. On that long walk out of Zebulun, Dad told me things I'd have to say.

"We're gonna be in Seattle," Dad said. "So there'll be cops all around." He paused, but I knew better than to say anything. "You know what to say if they ask you your name." Again, I didn't respond. I had my fake name down so well that it was my real name now. "But they might figure it all out. Those cops, they've got the devil on their side, and the devil's clever. They ask about your mother, you tell them she hurt you. You say she would hit you and scream at you, and that's why you chose to come with me."

Lying is a grave sin, some voice inside me whispered.

"Now, I know what you're thinking because you're a good girl. Isn't God against lying? But the law that gave you to her was an American law, a law that didn't recognize the truth about her death. Sometimes we have to lie to protect the truth."

"Yes, sir."

"Repeat it to me now, what you say if the cops have you and figure out who you are."

"I don't want to go back to my mother because she hurt me," I parroted.

"How did she hurt you?"

"She hit me and screamed at me."

"Good girl," Dad said. "Good girl."

Now that I was twelve, saying I wanted my daddy wasn't enough. I was going to tell those cops the lie that was actually protecting the truth. My mom was dead, and if they took me back to her, she *would* hurt me. She would get inside my soul and change me. She'd take away my righteousness and send me to Hell with her. If the cops took me back to her, I'd be dead too. You could come back from banishment, from a great penance, from anything else. But once you were dead, that was forever.

Once, my friend Jean's late aunt Rachel tried to come back. She was dead for three years, and then one day she drove into Zebulun in a new car with a trunk full of supplies, and she asked to be redeemed. She went to the Elders and renounced her worldly life and sins, and she offered to turn over her car and all her money to the church, but they wouldn't even listen to her. They acted like she wasn't there at all, because her earthly shell was just trying to tempt them. The real person was already gone.

So I was ready to step up and tell my righteous lies. But I never had to, because nobody found me. Dad and I made it to Seattle and lived there for more than a year, and nobody noticed that I was me.

There was never any danger of us getting caught until that day the cops hassled Dad on the street and searched his bag. Even then, they never took one look at me. I wasn't called to speak, but I was ready.

And right before the cops actually did come to take me, I found out that when you get older, God requires more of you than telling righteous lies. When you're older, you may be required to take action. Dad, Carlo, and I were all going to make sure nobody could take me from God. And maybe, if I did everything right, if I was quiet and good and sweet when I had to be, and if I took action when my great Trial came, I could go home.

18

Eugene

now

Mom takes me down to the school early for my test. I think about wearing the jeans I brought with me that I used to wear when Dad wanted me to blend in. But I decide I want to wear my normal clothes so I'll be comfortable. Even though I'm not going to actually go to this school for long, I want to do well on their placement test. I want to show them that I'm not stupid just because I'm a Citizen of the Word. I can almost hear Miss Sheila's voice in my ear, because I know what she'd say. *We women of the Word choose to fulfill our roles as wives and mothers not because we're less than but because we're more, because we choose to serve God. You're just as smart as any man. You're better educated than any American.*

I know all about history, about the prophets and the kings of Israel, and Jesus's life and everything he did on Earth, and also what he's done in the heavens. I know how to milk a cow and how to raise chickens and how to sew a dress and mend anything. I can do algebra and account for profits and loss and pick out a good mark from the not-worth-its on a city street.

But I'm guessing the only thing I know that's on the test is the algebra. A knot forms in my stomach as we get out of the car. These people are going to think I'm stupid, and so they're going to think all of us are stupid. Mr. Forest said I can't fail, but he was fudging the truth. If I don't do well, they'll put me in classes with a bunch of little kids.

We enter the high school through the front doors and walk down the empty hallway. This is the first time I've been inside an American school since I was seven years old. The school feels huge with nobody in it. I imagine it full of Americans in their jeans, girls with their bosoms hanging out, mixing with boys. I imagine walking among them, all by myself. With no Dad around. No Carlo. Just me and all these other kids. It would be like living in another universe. It's so far from here, from me, that it might as well be Mars. As I have this thought, I remember that Mars is, on average, 140 million miles from Earth. It was Mr. Doug who told me that. We looked up at Mars through the telescope he had set up on the side porch. He'd go on about how God created this vast universe for us to explore.

"Will you be okay?" Mom asks. "I'm going to go run some errands, and when you're done, we can head to the mall."

"Okay," I say. I'm standing in front of a table where a very pale woman with jet-black hair sits behind a laptop computer.

"Name?"

"Li—Alyssa DeAndreis."

She does something on the computer and then pulls a packet from a box beneath her seat. "You can wait inside. Just don't open the book-let until we start at ten."

"Thank you." I take the packet and walk inside the classroom. It must be a math classroom, because there are stylized equations all over the walls. It's easy stuff, like $x + 2 = 10$ or $7y = 48$. There's one boy in the room already. He's sitting right smack in the middle of the room, and he's wearing raggedy jeans rolled up past his ankles with a plain black T-shirt. His hair is long for a boy's, falling around his ears. On his face, he wears big wire-rimmed glasses.

"Have a seat," the boy says, patting the chair next to him.

Part of me wants to slide to the back of the room, but I don't. That's not what Becca would do, and today, I'm acting like her. Becca would just sit next to the boy and start a conversation about something normal. The trouble is, this kid doesn't look like a normal American. Even I can tell his clothes aren't in fashion and his glasses make him look like a dork. A cute dork, though. And not a threat.

I sit down. "Hi," I say. "I'm Lisa." The name just slips out. But no one else is listening.

"Technically my name is Pine Tree," the boy says, "but I go by Tree."

"Is that a joke?" I blurt.

He rolls his eyes. "No, it isn't. My parents, as you might assume, are hippies. Hence the need for me to test into school at age seventeen."

"I don't understand," I say.

"They believe in 'unschooling.' That's where you let the kids do whatever they want and expect them to just figure everything out. I didn't experience genuine reading until I was ten. A couple years ago, I enrolled in an online school. That's when I figured out how much I was missing. So I queried my aunt and uncle about whether I could come live with them in Eugene and go to real school. It so happened that the online school I was enrolled in wasn't accredited, so it didn't count." He presses a fist into the desk. "I'm hoping they'll let me be a senior."

"Oh," I respond.

He takes his glasses off and wipes them on his T-shirt. "What's your story?"

"Cult," I say. "Religious school." *God forgive me*, I think.

"Really?" He puts his glasses back on. "I love cults! Which one is it?" He looks me up and down. "Amish?"

"Do you see a bonnet?" I snap.

"Fine, don't tell me. I'll look it up." He pulls his phone out of his cross-body bag. "Let's see, cult, long skirt, bun, Northwest." He pauses for a few seconds. "Citizens of the Word!"

My eyes open wide.

He peers at me. "Am I right?"

"It's not really a cult," I say. "It's just a different sect of Christianity."

"Stupendous." He grins at me and sticks his phone back into his bag. For a second, we make eye contact. My heart skips. He's a boy outside my family. I'm not even supposed to be talking to him.

Stupendous? Is that good?

The woman from the hallway comes into the room. "So I guess

we're ready to start," she says. "There was one other kid, but his mom called to cancel. Does anyone need to run to the bathroom?"

We both shake our heads.

"Okay, then. Open your packets and write your name at the top."

I'm still reeling from Tree's smile, but I have to shake it off. I have to concentrate on this.

It turns out there are four sections on the test: English, science, math, and social studies. First is English, and I feel like I do okay on that. It's just reading a passage and knowing what the passage says, which feels obvious. I'm less sure about the science, because this isn't what Miss Sheila taught us. I could tell them all about how to deliver a calf or why chickens lay all those eggs, but that's not what they want to know. They want to know about the parts of a cell and how humans evolved from apes, which they didn't. So I just guess what they want me to say. Then the lady brings us box lunches. There's a ham and cheese sandwich on white bread, a red apple, and a carton of warm chocolate milk.

"Do you think you did adequately?" Tree asks. He's not smiling now, and that makes it easier. Behind his glasses, his brown eyes are nervous.

"On the English. The science was . . ." I almost say a bunch of nonsense, but I've already been too honest with him. "Not what I've learned. I learned farm stuff."

"Ah, *actual* knowledge," Tree says, nodding. "That's not what you need to get by in the world. You need to know what they want to hear." He stuffs almost the entire sandwich in his mouth at once.

"Tell me about it." I take a small bite.

Somehow, Tree has already swallowed. "I learned some of this stuff, but I cannot express how abysmal my online school was. At least I understood an iota."

"It sounds like you learned some big words," I say.

"Words are elementary if you're unschooled. You can read the dictionary all day long. Go on the internet and take word quizzes. Write lists of words. Try them out on your dog." He takes a large bite of his apple.

"I didn't know about word quizzes," I say. And it never occurred to me to read the dictionary, but it actually makes a lot of sense. That's one book we had in Zebulun that wasn't religious. I should have done what Tree did.

"I can send you some links," he says.

"Okay. They sound interesting." I finish my sandwich, and Tree finishes his apple in one giant bite, followed by one long swig that takes care of the milk. I can't stomach the milk at all, so I go to the water fountain and take a long drink. It tastes metallic, and that triggers a memory of me in another school, at another drinking fountain. I head back to the classroom thinking about that school and trying to remember things about it. Teachers' faces; my friends. They slide into my brain and out again.

The math goes okay, although there are a few questions I have to guess at. The social studies has questions about American history and where countries are located on a map. I have to guess at a lot of those. By the time the lady tells us our time's up, my eyes are almost filming over.

"You look blitzed," Tree says as we walk out.

"I have no idea if they'll say I'm a junior in high school or a third grader."

"They have to at least enroll you as a freshman if you're over fourteen. Believe me, I checked."

"Great," I say. I wonder if this is it, if I'm ever going to see him again. How can I, when I'm not actually going to go to this school? Mom is standing in the hall, looking at her phone. She waves at me.

"Hey, you want to exchange numbers?" Tree asks. "I can send you those links."

My heart leaps, and I half jump.

"Are you not allowed to engage in friendships with the opposite sex?"

"I can be friends with whoever I want to," I say. It comes out all wrong and snappish. But I don't know how to act around him. And I hate that I might have done so badly on that stupid test.

Tree doesn't seem bothered. He grins and hands over his phone.

"What am I supposed to do with this?"

"Put in your number. Then I'll text you and you'll have mine."

"Why don't you give your number to me," Mom says, "and I'll pass it on to Alyssa later today. We're about to get her a new phone." Mom hands him her phone, and he types something in.

"Great, thanks, Mrs. . . ."

"Lynn," Mom says.

"Thank you, Lynn. Stupendous to meet you, *Alyssa*. Text me soon!" He turns and walks away from us, bag slung over his shoulder. I like the way he looks from the back. He walks confidently, like he's not afraid of anything, but also like he's in his own space. He's unique. And smart. He figured out how to learn anyway. I catch myself smiling.

"He seems interesting," Mom says as we walk out.

"His name is Tree."

"Welcome back to Eugene." Mom laughs, and I smile with her, even though I don't really understand what she means by that.

"I'm not going to ask you how you did," she says. "I'm sure you did great. Let's just have a fun shopping trip."

As we drive to the mall, I try to imagine what Tree's life was like, just doing whatever he wanted all the time. I would have been at the library or at Becca's house. Maybe I would have been at an American school like the one I'm starting to remember. But then I never would have learned how to milk a cow or bake a pot pie or sew my clothes. Or how to steal and figure out which parts of a sandwich you found in the garbage were safe to eat.

"I'm sure you did fine," Mom says again, eyeing me. So much for not asking.

"I think I did okay on the English and math. Science and social studies, I don't know."

"They have to let you be a junior with English and math," Mom says. "Those are the basics."

But that's not what I'm worried about. There's no planet on which I'll be going to that school or be making friends with people who go there.

Still.

Later, after we're home from the mall and I've put away my new American clothes, I set up my phone. It takes a long time even with Liam's help. When it's finally all set up, I find a text from Mom with Tree's number in it.

I want to text Carlo and let him know I have a phone, but I'm not supposed to contact him again. I have no way of knowing where he is, and I don't want to think about that, so I flip back to Mom's text. I program Tree's number in as a contact.

I think about how he was nice to me even though he figured out where I'm from. Not everybody would be. A lot of people would have assumed I was stupid and brainwashed. And when I snapped at him, he didn't snap back.

I remember his smile and what I felt when our eyes met, and it comes back. My heart races, and I'm almost shaking.

I put the phone down. I can't like a boy. It's not okay. I probably only like him because he's the only boy I've met since I was twelve years old.

But in a few weeks, I won't have this phone anymore, and I'll have to cut off all contact with him. What could it hurt to just text him? To pretend I'm normal for a minute or two? A normal American could have a friend who was a boy.

Hi, it's Lisa, I text.

Good evening, my new friend Alyssa. Why did you give me a fake name?

It's not fake, it's what my dad calls me.

OH. Apologies. Apologies.

Your name sounds fake. I cringe as I read my own words. It was supposed to be a joke, but it looks harsh.

LOL true. I thought you wouldn't text me, but I'm delighted that you did. We strange people need friends in this world of normative assimilation.

Tree doesn't take offense easily, I realize. He takes weird things as if they're normal. He's not going to get angry. Tears come out of nowhere, and I have to close my eyes. It takes me a minute to reply.

It's the world that's strange, I write.

I honestly believed you weren't allowed to converse with boys.

We're taught that men are out to rape us or kill us. I've never said this out loud before, but there's something about this medium that makes it easier. That's only one of the reasons I'm supposed to watch out for boys. There's lots of stuff about the roles God has assigned to us. But the risk of being raped or murdered was the part Dad always hammered home.

I remember what happened after I ate the last of those eggs I bought that day I snuck off to the library with Becca. I tried to go out and get some more, because I knew Dad would want them, and if he saw that they weren't there, he'd be mad. But he thought I was going to see the man at the convenience store and I was a whore.

Some men, Tree says. *I promise you, not all of us.*

I remember Dad's hand against my throat, slamming me back into the wall.

I know that. Plus, my brother taught me how to fight.

LOLOL I'm terrified.

I remember Carlo showing me self-defense moves, and how that day I wanted to kick Dad in the nuts and claw his eyes out—go for the soft spots—but I didn't. I remember freezing like a cornered mouse. And hating myself for it.

You should be, I say.

You know what's really dangerous? Tree asks.

No, what?

Yogurt.

What?

Um, okay, I reply.

No, really. I read in the news that a woman died today in Boise after eating tainted yogurt.

I don't want to think about that. No talk about people dying. I want to be normal for a few minutes.

I hate American dairy products, I say. And I just used the word American, which isn't normal. So now I have to explain. My face burns. *I only drink real whole milk, like we had back home. If I ate yogurt, it would be homemade.*

You know how to make yogurt?

No, but butter and cheese and cream.

Stupendous!

I try to think of something to say next. I could tell him about other farm stuff. Maybe he'd think that was stupendous too. But it wouldn't be normal.

Oh Beelzebub, he texts before I can think of anything. *My aunt is yelling at me to take the trash out as per our agreement.*

Goodnight, I reply.

Goodnight (A)Lisa.

I sit in the dark staring at the phone for a while. Even when Mom and Dad were together, Dad wouldn't let me have friends who were boys. Playdates had to be both girls and Christian. My heart is still racing, but not because Tree scares me. Maybe because he doesn't. Maybe because he got me thinking about Dad and what he said about men and the convenience store and the eggs. And then he talked about someone dying.

I can't help myself. I search the internet for news about the woman who died from eating yogurt, and I find an article. *The woman's husband reports that minutes after eating the yogurt, his wife collapsed. The medical examiner has not yet provided the autopsy results.* I try to picture the woman and her husband. They're probably ordinary Americans, both wearing jeans. The article says they have two children, ages seven and eight. Now their mother is dead, but not like my mother is dead, dead in her body. That woman doesn't have any shell left.

I don't like thinking about that, so I put the phone down and go out into the kitchen to get a snack. It's dark, and everyone else has gone to bed. I feel like a criminal, opening the refrigerator, taking food. But I'm allowed to eat whatever I want here, Mom says. I see Mom's stack of yogurt, and I almost reach for one, but I stop myself. Instead, I pull out a block of cheese. I slice off pieces of cheese in the darkness, letting the sharp flavor roll over my tongue. I *wasn't* asking for permission, but I'm glad Carlo said I should eat the food. I'm glad no one will yell at me, or . . .

I remember being frozen with Dad's hand around my neck, my back pressed against the wall. I had tried to go back to the convenience store, and he had caught me.

Carlo was standing behind Dad. He was tense, like maybe he was getting ready to do something. But he didn't. He waited for Dad to decide to release me. Dad stepped back and let me fall. I dropped to my hands and knees.

"I'm going out to get some fucking eggs," Dad said. I heard the door slam, but I didn't see him go because I was coughing, my eyes facing the once-white carpet.

"Are you hurt, sis?" Carlo asked, kneeling next to me.

I just coughed.

"If you need something, you tell me," he said. "Don't just go out and risk yourself."

I nodded and lifted myself to my knees. I'd vowed not to go back to that store, and then I'd tried to do it. But I wanted to eat the eggs. I should have been able to eat the eggs. I just wanted to get more for Dad so he wouldn't be mad that I'd eaten them.

Carlo peered at my neck and touched it gently.

"I'm okay," I got out. "I'm okay."

Now I carefully wrap up the block of cheese. I put it back in the refrigerator exactly where I found it, and I tiptoe as quietly as I can back down the hall.

The cheese I ate sits heavily in my stomach.

I wasn't asking for permission, but I had it. I was allowed to eat the cheese. I could have even eaten all of it.

Mom just lets me do things.

I lie awake in bed thinking about all the eggs in the refrigerator, how there are so many that it seems like we could never run out. And how I could pick up my phone and call Tree. I could call Becca. I could try to find out Miss Sheila's number and call her. I could call anyone.

My phone pings. It's Tree. He's sending me links to online word quizzes, just like he said he would.

This one has the hardest words, he says.

Multitudinous ads, but worthwhile.

Most gamified.

I don't know what gamified means, and I don't know if I'll ever get a chance to look at these websites, but I do know that Tree is the third person ever to care what I wanted to learn. There was that old woman on the street, Becca, and now him. Even Mom wants to force me to go to American school whether I want to or not. But I told Tree I was interested in these links, and he sent them.

Thank you, I reply.

Sweet dreams, fair maiden.

There are footsteps in the hallway, and I can tell it's Mom. Already, I know what she sounds like. Maybe I remember from nine years ago. I bet she's going for a midnight snack, eating cereal or yogurt or cheese or crackers. I have the urge to get up and join her. Suddenly I just want to see her and know she's really out there and not a figment of my imagination. But she isn't really out there, I remember. It's only the shell of her. All of this is an illusion.

What's real is my living family: Dad and Carlo, and back in

Zebulun, Miss Sheila and Mr. Doug. Dad wasn't always angry. He didn't hurt me very many times.

I squeeze my eyes shut. I take the memory of myself getting up from the floor, coughing, after Dad choked me, and I slide it away. I grab a piece of another memory, of us eating cereal: me and Dad and Carlo, all together. Me eating all the cereal I wanted. I roll the memory back to the night before, to New Year's Eve, to when the snow started.

19

Port Angeles

age thirteen

It was New Year's Eve the year we moved into the house, and Carlo, Dad, and I were sitting on the couch watching the countdown on the little TV. As we got down to five minutes left, the flakes started falling, right into the light outside the sliding glass doors.

I got up from the couch and ran to the doors, and Carlo came and stood next to me. The flakes were big and thick, sticking to the overgrown grass in the backyard. We could see some stars up there too. The whole world outside had been transformed.

People started cheering on the TV.

"Come on," Carlo said. He slid the doors open, and we walked out into the snowfall. Someone down the street was setting off fireworks. The lights were shooting into the sky.

Carlo opened his mouth and let the snow fall in, and I did too.

Dad came out, and he opened his arms wide and opened his mouth, and we all three stood there in the snow and let it fall all over us. Dad was drunk, but that was okay. He danced around, catching those snowflakes on his tongue. The snow was all over my hair when we went back inside, and Dad laughed.

"My little snow princess," he said.

"Your majesty," Carlo said, giving an elaborate bow.

I twirled around, swishing my skirt, and the snow melted and dripped down onto my shoulders, and we all drifted off to bed.

The next morning, Carlo and I pulled some old cardboard boxes out of the garage, and we walked to the nearest hill we could find. It wasn't a huge hill, but it was big enough for a good slide. It was still snowing, but smaller flakes, and there were inches and inches on the ground. We crunched through the pristine sidewalks, marring them with our footprints. I didn't have boots, so I was just walking in my sneakers, which got all wet. Carlo was wearing work boots and that one burnt-orange coat he had, which he wore everywhere. It had been patched at the elbows already by the time we met him and had definitely never been washed. The snow caught on it and created dark spots, turning him into a human cheetah.

Carlo folded up the edge of the box and told me to sit on it. "Hold on now!" He grabbed the edge and got ready to push.

"Wait!" I cried. But he started to run with me, pushing our make-shift sled along. He gave me one last push, and down I went. I slid down the hill, twirling around on that box and screaming and laughing until I came to a stop at the bottom.

Carlo launched himself face-first onto another box and came

sliding past me, screeching and hollering.

"Again!" he cried. We ran up that hill as fast as we could, me dragging my box behind me. When we got to the top, Dad was coming toward us on the sidewalk, carrying another box.

"Having fun without me?" he said, dropping his box into the snow. "Try this one, Lisa. It's better."

I sat on it. It was better. It was bigger, and I could hold on to the front of it like a real sled.

"Ready?"

"Yes!"

Dad grabbed onto the back and gave me a running push. I flew down. As I got to the bottom, Dad and Carlo whooshed by me, propelled by their larger mass.

Two, three more times we went down that hill and ran back up.

The fourth time, Carlo pushed me so hard that I twirled and twirled and twirled, and I fell off that carboard onto the snow face-first.

"Lisa!" Carlo came running down the hill.

I sat up and threw snow at him.

"So that's what's what!" he said, throwing snow back at me. Dad made a huge cube and aimed it at Carlo. I made a ball, threw it at Dad, and ran away. Dad got me, but with a much smaller snowball. By the time we were done snow fighting, I was covered in snow and freezing water from head to toe. My hair was completely tangled up and wet, with whole blocks of snow sticking in it.

"Oh no, my snow princess is freezing," Dad said. He put his arm around me. "Let's get you inside."

We picked up our soppy cardboard and headed back to the house. By that time it had stopped snowing, and it was already warming up. The second we got home, I jumped into the shower. It was the best shower of my life; I was so cold.

I remember getting out of the shower and coming down the hall thinking it was time for me to make breakfast. The sun was shining in through the window, reflecting off the snow, so I had to cover my eyes with one hand. And Carlo and Dad were sitting there at the table with the cereal boxes and bowls and milk out. Carlo's old coat was draped around the edges of his chair, dripping onto the linoleum.

"You feeling better, sis?" he asked.

"Yeah." I felt better than better. I felt like I'd been wearing a coat that weighed a thousand pounds, and now it was gone. I felt like I could have flown up to the ceiling and eaten my Cheerios in the air.

"I love snow," Carlo said. "Wish we got more of it."

"It's great for a day, 'til it turns to slush and freezes," Dad said.

I just ate my cereal. There was plenty of it that day. We ate it with whole milk that almost tasted as good as the milk Mr. Doug got from the cows.

20

Zebulun

age seven

Whole milk straight from the cow is one of the best things you'll ever taste. And what makes it even sweeter, according to Mr. Doug, is when you don't have to milk the cows yourself.

It was only a few days after Dad and I were hiding in the basement that I tasted that milk for the first time. That was the first day Dad was going to start working on whatever projects the Citizens sent him to. And it was going to be my first day of Miss Sheila's school. I always liked school, so I was excited.

For the first few days, I'd wake up in that daybed in the little bedroom at the end of the hall on the second floor of Miss Sheila and Mr. Doug's house, and I'd be confused about where I was. I'd open my eyes and see the closet in front of me and know it was the wrong closet. And I'd sit up and feel the light on me from the window and know it was coming in the wrong way. And it would take me a few minutes to realize I was in Miss Sheila and Mr. Doug's house and not my mom's house. I was in a place with a big yard with fields behind it and not in Eugene. It was colder in that room, and the bed was different. It was actually more comfortable than the bed I'd had at Mom's house, but that didn't help. It confused me, in those first few moments.

But this day, for the first time, I woke up, and I knew exactly where I was.

I remember that I sat up in bed, and immediately I looked out the window. There was only a flimsy yellow curtain over it, so the light was streaming in. You could even see through it, and I saw the sky. I pictured what my mom would be doing, right then. She'd be sitting at the kitchen table in her bathrobe, a bowl of cereal in front of her. The radio would be on, playing morning news and Top 40 music. Her hair, now shorter, would be flat against her head, one side tucked behind her ear. In front of the table was a window that looked out onto a yard and a fence. I pictured her eating her cereal, looking out the window, looking up at the sky.

I looked up at the sky for a long time.

And then I shut my mind off. I closed it. I took that image and buried it. I wiped everything that had happened in my life before we came to Zebulun out of my head.

When I came downstairs for breakfast, Miss Sheila was stirring a big pot of oatmeal on the stove. Dad was sitting at the table reading the Gospel of the Citizens of the Word. I started to sit down, and Mr. Doug walked in. He was dressed in khaki work pants and a lumber-jack shirt, his sleeves rolled up to the elbows. He was tall and had thick arms and walked heavy in his steel-toed boots.

I shrank into my seat as he approached. He was so big, and I was so little.

There was already a glass set at the table in front of me. Mr. Doug leaned over me, picked it up, and poured milk from a glass bottle. "You try that," he said.

I shrank back.

Mr. Doug laughed and then softened his voice. "I didn't mean to scare you. That's milk straight from the cow. Every morning, some of the folks milk the cows, and some of us go around distributing it to everyone. Now, we still buy some milk from the store, but this is the good stuff."

I picked up the glass and took a hesitant sip. It was different from anything I'd ever tasted. It was warm, but that didn't make it bad. I looked up at him.

"Now you know what real milk is," he said.

I drank some more.

Mr. Doug gave me a little pat on the back. "We'll teach you how to milk a cow one of these days."

"Really?" I looked at Dad. Because I couldn't do anything fun without Dad's permission.

"Sure, why not?" he said, still reading.

"Really," said Miss Sheila, setting a bowl of steaming oatmeal in front of me. "Each week we do a unit where we teach the students life skills. How to milk a cow is one of them."

"Milking a cow is school?" I took another drink of milk,

incredulous. How could school involve actually *doing* something?

"You won't graduate from our school with book learning but no brains," Mr. Doug said, sitting down at the other side of the round table. "Thankee kindly," he said to Miss Sheila, who handed him a bowl of oatmeal.

"Not that we don't have book learning," Miss Sheila said, giving Mr. Doug a little bit of side-eye. "After breakfast, you'll come to the family room through there." She pointed through the living room to another part of the house that we'd only peeked in when I got the tour. "That's where we have our lessons. 8:00 a.m. sharp."

"Yes, ma'am," I said.

A half hour later, I had put on my long skirt and braided my hair and was ready to go. There were six other girls in Miss Sheila's school that day, plus a group of five or six who were living elsewhere but were watching us all on their computers. This computer in Miss Sheila's school was the only one I ever saw in Zebulun in all my years there, even though I assumed some of the men had them. I never touched it, and as far as I knew, Miss Sheila never touched it either except during school. We didn't like technology too much because the internet was a conduit to the outside world, which was full of sin. But we used it when we had to. We had electricity, and there were TVs in most houses, and some people had cell phones. And by people, I mean men.

Miss Sheila had set up desks for all of us, and mine was right next to Jean's. At that time, she only had two little sisters. And that day, she was holding her right arm against her body.

"Are you okay?" I asked her.

She shot a look at me. "Yeah."

"I'm Lisa."

"Jean."

"It looks like you hurt your arm."

"*I* didn't hurt it," Jean exploded, whisper-yelling. "It was Kitty."

Miss Sheila, who was fiddling with the computer, shot us a look.

Jean leaned toward me and whispered, "Kitty is my little sister. She's five, and she's a terror. She grabbed my arm and wouldn't let go, and I had to pull and pull and scream and scream to get her off me."

"Jean, what did we learn about our reactions?" Miss Sheila said, taking her place at the front of the class.

"I control them," Jean replied, her jaw set.

"That's right," Miss Sheila said. "Many times in our lives we'll encounter people who anger us. We must turn the other cheek as Jesus did and respond to provocation with sweetness. Of course, younger children are less capable of knowing right from wrong, so we must demonstrate for them, mustn't we?"

"Yes, ma'am." Jean sat quietly until Miss Sheila turned her back, and then she stuck her tongue out at me and rolled her eyes.

That's why we were best friends.

Miss Sheila's class wasn't just about milking cows. We also got to look through Mr. Doug's telescope and learn about the heavens. The first time I got to look through it was about a year after I got there. The other girls who didn't live there came back at night, and it was fall, so it was pretty chilly, and everyone was wearing sweatshirts or light coats over their blouses. A lot of the sweatshirts and coats didn't fit well because they'd borrowed them from siblings or parents. Nobody in Zebulun ever got anything new unless one of the women made it for them. I was wearing one of Miss Sheila's sweaters, which she'd knitted herself, and which was about five sizes too big for me.

All of us girls were excited, milling around in that classroom waiting for Mr. Doug, and as soon as he showed up and waved us through to the side porch, we exploded out of those sliding glass doors like a battalion of fire ants. We crowded around Mr. Doug while he explained where we should look and what we were looking for. He had the telescope pointed at Saturn, and we were all supposed to look at the rings.

One by one, hopping around excitedly, we got our turn.

Mr. Doug was talking about God and how he'd created the universe, and the mystery of all the heavenly bodies, which we might be able to visit after the world ended, when we were all heavenly beings, living in the firmament with Jesus. He explained that the rings of Saturn are made of ice. And then I stopped listening. Because I was looking at it, this beautiful and giant ball of iron and liquid and gas surrounded by ice and hurtling around the sun like we were.

"Lisa, it's Jean's turn," Mr. Doug said.

I stepped away from the eyepiece, and Jean eagerly moved into my place. Mr. Doug smiled down at me and winked.

An hour later, it was just us, and he was showing me the moon.

"The US government sent men up there," he told me. "Long time ago now, but I remember. I was about nine years old. We had a whole group of us in this very house watching on TV as Neil Armstrong stepped onto the surface."

"Are they still there?" I asked.

"No, they came back. But the government might send more people and build a town someday."

"I want to go!"

Mr. Doug laughed. "I don't. It's gotta be hard to live in a place with no air. It'll be different in the next life though. We can all go then."

"How come we don't see any Citizens up there now?" I asked.

"Well, they're there, but we humans can't see anyone in the next life. Not until we get there. It's supposed to remain a mystery to us mortals."

I felt like asking why, but I knew that too many questions could get me in trouble. A couple questions were good. That showed you were listening. But a lot of questions annoyed Miss Sheila. With Dad, sometimes one question was too much. So I just looked into the telescope again and examined the moon.

The next afternoon, during the practical part of the school day, I went home with Jean to help her watch her little sisters. We were eight by then, Kitty was six, Pauline was three, and Isobel was only a few months old. We'd all learned how to change a baby's diaper, so that's what I was doing while Kitty chased Pauline around the living room.

"I don't believe in people on the moon," Jean said. "Mr. Doug was being funny."

I frowned. Jean was always saying things weren't true. But I wanted to believe it. I wanted to believe I could go to the moon someday.

"If it's real, why can't we go there?"

"We can in the afterlife," I said, fastening Isobel's diaper. She waved her arms at me and smiled. At least, I thought it was a smile. It was hard to tell with babies.

Pauline rushed in front of my legs, followed by a screaming Kitty.

"That's stupid," Jean said. "Why can't we do cool stuff now? *If* it's real."

"We can help with the animals," I said. "That's cool."

"Yeah, way cooler than this. You're so lucky you're an only child." She caught Pauline. "Kitty, stop!"

Kitty let out a huge raspberry.

Jean pushed her away. "Go play!" She pointed to a blanket on the far side of the living room that had a pile of toys on it.

Kitty went over there, picked up a baby doll, and smashed its face into the ground.

"Let's read a book," Jean said, plopping Pauline on the couch.

I made sure Isobel was on her back in her crib and picked up one of the books. All of our children's picture books were hand drawn by one of the Citizens and photocopied. This one was about a little girl who met another kid in a park and explained to the other kid how to do penance. Not as entertaining as the author had hoped.

"I have a better story," I said, putting my arm around Pauline. "It's about the moon. Did you know people live there?"

Jean rolled her eyes, but she didn't try to stop me. Anything that kept Pauline's attention and separated Pauline from Kitty was good.

"There's a whole town, and it's a lot like Zebulun, 'cept everyone is wearing space suits," I continued. "And there's less gravity, so you walk like this." I got up and began bouncing around the living room.

Pauline followed me, and then Jean got into it, and finally Kitty noticed what we were doing, and she started bouncing around and laughing too. Later, I came up with all sorts of stories about the people on the moon, including a whole bit about space chickens. Jean always rolled her eyes. She never believed in any of it. She always said that someday she'd get a real book and prove that there were no people and no chickens up there, and nothing but dust.

Later, after I met Becca, I read all about the moon and the planets in one of her dad's books. Of course, there was nothing about invisible dead Citizens living there. Mr. Doug's story was one more thing that was true for us and not true for other people. But sometimes at night, I'd go outside and sit on a patio chair, or on the patio itself after Dad sold the furniture, and I'd look up at the moon and think about them, all those people who were free of this life and living in the heavens, able to go wherever they wanted.

I hoped our truth was the real one.

21

Eugene

now

In the morning, Mom suggests we go for a hike up Spencer Butte. I know why she wants to do this. It's because when I was little, she used to take me up there. Dad didn't like to hike, so it would be just us. We'd get to the top, where the forest dissolves into a bunch of large rocks, and you can look down over the whole city, and she'd take her hair down out of the bun. I'd take my hair out of the braid, and we'd dance around, hair flying free. We got some weird looks from other people, but we didn't care. Having long hair blowing in the wind seemed like the most fun in the world. Even though when we got back down to the car, we had to comb it, and it hurt like crazy.

For this I wear a pair of jeans Mom bought me. They're loose jeans, and they hang from my hips. Mom wanted me to try some form-fitting jeans, which I'm guessing are the cool kind, but I can't stand having anything gripping my body that way. So I cover the jeans with a T-shirt that I feel is too tight, that makes it look like I have large breasts. I pull my hair into a ponytail instead of twisting it into a bun or braiding it. I stare at myself in the mirror Mom has hung over the closet door in my bedroom. I've worn jeans plenty of times before, but doing it here feels different. My image seems to shimmer in front of me. I'm not sure if I'm seeing myself or if I'm seeing the person Mom wishes I would have been, the Alyssa who never left.

When Mom sees me, her face lights up. "Wow, you look so pretty," she says.

"Thank you."

She holds up a backpack. "I've got water, apples, a few cereal bars. Do you think we need anything else?"

I shake my head. We just had breakfast. I don't know if I'll ever get used to this.

"Barron," she yells back into the house. "We're heading out. Everything good?"

"Yepper!" Barron yells back.

We get in the car, and we don't say much until we reach the Spencer Butte parking lot. I look out the window to see if I remember any of the scenery, but I don't. I know I've ridden along this road before, but it's been wiped from my memory. We get out of the car and start walking up the path, but I don't really remember this either. All I remember is being at the top. We pass a few other hikers, and then Mom clears her throat.

"So, did you text that boy?" she asks.

"No," I say automatically.

"Oh." She sounds disappointed. "Well, there's always today."

"I mean, yes I did."

Mom gives me a raised eyebrow.

"I did," I repeat. "He was nice to me even with the way I look."

"Alyssa, you're a beautiful girl!" she exclaims.

"I meant my clothes. To Americans I look weird."

She winces at the word *Americans*. "Why did you say no at first?"

"It was just a mistake."

"Because your dad would get angry if you texted a boy. Because he didn't even buy you a phone. Because he kept you prisoner in that house."

"I wasn't a prisoner." I walk faster.

Mom keeps up with me. "I'm trying not to be frustrated," she says. "I can imagine what you went through, and I don't want to make it worse." But there's an edge to her voice. She *is* frustrated.

"Women just don't have phones," I say. "Girls don't text boys. Girls don't go out. It's not a prison; it's just how things are." There's an edge to *my* voice. I hate the feel of my legs in my jeans, the way the fabric scrapes against my skin, the way the waistband falls against my hips. Sweat is pooling behind my knees. My long ponytail flaps against my back.

"You didn't like it that way," Mom says, more quietly. "You had to live that way because of his abuse. You had to pretend it was okay with you so he wouldn't hurt you."

He didn't hurt me, I almost say. But the words don't make it out of my mouth. There are no police here, no social workers, no one who can do worse to me than what's been done. Of course she's right that I didn't like it, but I hate how she's making me sound like a victim. I did what I could to help myself. I learned anyway.

"I just want you to understand that you don't have to lie to me," Mom says. "Not about texting a boy. Not about what your life was like or what your dad did. No one here is going to hurt you for telling the truth."

I keep walking. She says she wants the truth, and that may be true when it comes to whether I texted Tree or what food I ate. But she doesn't want to hear about how old the Earth is or about the people living on the moon, that's for sure. She doesn't want to hear one good thing about my life over the last nine years. I'm guessing she doesn't really want to know about the bad stuff either. Nobody likes hearing a girl whine and complain.

Mom walks next to me in silence, biting her lip. It's like there are words and sentences and rants just behind her closed mouth. Things she wants to say about what Dad did to her and what she thinks he did to me and how stupid I am for believing in the Word. I try to appreciate that she doesn't say those things, that she doesn't want to be angry. People who want to change their flaws are better than those who don't. Miss Sheila used to say that when she was trying to get us girls to forgive each other for talking smack or pulling hair. But I hear what Mom doesn't say as clearly as if she said it.

If she didn't want me to believe in the Word, why did *she* teach me to believe it?

If Dad was so bad, why did she marry him and even have me?

If she cared about what he did to me . . . I don't know how to finish the thought. How was she supposed to help me? She didn't know where I was. But we were in the same house for years. She wasn't *really* looking. Just like she wasn't *really* trying to protect me from him when I was seven.

The knot in my stomach reasserts itself.

The day before I climbed out the window, Dad came to my school. He sat in his car on a side street and waited until Mom had dropped me off, and then he raced up to me and walked me half a block down the street. He told me what to do and when, and that I wasn't supposed to tell anyone, especially Mom. He said if I did what he told me, I'd get a big reward, and everything would be better.

I thought we'd all be together somewhere else and there'd be no more fighting. I thought if I did what he wanted, and if I kept the secret, then it would be Dad and Mom and me and Liam. Somehow, me keeping the secret and getting out without anybody hearing me was the key. I thought I had the power to change everything.

And I did.

But she did too. She could have stayed there in her car after she dropped me off and watched me.

We're at the final stretch of the hike now, where it gets steeper. We have to climb over rocks, and we're in the sun. I haven't hiked since I was seven, and I'm out of breath.

Because I kept the secret, all our lives changed.

But I was a child. She *knew* he wanted to take me.

But I wasn't stupid. I made choices for myself. My whole life, I've made choices for myself. I'm not some helpless little victim. I don't want her to treat me that way.

It's a weekday morning, so the top of the hill is almost deserted. There's just one older couple on the far end of the rocky area, sitting in the sun having a picnic. They have a blanket spread out on the rocks and what looks like sandwiches and fruit.

Mom and I sit on the closest group of rocks and look out at the trees. The side we're on has some houses, but there's a big forest that goes on into the distance. I almost forgot how much I used to love nature. All the way up the hill, I barely even noticed where I was.

"If you don't want to talk about this, it's okay," Mom says. "But I don't know if I can say it enough, because I know what it's like to be in the Word. I know how kind they can be, and how it can seem like a great community at first. I remember Sheila and Doug. We spent an entire month with them when we first got married, and they were so welcoming. They don't show you the bad side until you're already in. And they did rein in Art. Things didn't get bad between us until after we moved here."

I just listen and look out at nature. I try to appreciate the sun on my back. I don't want to think of her as a victim either.

"I didn't know him that well when we got married. It was just a few months. He said he wanted to take care of me, and he said he wasn't going to leave. He said he wanted to be with me forever. At the time, no one had ever said that to me. And someone who looked like him, wanting to be with me? I didn't have a lot of friends, so I didn't realize

I wasn't allowed to have any. I expected to be a stay-at-home mom, so I didn't know it was my only choice. I wanted something to believe in, and the Word had lots and lots of stuff for that." She pauses and chews her lip. "It was probably a year after we got married before he first hit me."

"Mom . . . " I trail off because I don't know what to say. *Did you hit back?* I want to ask. But I didn't. I tried to, but I was too small and too weak. I lay my head on my knees. I couldn't have hit back. But I wish I had.

"I'm telling you this because even though I was an adult, I still did what Art wanted me to do. He had me believing the Word was right about women having their place, and he also convinced me that *his* interpretation of the Word was right. And we both taught you that from when you were a child, so it isn't your fault you believed it. It was Art's fault, and it was my fault. I was married to him for nine years before I tried to break free. And I tried to take you with me. I went to court and got custody. But I never sat you down and told you that none of it was true. You saw all those things, and neither of us ever taught you it wasn't normal."

"Miss Sheila and Mr. Doug did tell me that," I say. "Mr. Doug said husbands are supposed to punish wives with kindness."

"I remember that. Did you ever see him force Sheila into penance?"

"Yes."

"Did you think it was kind?"

I start chewing my lip, and then I realize it makes me look like Mom, and I stop myself. "No. But he never hit her."

"What did she do to deserve penance?" Mom asks.

"Not having dinner ready. Or the kids in her school were being too loud. When that happened, she'd make us do lines until our hands fell off."

Mom turns to me and takes both of my hands in hers. The sun is blaring down on her, and sweat beads at her hairline. Several strands of her short hair plaster themselves to the sides of her face. "Alyssa, I need you to understand that none of that was normal. None of that was okay."

None of what? The penance, the lines, the whole town? Dad hurting her? Dad hurting me? Dad . . .

"Dad killed somebody," I blurt. "That's why they kicked us out of Zebulun. He caught this guy hoarding cash behind some bricks in the wall, so he beat him to death."

Mom sucks in her breath and releases my hands. Then she snatches them up again. "Oh my God, Alyssa."

"His name was Daniel Stevenson. Did you know him?"

"Yeah. Oh, he was a huge jerk. He had money?" Mom shakes her head. "He was one of the loudest when it came to lay preaching, all about the godliness of communal living."

"I remember that too." Mr. Daniel was old and his voice was scratchy, and you could barely hear him, but boy did he have a lot to say.

Mom releases my hands, but she keeps eye contact with me. "I hope you feel like you can tell me about other things that happened, too. I will *never* let him take you back. That will never happen."

"I know." I look away from her, and for something to do, I stand up. I walk along the top of the rocks toward the old couple and their picnic. I turn to the other side of the hill and look down on the city of

Eugene. She didn't stop him from taking me the first time.

Mom steps next to me. "They've given Art an ankle monitor," she says. "He can't leave the state of Washington. I talked to the prosecutor."

I stare down at the houses. I try to figure out where Mom and Barron's house is, but I don't see it. All the houses look the same, and I don't know the streets well enough. Even though I was born here, it feels like a strange new place. This is a place where people believe bizarre impossible things: The law protects people; an ankle monitor can stop a bad guy.

"I lied about texting Tree because Dad would say boys were dangerous. He'd say every man on the street wanted to rape me, and every boy who talked to me just wanted sex. But my brother Carlo wasn't like that. Mr. Doug wasn't like that. I knew it couldn't be everyone."

"You think of Carlo as your brother?" Mom's voice cracks a little. This is the first time she's asked about him. I think I know what she's afraid of.

"He would never hurt me." I realize that's what I said about Dad, so I turn to her and meet her eyes. "Really. He was just a kid who needed a family. And we needed him. He was there for me." I stop talking and picture him sitting across the card table, how his face lit up when he smiled. I know Carlo hurt people. I know he has a lot in common with Dad, and that's why they love each other so much. But the fact that he would never hurt *me* means something. It has to. And not just to me, but to Mom. Because he protected me when she couldn't. I change the subject, bring it back to something safe.

"I don't think Tree is dangerous," I say.

"I don't think so either." Mom's smile says she's glad I changed the subject too. Maybe she doesn't believe that Carlo didn't hurt me. Maybe she's not ready to hear what she thinks is the truth.

"Tree said, you know what's dangerous: yogurt. He said some lady died from eating it." My stomach twists. Why did I bring that up? I try to picture that lady, but I can't.

"I read about that," Mom says. "There were actually two women in Idaho. They're saying maybe it was poison." She puts a hand on my back. "But just because some nut in Idaho poisoned some yogurt doesn't mean we never eat yogurt again."

"Not all yogurts are poison, and not all boys are rapists. Check." The words come spilling out of my mouth before I even plan to say them. That's how I keep the truth in: push something else out. My heart is beating in my throat. I feel like I might explode. I cling to the second part of what I said: Not all boys are rapists. Not Carlo, not Tree.

"I want you to have a good life," Mom says. "I want you to be able to choose whatever you want to do. I want you to never believe that a man gets to tell you how to live your life."

"But you don't get to either," I say.

"Right. That's true."

"So I can go home to Zebulun?"

Mom sets her jaw.

"Then it's not true, is it? I can't choose." *Thunk thunk thunk.* My heart beats.

"You really want to go back to a place where they make an old lady kneel for hours? And women get married at eighteen and pop out babies and never leave town again? And you have to do everything Brandon says?"

I don't say anything. My teeth grind together. That's not all Zebulun is. But she knows that.

"I'm sorry. I know you lived there for a long time. I don't want to be dismissive of that." Mom sighs. "I just want you to see that we have nice things here too." She waves a hand over the city.

"I see it." I try to keep my voice calm. It has to sound like I believe it. As if I can just walk back down the hill and live in this world, as if Dad having an ankle monitor means anything, as if he can't touch me here, as if God can't see everything I do. As if I truly get a say in what happens to me. As if I'm not a victim.

Mom runs her hand through her hair and shakes her head. "It's not the same doing it with short hair."

I reach up and undo my ponytail. I run my hands through my long hair, which is already hopelessly tangled, and I let the wind have it.

"Oh, you really do have beautiful hair," Mom says. "Even the color."

"Thank you." I think about opening my arms wide and dancing around, but I don't do that. I just let the wind flow through my hair. I do like being up here on top of the hill. I like breathing the fresh air. I like deciding whether I'm going to take my hair down or not. I like that I have a phone and I can call whoever I want.

I look out over the city of Eugene, so tiny and far away. Those Americans with all their freedoms might as well be on the moon. I can't get to either place as long as I'm living. Yes, I can stand here with my late mother and pretend she isn't dead. I can hike in jeans and talk to Tree. But it's only temporary. It's only until the Trial is over.

"You'll get used to being here," Mom says. "I promise."

"I'm sure I will," I say. And I know I could, and I know I can't. My hand goes to the back of my head. I remember how it felt when it hit the floor, after I tried and failed to fight back. Nobody can do that to me here. I clench my fists and try to slow down my heartbeat. I know he's in Washington. Not because of some dumb ankle monitor, but because Carlo told me. Carlo wouldn't lie to me. He wouldn't tell me they were one place but come here instead.

"I'm so sorry," Mom says. She sets a careful hand on my back. "I shouldn't push you. I just wanted to have a nice walk together, like we used to."

"It was nice," I say. I try to smile at her. I force myself not to look behind me. Nobody's back there except some old couple having a picnic. Instead, I take off walking down the trail.

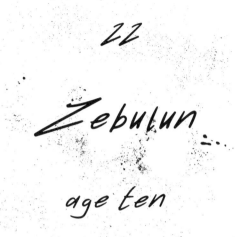

22

Zebulun

age ten

The day Jean's late aunt came back to town, Jean had stayed after school with me at Miss Sheila's house. Miss Sheila made us do some chores, like mopping the kitchen floor and dusting all the tables and shelves and things, but once we were done, she let us off. We went into the backyard and started a game with our favorite dog, a big happy mutt we called Bertie.

We were throwing a stick and getting Bertie to chase after it, and we also had a system of bases that we made out of rocks, and so we would throw the stick and then run, the goal being to get to the base before Bertie got to us.

Jean threw the stick, and it went really far, all the way to the edge of the road. She ran like heck.

"Come on, Bertie!" I shouted. "You can get it!" He made it to the stick, but he must have been tired out, because he paused with it in his mouth. "Come on, boy!"

Jean reached the base and threw her arms up. "Yes!"

Bertie dropped the stick and started barking. A fancy new car was coming up the road slowly. We didn't have a lot of cars that looked like that. It stopped right in front of Bertie, and the window rolled down. A lady I'd never seen before with a dark brown braid and sunglasses stuck her head out.

"It's okay, Bertie," the woman said. "It's me, Rachel."

Now Bertie got excited like he did when me or Miss Sheila or Mr. Doug walked in the door.

"Aunt Rachel?" Jean whispered. She stood frozen on those rocks.

"Jean!" the woman called. "Is that you?"

Jean didn't answer. I looked from her to Rachel. Bertie was still barking like his favorite person just came home. This lady couldn't be scary if Bertie liked her—that was a truth like chores and Heaven.

Mr. Doug came into view, coming from the direction of the front door. His shoulders were tight, and his face was grim. He walked up to the car window and patted Bertie on the head.

"It's okay, boy." He tapped his side. "Go on now."

Bertie whined, but he came walking back to me. I pulled him close. That stick was lying there at Mr. Doug's feet.

"Rachel, you got your answer," Mr. Doug said. "Go on now, and let's not make trouble."

"That's my niece over there," Rachel said, pointing at Jean. "I never got a chance to say goodbye. What if she thinks I wanted to leave her?"

I stared at Jean. She'd never once mentioned this aunt before.

She had lots of other aunts and uncles who she talked about all the time. Some of them lived outside Zebulun, but there was always gossip about who was fighting with who and which cousins were on which side. I thought I had the whole family tree down by now.

"Nobody wants to die, Rachel. She knows that."

Rachel stared up at Mr. Doug for a long moment. Then she leaned out the window. "Jean! I love you, honey! I'm going back to Portland. If you ever need anything—"

"That's enough," Mr. Doug said. "Let Jean's soul alone. She's a good girl." Mr. Doug said it sharply, like a warning.

Rachel pulled her head back inside the car. She lifted her sunglasses to wipe her eyes.

"Very smart, Sheila says," Mr. Doug said more softly. "Top of her class. Growing up real well."

Rachel looked back at Jean, her sunglasses up, showing her tired eyes. Then she looked up at Mr. Doug. She pulled her sunglasses back down, rolled up the window, and started the car. The tires ground against the pavement as she pulled out fast. She sped away from us, down the road out of Zebulun.

Mr. Doug walked over to us. His body was still tense, his shoulders hunched as he bent down to pat Bertie. "'Bout time to get cleaned up for dinner," he said.

We didn't say anything else about Rachel until dinner was almost finished. Dad was working late that day, so it was just Jean, me, Miss Sheila, and Mr. Doug. Jean hardly said a word the whole meal except *please* and *thank you*. I knew I should have kept quiet since everyone else was. But I couldn't stop thinking about her. The question came bursting out of my mouth.

"What happened to Jean's aunt Rachel?" I asked.

"She died about three years ago," Miss Sheila said. "Right before you and Art came." That was all anyone said. Everyone else just went on eating. Except now Jean's eyes were filling up. She pushed the remains of her potatoes around her plate.

"But what happened?"

Miss Sheila put a hand on my shoulder. "Sometimes when people die, it happens slowly. We all failed Rachel by not seeing the signs before it was too late. She became willful, dressed more worldly, talked back to her husband. Then one day, it happened. Rachel was gone. She left her husband and the Word. Her soul was lost. That woman who came back today, she wasn't Rachel. She was the shell of Rachel that remains."

Jean was full-on crying now. She wiped her face on her sleeve.

"Like my mom," I said.

"Yes," Miss Sheila said. "Jean, we're so sorry. We know how hard it is. Why don't you clean yourself up?"

Jean leapt up from the table and ran up the stairs.

"May I be excused?" I asked.

"Sure," Mr. Doug said. "You go help your friend."

I found Jean in the bathroom crying her eyes out.

"It looked like her," Jean said through gasping breaths. "It looked *just like* her."

"She didn't look dead," I said.

"But she is," Jean said. "I dream about her. I see her where she is, Lisa. In the brimstone. She cries. She calls out to me. Like she did today, only she says other things. She wants me to come to her. In the dream, one time I did. I went to her, and she pulled me in. I was in the brimstone, and it was so hot. It was burning. And I ran, and I woke up." She blew her nose on a piece of toilet paper.

"She can't get you if you don't go," I said.

"I won't go," Jean said. "I won't go."

I didn't know what else to do, so I sat on the toilet lid while Jean wiped her eyes. Jean was always telling me things she didn't believe. She thought lots of stuff we learned in church was stupid. Like the people on the moon and how only men could be Elders. But Jean believed this. She knew her aunt was dead even though she was just driving down the street.

We all knew shells could come to you in your dreams. We all knew we had to be vigilant in case one came for you, but we also knew we had control. We could always say no, refuse to travel with the devil and his companions. Shells could be turned away, sent back to where they came from. But the fact that it happened to Jean, that was something new for me. If Jean believed it, it must really be true. Rachel was dead, and so was Mom.

That was the moment I truly understood Mom was a shell. She never was my mom after she left Dad. That woman with the trimmed hair in jeans who read me the bedtime story would have dragged me down with her. I knew if I ever saw her again like Jean had seen Rachel, I had to be strong. I had to resist the temptation to believe it was my mother I saw. I had to take all my actions knowing the truth.

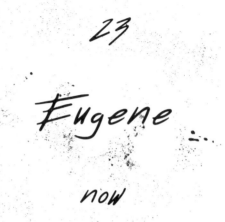

23

Eugene

now

Back at Mom and Barron's house, I carefully comb out my hair. It's so long and so tangled that it feels like it takes hours. I wind it into a bun, and the face in the mirror takes shape again. It's me, Lisa, staring back.

The knot in my stomach tightens. Around the knot, something churns. I came too close to saying bad things about Dad. I came too close to letting myself think of Mom as alive, and too close to forgetting what will happen if I do.

Men have a right to punish their wives and children. The Gospel of the Citizens of the Word says it, and American law says it too. Dad never went to jail for hitting Mom. All he got was a restraining order. He never went to jail for killing Daniel Stevenson—he just got banished. He didn't even get declared dead. But he could declare me dead as easily as he slammed me against the floor. He can make sure I never go home again and send my eternal soul to Hell.

I shouldn't have said anything to Mom at all. I shouldn't have listened. I don't know what being in this house is doing to me. What Mom was saying made sense, but it's not what I know to be true. Listening to her is going to kill me in one way or another. I can't stay in this house right now, or my mind will break, and I won't be able to make sense of anything.

If I was in Port Angeles, I'd sneak away to Becca's. I still want to talk to her about what's happened. But nothing has changed. She'd never forgive me if she found out the truth—the American truth.

I want to smash something. I grab my pillow off my bed and throw it down as hard as I can. It doesn't make me feel better.

I *did* tell her the truth. According to the Word, Mom *is* dead. When you get kicked out, like Dad, you're in a state of limbo: not a Citizen, yet still redeemable. It's understood that you may be able to come back someday, that you still have a life, that if you do enough penance, you may be able to reach the firmament. But Mom *left*. She voluntarily rejected everything that was true. She died.

But not the way Becca's mom died, and she won't see it the way I do.

I want to call her, but I can't. Not yet. Not until all this is over and I'm back home.

I pace around the room. I just have to get out of this house. And Mom wants me to see Tree. She thinks talking to boys is good. But I'm not doing this because of what she thinks. I don't trust what she thinks or what she says. I just have to do something that's possible.

I pick up my phone and press his number.

"Hola."

I freeze. "What?"

"Buenos días, mi amiga."

"Why are you saying that?"

"The question is, why not?"

I take a deep breath. "No reason. I'm sorry." Tree's voice sounds nothing like Carlo's. Lots of people must say *hola* when they pick up the phone. It's just a coincidence, or it's a sign that I'm supposed to stay on track. It's a sign that I'm doing what God wants me to do.

"Well? You phoned me."

"Do you want to hang out?" I'm gripping the phone as if it might fly away from my face.

"I thought you'd never ask. Do you have a car?"

"No." I try to relax. I try to act normal. "I don't even have a license. I live . . ." I try to remember exactly where I am. "There's a Safeway a couple blocks away."

"Fortieth Avenue?"

"Yeah, that sounds right."

"Meet me there in half an hour?"

"Okay. Goodbye." I hang up the phone, and I know that was weird. But maybe he's weird enough himself that he doesn't care.

I'm still wearing the jeans. They don't go with the bun. I was about to put on my skirt, too, to complete the transformation back to myself. But now that I'm about to leave the house, I realize I need to keep the jeans. I need to keep on being Alyssa. At least, half Alyssa. Enough Alyssa that no one will recognize the Lisa inside.

I grab the phone and stride down the hall toward the front door.

Mom is standing in the kitchen.

"I'm going to meet Tree at the Safeway," I say. I stand straight and still and brace myself.

"If you're sure you'll be all right," she says. Her eyes say that she's worried.

"I will be." The churn from my stomach has reached my throat. I feel like I'm going to barf.

"You have your phone?"

I nod.

"Then I have to put my money where my mouth is," Mom says. "Just please be home for dinner so I don't worry about you. And call if you need anything. Any little thing goes wrong, you call." She plucks her wallet off the counter and hands me a twenty-dollar bill.

I take it, stare at it in my hand.

"Never meet a boy without money of your own."

"I'm not *meeting a boy*; we're just hanging out."

"Okay." She tilts her head and smiles. "I thought I saw a little spark there."

"Mom!"

Mom puts both hands over her mouth, and I can hear what she's thinking. I just acted like a normal teen. Fine, if that's what she wants. I roll my eyes.

"See you later," I say. I put the cash in my pocket, and before she can change her mind, or I can, I open the front door, push away the screen, and step out into the driveway. The screen closes itself with a clatter, and my insides jump. I walk slowly to the edge of the driveway.

I haven't been this far from home by myself for years. That convenience store was as far as I ever went. And how many times did I do that?

Is Tree *a boy* the way Mom thinks he is? Yes, but no. Yes because I like him, but no because I can't. I can't want a boyfriend, only a husband. Only the husband my father chooses, unless he's not around for some reason, and then Miss Sheila could help me. Then I could be interested in a boy, but not now. It's not okay.

So I tell myself we're just hanging out. I'm just getting out of my mom's house.

But the outside world is a dangerous place. In every one of these houses, there's someone who would as soon rape me as give me the time of day. I'm only safe when I'm with Dad or with Carlo. Or with Becca. Becca somehow made me feel safe too. Because she was never afraid to walk down the street. Her lack of fear was my armor, extending like a bubble around me.

Now I don't have any bubble. It's just me in these strange clothes. My feet hurt a little from the hike. I stand at the edge of the driveway, frozen. There's no one else on the sidewalk. Down the street, on the opposite side, in the direction I have to go, there's a man pushing a lawn mower. He's wearing long shorts and a ratty T-shirt.

I know this man is not going to hurt me. I *know* that.

I step onto the sidewalk and turn right.

Hardly anyone gets raped or murdered while walking down the street in the middle of the day. Especially in a reasonably nice middle-class neighborhood in Eugene. I know that. My pulse beats in my ears as I walk closer to the man.

He raises a hand to me. "Howdy!"

I raise a hand and walk faster. I zip around the corner away from him. I'm walking so fast that I'm in danger of breaking into a run. I'm in danger of running and running and running. Instead, I walk even faster. I turn left at the bigger street, and now I can see the Safeway parking lot. A couple of cars go by, and nobody stops. Nobody jumps out of their car to drag me in. I race into the parking lot and make a beeline for the doors. I stand outside by the sad-looking plants and look around for Tree. But I'm early. He won't be here yet.

I watch people come in and out, and I can't help but size them up. That man has his wallet in his back pocket. I could take it in three seconds, and he would never realize. That lady's wallet is in her purse, which is hanging open inside her cart. I'd just need to wait for her to walk away from it.

Stealing from people was more dangerous than walking down the street. But I never did that alone. Carlo was always with me. What if I had to do it myself? What if all I had was me? What if I was living in that tent alone?

Nobody I've met here has ever done the things I've done. My vision blurs as the thoughts run through my head. I lived in a tent. I picked pockets. I lived right next to crazy people whacked out of their minds on drugs. Nobody ever hurt me. And it wasn't just because of Dad or because of Carlo. I knew how to pick out a violent person from a harmless one.

I'm trying to convince myself that I'm safe. I'm trying to

convince myself that I can stand here and do nothing and it will be okay. This is my Trial, after all. Being on my own is part of the road to becoming a Citizen. I can get through this with God's help. I am *not* a victim.

Tree comes through the automatic doors. "Hey, hey!" he says, walking over to me. He's carrying a grocery bag. Inside the bag are maybe seven yogurts and two spoons. He grins. "I thought I'd walk on the wild side. Take some risks. My parents were content to allow me to smoke and partake in psychedelic mushrooms, but those pastimes are so blasé."

I let out a tiny burst of laughter. There's a part of me that wants to cry. Another part of me is breaking apart.

"Shall we take a walk and partake in a game of yogurt roulette?" He inclines his head toward the edge of the parking lot.

"Sure."

We begin walking. I realize I probably haven't walked this much in one day since we left Seattle, and I don't know how long I'll be able to go.

"Did you have lunch?" he asks.

"No. I didn't think of it." I don't realize I'm hungry until he says it. I always try to pretend I'm not hungry until it's dinnertime. The yogurt is looking good now.

We walk for a few blocks until we reach the entrance to a park. As we leave the main sidewalk and head into the green space, I have some kind of déjà vu. I feel like I've been here before, maybe when I was little.

"Is there a merry-go-round down there?" I ask.

"Yes. Merry-go-round. Teeter-totter. Monkey bars. Swings. It's a cornucopia of potential injuries for small innocent children."

"If we're taking risks, that sounds like the perfect place to eat our yogurt," I say.

"Verily, it does."

We stroll down a hill and come out at a playground. Sure enough, there's a lot of equipment set in sawdust. A few kids are on the swings, but the merry-go-round is all clear. I sit down on one edge and press my legs together.

Tree sits near me, one handlebar between us.

I take a deep breath and silently thank him for leaving space between us. The line between safety with another and danger is thin and unclear. A man is supposed to protect you. All men want to rape you. Trust your father and your brother. Trust no one. *A boy* versus *just hanging out.*

My mom is dead, and she's waiting for me at home. Being obedient can save a soul, but some things you can't come back from. Keep sweet, and take action.

Tree sets the bag in the middle of the merry-go-round and pulls out two yogurts. Carefully, he picks at the foil around the top of both yogurts, making sure they're sealed tight. "It appears we won't perish today," he says. He hands me a yogurt and a spoon.

"What's life without risk?" I say, opening the foil. I dig in my spoon and stir. It's the kind that's already pre-stirred, but I like to stir mine good anyway. We so rarely had yogurt that when we did, it was a whole process. I take a bite. It's peach. Sweet and gooey and delicious. And not poison. I'm sure of it. God wouldn't take me before my Trial is complete. Even out here alone with a stranger.

Stop! a tiny voice inside me screams. *Stop everything.*

Tree presses his feet against the ground and the merry-go-round begins to turn. I add my feet and we turn faster.

"Really fast and then raise our feet!" Tree says.

We push off and push off and push off, and then we lift our feet and let the merry-go-round spin. I keep eating the yogurt. I knock the spoon into my mouth, and some of it dribbles against my cheek. We spin and spin. Finally, as we slow down, I stumble off. My stomach is churning. I wipe my mouth with the back of my hand.

Stop!

"Are you all right?" Tree appears next to me.

I hold up the empty yogurt container. "Victory over fear!" I cry.

"Victory over fear!" Tree raises his yogurt in the air as well.

I lower my hand slowly. I think about that woman in Idaho who died. I try to picture her, but I still can't. I'm standing in the sun, but I begin to shiver.

"Hey, too much excitement?" Tree gently puts a hand on my back and guides me over to a bench that's set back from the sidewalk. It faces the merry-go-round, one of those places where moms are supposed to sit to watch their kids play, making sure the kid is never out of their sight, never in any danger.

"Hey, we can check our exam scores," Tree says. He pulls out his phone and navigates to a website. After a minute of passing through screens, he leaps to his feet. "Senior! Score one for shitty online school!"

"Congratulations."

"Don't you want to check yours?"

I pull out my phone and stare at it. I remember all the directions and the password. How I had to put in Mom's email address as the username because I've never had an email account. Part of me thinks there's no point, but I do want to know how I did. What if I did end up going to school here? How stupid do they think I am?

I navigate through the screens. I know how to do this thanks to Becca. Who must be worried sick about me right now. After typing the password wrong twice, I finally get in. I have to blink a few times to be sure I'm seeing correctly. "Sophomore," I read. "Isn't that only one year behind?"

"You're sixteen?"

I nod.

"Verily, it could be worse. Plus, my aunt talked to the principal, and she said it would be possible to advance early if I did well. So maybe you can still end up graduating on time."

"And then what?" I try to picture myself graduating from high school, but I can't even see it. This would be my last year of Miss Sheila's school. If I was still in Zebulun, I'd be mostly helping the younger kids and working. Dad or Miss Sheila would be matching me with a husband. How can I possibly find a husband here?

"A question I've often asked myself." Tree sits down again and slips his phone into his pocket. "I decided to move in with my aunt and uncle and go to normal school so I could get accepted to college. Now I have to apply. And pay for it." The smile fades from his face. He grips the bag with the remaining yogurts.

School starts in less than two weeks. The future is barreling toward us. For him, it's going to extend forward, into college and a career, into a million different possibilities. Maybe he'll get married and maybe he won't. Maybe he'll be a doctor. Maybe he'll be a writer. Maybe he'll travel around the world. My future fragments before we even get to high school. I can't see anything beyond today clearly. Behind a pane of cloudy glass in my mind is an obscure vision of myself, back in Zebulun, carrying a baby I can't quite see, near a husband outside my peripheral vision. I want to see Carlo there, but I can't. I don't see him in that future. I don't see us meeting ever again. Everything we're doing now is so that we can be together, but I can't see it. I see blurry fragments of terrible things. And the version of me that goes to high school? It's somewhere to my far left, past all the glass, beyond imagination.

"So how come you moved to Eugene?" Tree asks.

"My mom has custody of me, but I was with my dad. The cops came and took me back."

"Oh. Oh." He nods as if something is all coming together. "That's why your mom wears normal clothes, not the cult stuff."

"She used to wear the same clothes, but she changed."

"Is that why they got divorced?"

I almost laugh. That's the reason Dad would give. It would all be Mom's fault. Nothing to do with the ways he broke the tenets of the Word. "Yeah, she left the religion, and she wanted to take me away from it too. But in our religion, you can't just leave. Especially if you're a woman. The man, the father, his word is the law, even if it goes against the law. My mom had a restraining order, but he came to my school—I was in second grade—and he told me to climb out my window and meet him, so I did. Because you have to— whatever your dad says, you have to do it, no matter what. And if you do it, the religion says, life will be good." I pause to take a breath. I can't believe all that just came out of me. I haven't even said that to Mom, or to Becca, or to anyone.

"Whoa, second grade?" Tree whistles. "That's tough."

"It was," I say. "But also it wasn't."

Tree tilts his head and waits, as if he expects me to say more.

"We went to this town—"

"Zebulun?"

I grip the bench in surprise. "You've heard of it?"

"Sure, I Googled the Word after I met you. It's all on Wikipedia, how they live in a town called Zebulun out in Eastern Oregon, and they farm and the whole town is owned by this one guy."

"It's not like that," I say, even though I have no idea what something called Wikipedia says. I just know that whatever Americans say about us, it's a lie, because Americans don't even want us to exist.

"They don't farm, or it's not owned by that guy?"

"No, they do farm. The guy's name is Mr. Brandon. That's just how kids speak to adults. Everybody's Mister or Miss. What I mean is, it isn't a bad place. The people are good. Mr. Brandon legally owns everything, but really everyone owns everything together."

"Oh, like a commune! My parents would love that."

"Why did you move here?" I ask. "Was it just for school?"

205

Tree shrugs. "Not really. My parents . . . " He picks up one of the yogurts and tosses it from hand to hand. "They mean well. But they have this philosophy that kids are better off learning by 'being free.'" He makes air quotes. "Basically, they didn't supervise me at all. I didn't go to school, yeah, but I also didn't learn how to interact with people. It was just me, my parents, and my two sisters. I started going to this sports camp for homeschoolers, which my parents hated because sports are way too organized, and the kids were terrible to me. They'd make fun of my clothes and my hair and my glasses and the way I spoke. I was too weird for homeschool."

"So you wanted to be normal?"

"Don't put it that way!" Tree adjusts his glasses. "I just wanted to be part of the larger civilization."

"I wanted to read books," I say.

"You couldn't read?" Tree almost shouts it.

"Just religious stuff. So I'd sneak over to my friend's house and read her books."

"Good for you!" Tree high-fives me. "You gotta find a way to learn anyway."

I stare at him.

"What?"

"Someone else said that to me once."

"It's good advice. At least my parents let me learn if I wanted to. They're not happy about me moving in with my aunt and uncle though. They think I've become a capitalist."

I don't know what he means by that, but I can see in his face that it hurts him. And I can see that his parents are wrong. Tree did the right thing by leaving them. They were wrong. He had to leave. He's better off now that he got away.

"I keep telling my parents they need to send my sisters to school." Now he holds a yogurt in one hand and spins it. "But they won't even consider it. And my sisters—they're twelve and ten—they don't understand what the big deal is. By the time they realize how inferior their education is, they'll be like me."

"There's nothing wrong with you," I say.

"Thank you. It's hard to tell sometimes." He taps his head. "What would be up here if I'd gone to school?"

"You'd be a different person."

"My sisters deserve a chance to be—*not* normal, just . . . " He shakes his head. "Well, I call them every couple days. I hope I can get through to them."

My brother Carlo deserved a chance to be normal, but I couldn't help him. By the time I met him, he was already out of school. He already had to take care of himself, and then he had to take care of both Dad and me. Maybe he would have liked to read books besides the Gospel and graduate high school. I can't say any of that. Tree may be different from all the other Americans, but I'm even more different. I can't call my brother. There's no getting through to him. I have to obey.

Suddenly I can't sit here anymore. My ability to act American is breaking.

"I told my mom I'd be back for dinner," I say.

"Shall I walk you home, then, m'lady?" Tree stands and sticks out his elbow.

I carefully set the ends of my fingers on his arm. I want to put my arm all the way through his, to move closer, but I can't do that. I'm not even supposed to be out here. I just did it for my late mother, I tell myself, so she'll think I'm acting normal. But that's not really true. Without Becca, I don't have any friends at all. When Tree spoke to me at the exam, he was the first person my own age besides Becca I'd spoken to since we left Zebulun. I just wanted to talk to someone. Anyone. And then when we talked, something happened that wasn't supposed to. I stumble and grab on to Tree's arm.

"Is m'lady about to swoon?" he asks. "Maybe we should sit down again."

"No, I'm okay." I keep gripping his arm, and we walk slowly. Tree isn't just anyone. He's a good person. I can feel it like I could feel it with Becca, like I could read those people on the Seattle streets. I can tell that he's never punched anybody, that if I were to look down at his knuckles right now, they'd be soft and not scarred. It's not just his sisters he wouldn't hurt. I know he would never hurt *anyone*.

"Methinks I've found a lady stranger than myself," he says.

I try to laugh. Slowly, we make it to the top of the hill where the path intersects with the street. There's a trash can on the corner. We stop for a minute, and I steady myself. I try to re-center my brain and my heart. I try to focus on what I'm supposed to be doing, not what I want. "You can toss the rest of the yogurt," I say.

"Well, my aunt likes it. I should keep it for her."

"It's probably gone bad from the heat."

Tree shrugs. He lets go of my arm, walks over to the trash can, and throws out the yogurt.

I stand still. A car is coming up the street. It seems to be moving in slow motion. It occurs to me that I could step in front of it. Then there'd be no more futures. No more things that are both true and false. No more people who are dead and alive. No more pretending I'm someone I'm not. No more seeking a way out. No more Trial to complete.

I take a step off the curb.

"Whoa!" Tree grabs my arm and pulls me back.

My heart is trying to escape from my chest.

"Another thing that's more dangerous than teenage boys," he says. "Cars!"

"Riding in cars with boys?" I say. I saw a movie at Becca's. Not the actual movie, just the title, flowing across the TV screen with all the other titles I never had a chance to watch.

"Better to be inside than in front of."

"Right." We begin walking again. This time it's Tree who clings to my arm rather than the other way around. And I'm grateful. Because I don't want to die. I didn't want to die just now. It was an impulse, a sudden solution. But I don't want to get out that way. I want to get out of completing my task. Or get through it.

We walk all the way to Mom and Barron's house. He lets me go at the end of the driveway.

"Thanks for calling me," he says. He stuffs his hands in his pockets. "I hope you didn't think the yogurt thing was dumb."

"No, I had fun." Fun is the opposite of everything right now. I'm sweating and my pulse is pounding, and I'm feeling faint. I'm trying not to fall down. I'm trying to act normal. Like Becca would act. How would Becca act when saying goodbye to a boy at the edge of a driveway? If he was a *good* boy, the kind who didn't hurt people?

I step forward and wrap my arms around him. He's not tall, but I'm so short that my head presses against his chest. Quickly, I step back again.

He's blushing, and he steps back too.

"See you later," I say, and I turn and walk toward the house. My vision blurs, but I stay upright. I turn around when I get to the door, and I see him walking back in the direction of the Safeway, hands in his pockets. There are no cars in the street. There's nowhere to run. There's nothing to distract me from what I'm feeling. I like him. I want to be able to like him. I want to be able to be like Becca, and just thinking about that makes me feel sick. My stomach twists and turns and tumbles. Becca was different from me. She was able to do things that I can't.

24

Port Angeles

age fifteen

By the time I was fifteen, Miss Sheila's school, for me, mostly consisted of reading from printouts of books and pamphlets written by Citizens for other Citizens. I couldn't participate in the chores portion of the day, where the girls back in Zebulun would take care of cows and sheep and chickens, or learn how to grow vegetables, or help with cleaning and cooking and childcare.

I'd do chores anyway, of course. I did all the cooking and cleaning. But mostly, all I had to do was read stacks and stacks of printouts. A lot of it was scripture, interpretation of scripture, or meditations on how to live an appropriate life. There were pamphlets on family relationships that discussed how a man should direct his wife's activities, how a wife should manage the home, and how couples could avoid conflict and live in harmony. There were how-to manuals on everything from unclogging a drain to folding one's underwear.

There were pages stapled together that described how the Earth was created and how the dinosaur fossils came to be, and how the people living on the moon arranged their towns.

There were cookbooks. Miss Sheila wrote one herself, and some she compiled using recipes from other women. I once heard Miss Sheila telling Jean's mother that some of the women didn't want to give away their best recipes, so they purposefully wrote them down wrong. Miss Sheila said that she was too smart for that and changed them back.

But I couldn't do much with the cookbooks because Dad wasn't going to buy all the ingredients we needed.

The other thing I had to do was math workbooks. They were about fifty years old, but that was okay because one plus one equaled two even back then.

Point being, there was only so much time I could spend reading those printouts and doing the same old math problems. So I started sneaking over to Becca's house more and more. Her parents were gone during the day, but Becca would leave the sliding door unlocked for me. So while Dad was sleeping, I could sneak over there and read for a while.

This one morning, I was pretty much done for the day, even though it was only 10:00 a.m. Miss Sheila had assigned me to write a reaction to a pamphlet by Mr. Brandon about the sacred role of the Council of Elders, which was him and those other two men who'd banished us. But that was easy enough, so I had plenty of time. Just like I had about a thousand times before, I slipped out our back door, through the hole in the fence, and over to Becca's yard. Pretty soon I was in Becca's room picking up where I'd left off in this great big hardcover she'd checked out from the library that had to do with fae and magic and enchantment. That book took me away from the world so well that I lost track of time.

I looked over at the clock, and it said noon. I slammed the book shut. I'd been gone way too long to be safe. I hightailed it out of the room, and I was almost to the end of the hall when I heard the creaking of the front door opening.

I pressed my back against the hallway wall. Listening again. Pretending I didn't exist again.

Becca was laughing as she came inside. There were two people's footsteps. A male voice laughing as well.

I slid along the wall and peeked around the corner. Becca was standing in the middle of the living room with a boy. They were kissing. Becca was tall compared to me, but he was much taller than she was, a beanpole with short hair that stuck up on the top of his head. She was standing on her toes tipping her head back. He was running his hands through her long red hair. They were both wearing jeans, and she had on a tight green sweater that left a swatch of skin showing above her high waist.

Isaac, I thought. This must be him. The guy she couldn't stop talking about. But she hadn't told me they were actually a thing. When had this happened? Was this the first time? I stood there, frozen, as he picked her up and swung her around. She laughed and trilled at him to stop, but it was obvious she didn't mean it, so he swung her again.

"No, really! Omigod, I'm gonna barf if you don't put me down."

He stopped swinging her and set her down on the couch. He was on top of her, and she wrapped her legs around his body.

I didn't know she'd even kissed him before, or anyone. I put my hand over my mouth to keep from reacting, but I couldn't stop watching. They kept making out on the couch, grinding against each other. The only time I'd ever seen something like this was when I was watching TV with Becca. She'd laugh, and I'd be uncomfortable. I thought she was uncomfortable too, because it's not okay to do this. What kind of woman would even want to do this? Not the person I knew. But here she was.

A long time seemed to pass, and then the boy who must have been Isaac sat up and looked at his phone. "Shit, we have to get back."

Becca leaned over the couch and finger-combed her hair. She flipped it back. "Does it look okay?"

"Does it ever!" Isaac kissed her and then took her hand, and they hurried out the front door. Even through the closed door, I could hear their laughter.

I stood there in the hallway for a long time trying to process what I'd seen. I felt sick to my stomach and uncomfortable from head to toe, and I wasn't sure why. Becca wasn't a Citizen, so she didn't have to act like one. I knew in my heart that I shouldn't judge her for acting just like any other American. Her behavior didn't affect me. It didn't hurt me or put my soul at risk. The worst feeling was knowing she'd been hanging out with Isaac and not telling me about it. Maybe she thought she couldn't tell me about this because she knew I'd feel this way. I wanted not to feel it, but at the same time, I had to feel it, or I'd go down the same path.

I had been away for hours now. Dad could have gotten up. I broke from my stupor and slipped back out the sliding glass doors, went through the fence, and got inside our house. Everything was silent, and I heaved a sigh of relief. Still, behind my eyes I was replaying the vision of Becca on the couch with the boy.

"Lisa."

I jumped.

Carlo came out of the kitchen holding a bowl of cereal.

"Oh, hi," I said.

He stared back at me.

"I didn't know you were coming home."

"They cut my hours," he said.

"What, why?" That meant even less money. We were paying almost everything in rent to the guy Carlo knew who had set us up here, and also for things Dad wanted, like alcohol, so how were we supposed to eat now?

Carlo shrugged. "I guess business is bad."

I tried to think of something encouraging to say, but all I could think about was being hungrier. Not having dinner or not having breakfast. Having to give all the eggs to Dad.

"You were next door," Carlo said. He took a bite of his cereal, but his eyes never left mine.

"Shhhh!" I put a finger to my lips and went over to him. I grabbed him by the arm and pulled him into the kitchen, the farthest point in the house from Dad's bedroom.

Carlo set the cereal bowl on the counter. "Sis, you can't just go doing that."

"It's not hurting anyone. I just wanted to read something other than those boring pamphlets. Would you want to sit around reading them all day?"

Carlo laughed. "Well, no. But it's my responsibility to look out for you."

"There's no one there."

"But you've been seeing that girl." He folded his arms and looked down at me.

I didn't want to lie to him, so I said nothing. I knew he had to have figured it out. Even though Dad was always looking for reasons to be afraid I was going to be raped or murdered or drawn to sin, Carlo was a lot more perceptive. We'd walked by Becca's house together, and I'd looked at her.

"Listen, Lisa, I trust you. I know you're a good girl. And I know it's hard to be here all alone. Everyone's gotta have a friend. So don't let Dad see you. I don't want him to think I'm neglecting my responsibility." He looked serious. Sincere. He wanted to look out for me. Guilt sprang roots in my chest.

"I can't stay inside here forever," I said, almost a whisper. "I can't just be alone all the time."

Carlo wrapped me in a hug. "I trust you."

"I'll be careful," I said into his chest.

He patted my hair. "I know. Now can you go back to pretending to read all those papers again?"

"Yeah, okay." I went back to my ancient computer and my stack of papers, and Carlo sat at the kitchen table eating his cereal.

I thought about Becca and that boy, and thought about it,

and thought about it. I replayed that scene so many times that I wasn't even sure what was real about it and what I was making up. I kept seeing him bend down to kiss her and her standing on her tiptoes. Him picking her up. What would it feel like to have a boy pick me up that way and spin me around? What would it feel like to have a boy kiss me? Why didn't I get to have that?

I put my hand over my mouth, as if the thought would come screaming out. *No no no no no*, I told myself. *I don't want that. I could never want that.*

I tried to read and work on my paper about the Council of Elders, but I couldn't see anything but that boy and Becca, Becca and that boy, and me standing silent and hidden against the wall. Because that was the only place I ever was. Why couldn't I be anywhere else?

I was so distracted by replaying that scene in my head that I almost missed that Miss Sheila was back online and talking again. But the sound of Jean's name pulled me back.

". . . will be serving penance for the foreseeable future," Miss Sheila said.

I looked up from the papers, wishing I could see the class. But the screen, as usual, was black.

"Normally I would not think it appropriate to discuss a student's private issues," Miss Sheila continued, "but since you girls have been talking, I think it's important that everyone knows the truth rather than relying on rumors. Jean was discovered alone with a boy in the loft of one of the storage barns."

I listened for any reaction from the girls, but there was no sound.

Everyone must have been holding their breath, like I was.

"Fortunately, the situation was addressed before permanent damage was done. But Jean has committed a grave sin and must face the consequences of that. She will not be allowed visitors until further notice. I hope everyone understands how serious this is."

There was no response from the girls. All I could do was imagine their faces. If the sin had been less grave, there might have been eye rolls, smirks, or whispers. But they knew better than to show their minds now.

I had tried to write to Jean like she said. I couldn't write from Seattle, with us being homeless, but once we got to Port Angeles, I scrounged up some paper and a stamp. I didn't have her exact address, so I sent it to Miss Sheila's house instead. But I'd never gotten a letter back. I didn't know if Miss Sheila had given the letter to her or not, but I had to assume not. I knew Jean would write to me if she could. Now I realized I should have tried harder. What if Jean thought I'd forgotten about her? Now she was trapped inside that house with those terrible sisters, and she'd probably be married to the first man her father could get to agree to it. And it wouldn't be whoever she'd been in the barn with, that was for sure.

Miss Sheila switched to talking about something in the scripture, and now the pictures in my mind were all mixed up. Becca and Isaac on the couch. Jean with some boy in a barn loft. Jean chasing Kitty around her living room. Becca and her bedroom full of books. Jean saying all those things about how she didn't believe. I knew Jean was wrong, but I also knew she didn't deserve whatever was going to happen to her. She deserved to be able to sin without giving up every-thing in her life, just like Becca.

And for me, there was no chance to sin. I didn't even know any boys. I wasn't allowed to even think about them. But I did. Inside my own mind, where I could think whatever I wanted and nobody would ever know. I thought about boys: Isaac, whoever Jean was with, people I saw on TV, boys I made up in my head. In secret, I thought about what sin could be like.

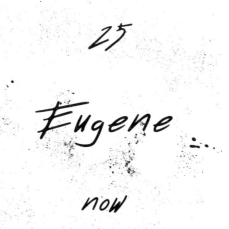

25

Eugene

now

I manage to get inside and have a couple minutes to myself before Mom realizes I'm back. When she notices I'm in the kitchen, she rushes in and throws her arms around me.

"Oh my gosh." She pulls back. "I'm so sorry to worry like this. I know your dad kept you in the house, and I never want to do that. I just don't know what's going on inside your head."

I have to look up to make eye contact. Even though everyone is taller than me, I'm not used to looking up at people. I'm used to looking demurely down at the ground. "It was weird being outside by myself, but once I was with Tree, it was okay. He's a good guy."

"I kept staring at my phone." She laughs nervously. "I guess that's what being a parent of a teenager is supposed to be like. Always worrying for no reason."

"I can take care of myself," I say. More to convince myself than to convince her. "We were homeless for a year in Seattle."

"A year!" She steps back and puts both hands over her face.

"It was okay." That's when we met my brother. That's when things started to get better. I can't say that though. There's another part of me thinking, that was before Dad ever put his hand around my neck. I hate thinking about how having Carlo with us and Dad hurting me went together, and I couldn't have one without the other. I can't have anything good without something bad.

"Oh Jesus. Alyssa." She turns her back on me and moves her hands to her head.

Barron, in the living room, hears the distress in her voice and comes over to us. He wraps his arms around Mom and raises his eyebrows at me over her shoulder.

"I told her about us being homeless after we got kicked out of Zebulun." I chew my lip. I already told Mom, so it doesn't matter if he knows too. "Dad killed someone, so they kicked us out. We went to Seattle, and we were street preaching. We lived in a tent." I decide to skip the part about learning how to pick pockets. But talking about that time makes me feel stronger. Before Carlo, I had to deal with people out there. Dad didn't do everything. He couldn't do everything, and besides, he'd drink when he could.

"I'm sorry," Mom says. "It's not about me. The social worker said I'm not supposed to be judgmental or angry!" Her voice rises as she says this. She plants her fists on Barron's chest.

"She hates that you were hurting and she couldn't help you," Barron translates. "I hate that too."

I can see why Mom couldn't handle being a Citizen. Citizens have to control their emotions, at least if they're women.

"I hate him." Mom presses her face into Barron's chest, so her voice is muffled. "I hate him so much."

"I'm all right," I say. "I got my test results. They're going to make me a sophomore."

"That's not too bad," Barron says. "You'll only be a year older than the other kids."

Mom is silent, her fists still balled, her forehead still pressed against Barron's chest. I guess I'm not supposed to be judgmental or angry either if I want to fit into this family. I should keep sweet here just like I always did with Dad. And I always will, on the outside. I'll never let her know that I think she's uncontrolled, that I think she should be able to turn around and face me. Always keep the inside separate from the outside.

"I can make dinner tonight," I say.

That does it. Mom turns around. "You will *not* make dinner," she says. "You are a teenager. You're supposed to lie on the couch watching TV while your mom makes dinner for you. You aren't supposed to have to work in your own house like a servant." She wipes tears away.

"How about we let her help out?" Barron says. "Maybe Alyssa's bored with lying around."

"That's all it is," I say. "I might as well do something."

"Fine." Mom takes a deep breath. "I'm sorry. I can't seem to get control of myself like a good woman. I'm glad about your test results. I'm glad you had a good time with Tree. I shouldn't have snapped at you. I'm gonna have to make a whole wheel of apologies. Just turn the dial to the right one." She opens her arms, and I step into them. I wrap my arms around her but only touch her back lightly.

"It's okay," I say. "I know it's hard." *I thought about you*, I think but don't say. *I thought about Liam. I wondered what you were doing.*

But every time I had those thoughts, I shut them down again. My mind would wander. It would create pictures of her and of Liam. They would come to me at random times. When I was trying to fall asleep, when I was cooking dinner, when I was sitting on the patio, when I was reading a book at Becca's. I missed whole pages of books because she'd pop into my mind. And then I'd have to close my eyes and focus on the Word, and pray, and try to stop the images and memories and thoughts. Now she wants me to remember and just let my mind go. She wants me to pretend the last nine years were the dream and this is the reality.

I pull away. "I saw some chicken in the fridge. Is that okay?"

"That will be wonderful, honey," Mom says. "Thank you." She slips past me and hurries down the hall in the direction of her bedroom.

"I guess you're the voice of reason," I say to Barron as I dig through the refrigerator for dinner ingredients. I see red peppers, broccoli, celery—all sorts of fresh vegetables. I think I'll stir-fry the chicken with it.

"She's the voice of reason for me too," Barron says. "That's pretty much marriage in a nutshell. Help each other get through stuff and don't make things worse."

"Don't make things worse. I'll remember that."

"You need any help?"

"No, sir, I'm just fine."

"I can chop up those vegetables." He holds out a hand.

I give him the bags of vegetables, and he takes out a cutting board and begins chopping them. I fill the rice cooker, and after a minute of silence, he turns the TV to a news channel.

As I chop up the chicken, I listen to a report on the midterm elections and a piece about funding for art teachers in schools. Then they start talking about yogurt. "A third death related to allegedly poisoned yogurt has been reported, and this one happened in Portland. Could this be related to the deaths in Boise?"

"Wow. We're gonna have to throw out our yogurt," Barron says. "Your mom loves that stuff."

"A fourteen-year-old boy has died in Portland after eating a store-brand yogurt, and the symptoms were very similar to what happened in Idaho. Do we have a serial yogurt poisoner on our hands?"

My stomach churns. I think about how much I enjoyed that yogurt today, how hungry I was, how it hit the spot. How we acted like it was a big joke. But three people are dead. Three.

"Yeah. That's crazy. Why on earth would someone do that?"

"Lotta nuts out there," Barron says.

"Tell me about it. Half of them live in Seattle."

Barron is silent for a minute as he finishes the chopping. The TV moves on from the yogurt news and goes into sports. "Hey, if you ever want to talk about that stuff to someone who won't freak out, you can always talk to me," he says. "I promise I'll just listen."

"Thanks," I say. And I mean it. Barron seems like a nice guy, for an adulterer who's going to Hell. He's the first man to ever help me make dinner. But I won't be talking to him about any details of my life. Where would I even start? I'm glad he's not like Dad though. I'm glad Mom has been living a good life. I dump the chicken in the wok and turn on the heat. I'm glad she hasn't been suffering for her sin in this earthly body. There's been plenty of that in the spirit world.

As I stir the vegetables in, I realize there was something missing from the refrigerator. There wasn't any beer. And I haven't seen any wine either, and no whiskey, and no huge bottles of cheap vodka.

"You guys don't drink at all?" I ask Barron.

"Nope. I used to drink some, before your mom. But after what she went through with Art, she'd get real nervous when I had a beer. So I thought, why put her through that? Nobody needs a beer to be happy."

I almost say, *Dad did*. But the beer and vodka didn't make him happy. He wasn't happy to start with, and the drinking just made him angrier. He wanted to be an Elder, and that was never going to happen. His best hope was just to be able to go back some day. He started street preaching in the hopes that he'd get that, or maybe so he could be the important one, telling people what to think, acting as much like an Elder as he could. One good thing about the time we were on the street was that it was harder for him to get alcohol. Maybe he didn't want to drink as much because he had a purpose. Maybe his drinking got worse in Port Angeles because it just did.

"That's good," I say instead.

"What's good?" Liam asks, suddenly behind me.

I scream.

"Sorry, I didn't mean to scare you again!" comes his high voice.

"Heavenly Father, give me strength," I say. I'm shaking, and the wok wiggles under my hands. The chicken is almost done. This meal cooks quickly. That's why I like it. When a man wants his meal now, you find a way. I breathe in and out. "It's not your fault, Liam. I'm just a jumpy person. Especially when I'm cooking."

"Why?"

Carefully, I pick up the wok with an oven mitt and pour the contents into a large bowl. "My dad used to come up behind me like that."

"Oh. You want me to set the table?"

"That would be really nice of you." I have to step aside while Liam clumsily pulls the plates one by one out of the cupboard. What a nice, polite kid. Mom and Barron must be teaching him to act that way. They're teaching him to be good to women and help with chores and act like he's not entitled to be in charge.

My heart is still beating quickly. I try to remember when I last jumped like that, and I don't think it's happened since the day we moved into our house. Because Dad never surprised me. I was always ready for him. My heart would already be beating. I'd already be braced for something to happen. Here, I must have relaxed. I thought I was safe.

I need to stop myself from feeling that way. This is the part of the story after the worst has happened. This is the part where the warrior or the saint or the chosen one fights against insurmountable odds to regain what's been lost. There's no such thing as safety. There's only following the plan.

I carry the bowl over to the kitchen table. Liam is setting out glasses for everyone.

The rice cooker dings. I turn back to dish it out, but Mom is already there, spooning it into another bowl. So I sit down at my spot at the table and wait for her to bring the rice over to us. I wait for Mom and Liam and Barron to all sit down.

"Is it okay if I say a prayer?" I ask.

Mom's eye twitches. "Sure, honey. Go right ahead."

I bow my head. "Dear Heavenly Father. Thank you for this bounty you've set before us. And thank you for sending me back to this loving family, who I have missed so much over the years. We pray that you also grant your bounty to those who can't be with us today, and protect those who do your will. May your plan be realized on Earth. Amen."

Barron clears his throat. "What a nice sentiment."

We pass the dishes around the table. Nobody starts eating until everyone is served. Even me. Even Barron waits to make sure I have food before he eats. Liam takes a big bite of chicken.

"This is really good," he says with his mouth full.

"Thank you." I beam at him.

This is the perfect painting of an American family. Everything seems nice on the outside. It's too normal to be real, too good to be true. This is the illusion that's been waiting for me for all these years, as inevitable as sin. Some version of this was always coming, and we always planned for it, one way or another.

26

Port Angeles

age sixteen

After we got to Port Angeles, Dad stopped talking about what we'd do if the cops found me. We were living our lives as if it wasn't going to happen. But then, not long before the cops actually did take me, Dad brought it up again. He had been going online on his phone and looking at Mom's social media accounts. She often posted things about me—lies, Dad said.

We were all at the table after eating dinner when he started ranting.

"It was a picture of Lisa that was supposed to be aged up, using a picture from when she was little. Didn't look anything like her, of course. There's this pathetic kid looking all skinny—they had to CGI that shit for sure. *Have you seen this girl?* And then there was a picture of me, which was also supposed to be aged up. Gave me gray hair and bags under my eyes. Considered armed and dangerous. Me! Armed and dangerous! Know what this goddamn picture didn't say? That I'm her *father*. They left that whole part out. Bitch is putting out like I'm a danger to my own kid."

I got up and started cleaning plates off the table.

"Lisa, pour me a glass of vodka," Dad said. "On ice."

I set the plates in the sink, got out a short, round glass, dumped in ice, and poured the vodka from the giant bottle that lived in the corner between the stove and the refrigerator. I walked back to the table and set it in front of Dad. "Carlo, you want anything?"

"No thanks, sis."

I retreated to the kitchen, fiddling with the dishes.

Dad's glass clinked against the table. "Now, we got a good thing going here. Ain't nobody know about us. But that could change. The devil always knows things. There's always another Trial, son. It could be that we have another one coming. With all this social media stuff, it could happen. It could happen."

"Lisa don't go nowhere," Carlo said. "Nobody's gonna see her."

"We have to be *ready*." Dad's voice lowered. "I feel a Trial coming, son."

"We won't let anybody take Lisa. I don't even want to talk about it." Carlo got up from the table and began pacing around.

I ran a sponge over a plate, trying not to think about what they were saying, what it meant.

"All we need is two years," Carlo said. "She'll be eighteen, and then nobody can take her."

"I'm telling you." Dad slammed a hand down on the table. "I feel a Trial. I feel it deep inside me. Something's coming, and if we don't have a plan, the devil will take her and keep her. She'll be lost to us."

"What plan?" Carlo asked.

"We need to defeat the devil. We need to remove the devil from the picture."

"How're we gonna do that?" Carlo sat back down at the table. He tapped his fingers against it like he did when he was agitated.

"There are multiple potential scenarios," Dad said. "But if they ever do come for Lisa, most likely, they'll arrest me. I'll be in jail for a day or two. Then it'll be a while before there's a trial, but I'll have some kind of restriction on my movement. But they won't arrest you, son. You got nothing to do with it at all."

"I've known she's kidnapped," Carlo said. "Ain't said nothing."

"Yeah, but you never met us until the deed was done. The law won't care about you that much. That means the Trial will fall on you."

"I'll do anything to keep Lisa safe," Carlo said. His voice was raw.

I closed my eyes to try to stop myself from crying. I'd also do anything to keep him safe. It *was* possible that he'd go to jail too if the cops ever found me. I could never let that happen.

"I've been thinking," Dad said, glass clinking. "About a way to make sure the devil won't have Lisa for long. A way to make sure she'll come back to us. We all have to be ready if the time comes. We all have to know how to play our parts. Lisa, put those dishes down and come over here."

I let the bowl I was washing slide into the soapy water, dried my hands on the old towel hanging from the oven door, and went back to the table. Dad's glass of vodka was half-empty but he didn't look drunk.

He looked more focused. His eyes glinted, and he spoke with an urgency and a purpose.

"Lisa." He turned to me. "Should this Trial be assigned to us, you'll have to carry out your task alone. Are you prepared to do that?"

"Yes, sir."

"Your work, your solidarity with God and your devotion to Him, will determine whether the devil lives or dies."

I glanced at Carlo, who was leaning his elbows on the table, eyes hard. "Yes, sir," I repeated. How could I do anything to the devil? I wondered. But even as I had the thought, the answer dawned on me. What Dad really meant by *the devil* exploded into my brain. I didn't know yet what he was going to ask me to do, but I knew it would be a Trial, all right. I knew if God ever saw fit to take me away, I'd have to do something I'd never dreamed of.

"Here's how it will happen," Dad began. He took a long drink of vodka and handed me the glass.

I refilled it, set it back down in front of him, and listened.

Dad told us what our plan was. He explained every step of what would happen if the police ever came for me and sent me back to my late mother. He swore that if we completed this Trial, we'd all be together again, and furthermore, we'd be welcomed back to Zebulun, having completed just the kind of great Trial that would count as penance grand enough for his crime.

I knew the plan was crazy then, because I'm not stupid. I knew the law would be out there waiting for us. I knew it would take all my strength to do what he was asking of me, and in the end, it might all come to nothing. I knew they'd never let Dad back into Zebulun. But they might take Carlo and me. I might be able to go home again. And if I did, then Dad couldn't touch me. Mr. Brandon and the other Elders and Mr. Doug would keep him from entering the town.

Carlo rested his head in his hands as he listened.

I reached out and rested my hand on his arm. I dug into his arm with my fingers. *We're in this together*, I tried to say with my touch. *You won't lose me.*

He lifted his head and smiled at me through watery eyes. *Together*, he seemed to say.

We sat and listened as Dad's plan drifted into a rant about the devil and all the pictures Mom was posting. I closed my eyes and tried to imagine what it might be like if this all happened, if God did choose to send us down this dark path. But I couldn't see anything. I couldn't imagine it actually happening: me seeing Mom again, me being alone, me being anywhere but this house.

It was like Carlo said, I just had to make it two more years, and then I'd be eighteen. And then what? Then I could keep on staying in this house alone, but without any fear the law would take me?

I got up from the table and went back to the dishes. I had to do something with my hands or I would go crazy. That was when a smidge of a plan started forming in my own mind, when the devil needled his way in. When I started thinking, what if I've been keeping good and quiet and sweet for too long? What if I have to take my own actions if I want to get out of this?

I washed those dishes as quietly as I could.

27

Eugene

now

All I have to do is follow the plan.

Dad's plan.

My plan.

God's plan.

My plan.

Dad's . . .

After cleaning up our dishes together, and after Barron has loaded the dishwasher and turned it on, the four of us are sitting at the table again. Barron has suggested that we play a board game as a family.

And then . . .

The only game I know how to play is poker. Carlo and I, and sometimes Dad, could play poker all night long. Texas Hold'em, seven-card stud, lowball, five-card draw. You name the variation, we played it. For beans, for pennies, for drinks. Dad and Carlo drank alcohol, but I drank pop. Not because they wouldn't let me drink. There's no rule against women drinking, specifically. Nobody's supposed to drink at all.

And then the devil's illusion will fall apart.

And then only one thing will be true.

And then . . .

Mom opens up the board for a game of Sorry! The box is beaten up at the corners. The board has nicks in it. The cards have been bent and folded and mangled. This game has been played with, and I remember it, but vaguely. A memory of moving these little red plastic pegs around swims in my mind.

The news is on the TV in the background.

. . . the law will have its say, if it can.

And then . . .

The dishwasher swishes, magically doing the work I used to do every night. Replacing my hands. Saving me work.

This is my work now: playing a game I don't remember. Pretending I care about whether I win. Not trying to picture what comes after. Not trying to fill that blank space in my brain. Because I can imagine the future, and I can't. When I think past the end of this moment in time, the pictures blur. The second I see something that seems true, it evaporates. And there's never an end point. What happens when it's all over? I silently pray to God for clarity. I wait for an answer, even though I've never heard from Him directly. If there's ever a time for Him to pass by Dad and speak to me, it has to be now.

Liam sits to my left. Barron sits across from me. Mom sits to my right. There are no drinks anywhere, no beans, no pennies. The table is sparkling clean under the game board. I used to clean our table, but it never looked clean like this.

I am one person inside; outside, I'm another.

Liam squirms in his seat. "I want to go first!"

"We have to draw," I say. "Right?" I cut the deck. "Highest number goes first?" I set it in front of him. He draws a three. "Ouch." Barron draws a six. Mom draws a ten. I draw a twelve. "Whatd'ya know?" I shuffle the cards and replace the deck.

"No fair."

"Sorry!" I draw a two and immediately take a red man out of my start.

We play. Drawing cards, moving men, knocking each other off, laughing our *Sorry*s. In the end, Liam and I both have our last man in our safety, but he draws the right card first and wins.

"Yes!" he exalts, pumping his fists.

"Oh no!" I say dramatically, pressing my face into my hands.

"Play for second?" Barron asks. So we keep playing, and I make second. Barron insists that he and Mom continue, until finally Mom comes in third. She begins packing up the pieces, putting the cards together.

"Jesus," Barron says. "Did you hear that?"

"Hear what?" Mom asks.

Barron picks up the remote control and turns the sound up on the TV.

". . . Salem. This is the fourth death linked to yogurt. And we have confirmation that at least six additional people were sickened in Washington, Idaho, and Oregon. Do authorities believe all these incidents are tied together?"

"Nothing is confirmed yet, Shelly, but we're hearing reports of similar symptoms. The victims all became violently ill as if with food poisoning."

"Is foul play suspected, or could this be a case of bad yogurt?"

"We do have autopsy results from the two Idaho victims, which reveal, according to authorities, the presence of poison. Three major brands of yogurt have now released statements advising customers to be sure that the seals on their products are unbroken."

"All right," Barron says. "We're getting rid of all our yogurt." He goes to the refrigerator, pulls out a few containers, and throws them in the trash.

"Did you even check the seals?" Mom asks.

"No sense risking your life for some cheap dairy product." He pulls Mom into a hug. "You're worth three times the cost of those yogurts."

Mom laughs.

The news has moved on to national politics. One candidate is up by sixteen percentage points in the latest poll. Can the other candidate come back? Such and such may gain points if he can get his message across.

Four people dead is nothing to them. Thousands of people are murdered every year. Thousands of Americans die every single day.

Thousands of kids end up in emergency rooms, and those people they're talking about on TV send them back to their parents. If they die, they'll just be one more among the thousands. When you're a girl, you belong to your father, or whoever the law says you belong to.

If a man says he owns his daughter, no one even makes him prove it.

I remember waking up in a hospital bed. Carlo's voice. A woman with long, straight brown hair and a large blue purse.

Did anyone hurt you?

Yes, I said. I said yes.

I didn't tell her the whole story. I couldn't. Not with Carlo there and Dad close by. I couldn't tell them:

I was standing in front of the sink washing the dishes.

I heard his footsteps, and I stiffened. I knew the way he walked when he was angry. *Stomp. Stomp.* I stopped the movement of my hands. I got ready to fight him.

His hands grabbed my waist.

I tried to get his hands. I used my elbows. I tried to kick.

He pulled me away from the sink and then threw me back against it. I was still using my elbows. I was trying to fight back.

He slapped my face with an open hand. *You were next door with that bitch. You're a whore. You're a slut.* I don't remember it all, just some of the words. He said them over and over again. *Whore bitch next door slut.* He must have seen me coming back.

He grabbed my body, and I kicked, but he threw me down. He must have kicked, too, and I kept trying. I tried to go for the soft parts, like Carlo showed me. But I couldn't reach him. He slammed my head into the ground.

There was a break. I think it was a short one. I woke up to blood in my mouth and in my eyes. Dad was moving backward, being pulled away. By God? I thought. But it was Carlo. Carlo pulled Dad away from me, and I heard fists crunching flesh, and then there was crying.

Dad said the word *son.*

They were both crying. I wasn't crying. I could barely see. I was gasping for breath. I pressed my hands against the ground, because I wanted to get up. I wanted to be able to fight back. *But Carlo is here now*, I thought. *Carlo won't let him come back.* And I let myself go.

And I woke up in the hospital, and the woman asked me, did anyone hurt you, and I said yes.

But Carlo and Dad came for me together. Dad must have told the people at the hospital something, and they believed it. Carlo held my hand in the back seat, and Dad drove, saying nothing. He didn't have to say anything, because he didn't owe me, he *owned* me.

The cop who walked into my bedroom said they were looking for me, but it wasn't true. Nobody in that hospital had my picture. Nobody checked Dad's story. Nobody knew I was a missing person, that really, according to the law, it was my mother who owned me. Nobody asked me where I wanted to go.

The TV in my late mother's house is blaring nonsense. I can't understand anything. I'm thinking about that car ride back to our condemned house, and I move my whole brain. I move it to Zebulun. I think about Miss Sheila.

I remember being in a kitchen with her, baking a chicken together, preparing greens, cleaning dishes. I picture us at her sewing machine, when she patiently showed me how to make a stitch. I think of us outside the chicken coop, and how she taught me how to gather eggs. I see her eyes crinkle as she smiles and hear the kindness in her voice.

I remember her sitting by my bed, telling me about God's love. *I'm so blessed to have you here,* she said. *God never saw fit to give me children. I believe God will bless you, and you'll have great joy in your life.*

Nobody asked me who I wanted to belong to. Nobody asked if I wanted to be with someone who was kind and loved me even though she didn't own me at all. Who wouldn't want that? Who wouldn't try to get back there? I try to keep my brain with Miss Sheila, but it moves sideways.

I remember lying in my sleeping bag in that tent with Carlo on one side and Dad on the other, facing Carlo, and him facing me. I knew nothing could hurt me while he was there. It wasn't the same as being at home with Miss Sheila, but it was something. Carlo was someone. I think about the scars on his knuckles and the adoption ceremony and the way he and Dad hugged, and how after they took me back from the hospital, Carlo slept on the floor next to me. I would wake up all the time, every hour, and I'd check to see if he was there, and he would be.

My mind swims on all of it. The hospital. *Yes.* Miss Sheila. Carlo pulling Dad off me. My bruises changing color and fading away. Riding those cardboard boxes down the hill in the snow. And the future. What if they put handcuffs on those scarred knuckles, and that's the end?

My phone pings. I'm in my late mother's kitchen. Now, not then.

I jump and swipe the phone from the counter.

Did you see the news? Tree asks.

Yes, I reply.

Appreciation for making me throw it out!

I remember Becca kissing the boy, Isaac. She told me later that they were dating. She told me when they had sex. How I'm not supposed to want that, but I do. With Tree maybe, or maybe just with someone. Maybe I want to stop forcing myself not to feel what I feel and not to say what I think. Maybe I just want something, anything, but what's before me.

The library.

Going there with Dad and Carlo because Dad wanted something, and they didn't want to leave me at home. It must have been a few months after I went with Becca. The lady at the desk watched me but didn't say anything. And when Dad and Carlo weren't looking, she slipped me a business card that said Washington Child Abuse Hotline on it. And I slipped the card back and shook my head.

"We just wear weird clothes," I said to her. "But thank you."

I didn't say yes.

But that was before he held me against the wall by my neck. That was before he slammed me into the floor. And no one did anything. God didn't do anything. God says I have to obey my father, no matter what.

Four people dead.

"When it's all over the news, and there are at least four people dead," Dad said. About four months had passed since he slammed my head into the ground. My bruises had faded, and my brain had mostly healed.

The next day, I went over to Becca's house for the last time.

I'm not supposed to be here, interacting with my late mother. I wasn't supposed to go to Becca's house. I wasn't supposed to say *yes*.

I can't go back and change things, and I can't change the future either. I can't change the Word or who's dead and who isn't.

"Alyssa, honey, are you all right?" Mom is watching me as I hold my phone. I've been staring down at Tree's text for so long that the screen went black. "Did he say something?"

"No, it's not him."

"I appreciate you playing that game with us," she says. "It means a lot to Liam to have a sister. He just lights up when you're around."

"It means a lot to me too. I thought about him. Wondered how he was growing up." That's true. I remember imagining him. How he'd look. What he'd sound like.

Mom looks like she's about to try to hug me, but she doesn't. "Well, goodnight, then."

"Goodnight."

"'Night," Barron says.

They head down the hallway toward their room. Liam is in the bathroom brushing his teeth. Singing. I can't understand the words. Joyful singing as he brushes.

I can wait until tomorrow to make a decision. Before I do anything, I can take one more walk. I can leave this house if I want to. In this brief moment, I'm allowed.

Meet me at the park, I text.

As you wish, Tree replies.

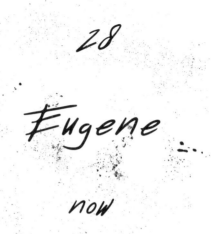

28

Eugene

now

In darkness, the Word says the monsters come. Women should stay inside, in the light.

There was a light right behind me where I stood washing the dishes. The fixture was broken, so it was too bright.

The whole time Dad was hurting me, there was light.

I walk under the streetlights as best I can until I get to the park. It's well lit too. They care about safety in Eugene. If you're walking down the street.

What about if you're inside? What if your husband beats you while you're pregnant? Will he go to jail? Or will there be a court order telling him to stay away? A piece of paper with words printed on it means less than the words. It means that everything you did was okay, and you can do it all over again, and nothing will happen. It means that you will walk free no matter who you hurt, as long as you hurt them inside the home, in the kind of light that falls from a ceiling and illuminates the color of the bruises as they grow and fade.

I know it's all wrong.

That's America. This is living among the dead. That all happened by American law.

If Dad had beaten me in Zebulun . . . I can't finish that sentence. I never saw it happen. The worst thing that could happen did happen: he got banished. Well, there's one more thing. They could have declared him dead. Maybe they'd do that. Maybe, if I told them what happened, they'd still do it. Hurting your child is worse than killing another Citizen, especially if that Citizen committed a deadly sin. *Let no man abuse his wife or his child, but only punish in proportion to the offense. Let each man show mercy and kindness in relations with his dependents.* But also: *A man is master of his home and hearth and has dominion over his wife and his children. Let every son obey his father and let every woman obey her father and brothers, for the path to salvation is obedience.*

The devil ties me to this place, to these American laws. The devil keeps me from going home.

But that's wrong. It's all wrong.

The merry-go-round glints in the glow of the streetlights that dot the path through the park.

I have to choose if I want to go home or not. If I can be American or not. Who I want to belong to, and who can protect me. Who has protected me before?

Tree is coming toward me from the direction of the street. He lopes along, hair flopping in his face.

When will I ever get this chance again? When will I ever be alone with a boy before I get married? When will I be able to do this without being hurt?

"I knew you couldn't stay away," Tree says in some weird fake British accent.

"Do you like me?" I face him. There are three feet between us. I look up at him and meet his eyes.

He laughs nervously. "Yes?"

"Yes or no."

Tree drops the accent. "I meant, yes. Period. Sorry." He lifts a foot as if he's going to take a step closer, but then he doesn't. "Are you okay?"

"No."

"Um. What's wrong?"

"Four people have died from poisoned yogurt."

"Yeah, that sucks."

"A few months ago, my dad beat me up so badly that I ended up in the hospital."

"Oh my G—"

"But I have to honor my father and obey him."

"Uh."

"I miss my grandma, Sheila. And I can never see her again unless I follow the Word."

"What—"

"And I'll never see my brother again either. He saved my life. He got us food. He got us a house and my dad a job. And if he hadn't pulled Dad off me, I might be dead. He'd do anything to protect me.

And I owe it to him to protect him. I have to obey my brother like my father." I pause to take a few breaths. The night is warm, but I'm hot. I feel like I'm in a furnace, like I've already landed in the fires of Hell. Because what I did, what I already did, is terrible enough to land me there. And maybe this is the beginning. Maybe this playground is the top of the tunnel that will take me down.

"Lisa, I don't understand. Is your dad threatening you? Should I call the cops?"

"My dad isn't here. I live with my mom."

"But he wants you back?"

"Exactly. The law rescued me from my dad. But the *law*, God's law, says I can't be rescued."

"That God stuff is bullshit, Lisa. Nobody gets to beat you up."

I run my hands over my hair, feel my bun. Tree lives in a different universe. Where he lives, there's no devil to come for you. There are no Trials that you can fail that will destroy your family forever. If somebody killed Tree, someone would care.

"You said you like me. What does it feel like?"

"Um, I mean . . ."

"Do you want to hurt me?"

"What? No! I want to. Um. Hang out."

"And have sex with me."

"No! I mean, if you want to."

"If *I* want to?"

"Yeah, that's how it works. You both want to."

"And so you just do it."

"Uh . . . with a condom."

"I can't *just do* anything," I say quietly, mostly to myself.

Tree takes a step forward. Gently, carefully, he pulls me into his arms. "This cult stuff really has you messed up."

I press my face against his chest. I'm getting sweat on his T-shirt. He smells like soap. Clean. Fresh. Normal. Safe. "Maybe," I say.

"I don't know what's going on," Tree says. "All I know is, the guy who beats you up is bad. If you're thinking about running away and going back, you shouldn't."

"That's not what I'm thinking about."

"Are you sure? Because it sounds like you're thinking about it."

"It's not him I want to go back to, it's my grandmother in Zebulun. But my mom would never let me go."

"I don't want to insult, but it doesn't sound stupendous. We couldn't be friends there."

My stomach twists. He's right. We couldn't be friends. I could never think about doing with him what Becca did with Isaac. I wouldn't be allowed to stand here with my face against his chest and have someone talk to me like I'm a human being.

"Do you like *me*?" he asks.

"I don't know what that means." I pull back a little bit. I'm still in his arms. "I'm not supposed to feel anything like that until after I'm married." My feet are planted on the concrete path, connected to the ground, connected to the heat.

He sets a cool hand against my cheek and looks into my eyes. He's asking me for permission. I'm not supposed to know that. I'm not supposed to be here. I look back at him. I don't know if I'm giving him permission or not. He leans his face down, and it's a long time coming. I could pull away, but I don't. His lips connect with mine, and then his face is pulling away again, up and up until he's standing straight. My heart beats faster. I wait for something to happen. Something bad. Something good. I don't know.

"Was that okay?"

"I think so." I'm thinking about Becca and Isaac on the couch. Him kissing her, her legs around him. Changing it to me and Tree. Him on top, my legs around him. Me kissing him. What if I kissed him right now, like Becca kissed Isaac? I try to wipe the image from my brain, but I can't. I want to do it. I want him to kiss me again. Except I'm not supposed to want that. If I go down that path, I've made a decision.

"It's okay if you don't like me," he says. "We can still eat yogurt together. You know, once the poison stuff is over."

I stand on my tiptoes and kiss him. I press both of my hands against his face. I touch my lips against his for several long seconds. He wraps his arms around me, and I fall back, and now our bodies are closer.

He runs a hand over my hair. "But if you do like me, well, *that's* stupendous!"

"I do like you."

He smiles, and he leans toward me again, and now we're kissing for real. Like Becca and Isaac, except quieter. As if we have all the time in the world. As if he doesn't want to hurt me, as if boys aren't terrible, as if this is something I'm supposed to do. As if I get to choose whether I do it.

Finally, he pulls away from me. "Wow."

"Yeah." I've stepped into another universe. The streetlight casts a glow over the right side of his face. Next to us is the merry-go-round. In front of us is a grassy field, and then the street. Behind us is the path back up the hill toward my late mother's house. My feet are solid on the hard ground. I wasn't supposed to do that. I can't go any deeper, or everything Dad said about me will be true. I don't get to be here. "I need to go."

"Can I walk you home?"

"Thanks, but no. I'll be okay."

"Do you want to talk more? I can sit over here." He points to the merry-go-round.

"No, I'm good. Thank you for listening. I'm sure I sounded pretty crazy."

"Just tell me you know you deserve to be treated better."

"Yeah. I do." I stand on my tiptoes and kiss him again, and then without saying anything else, I turn and walk back up the hill. I'm being propelled away from the merry-go-round, away from Tree. I'm walking deep into the universe I belong in. The memory of the kiss with Tree plays in my brain, and my stomach churns. I can't hold both universes in my brain. I can't live in both places. I have to exist in one realm or the other. I have to get my life and my soul back. I can't keep doing the wrong thing just because I want to.

The day after Dad explained his plan to us, I wanted to get away. I didn't want to have to obey. I was scared, and I was willful, and I did the only thing I could think of.

29

Port Angeles

age sixteen

The day after Dad told us what we had to do if the cops came for me, neither Dad nor Carlo went to work. Dad was off because he never worked during the day. And Carlo was off work, too, for some reason. Maybe something to do with the plan. I didn't know. They didn't tell me. All I knew was, around 7:00 p.m., they both went out and left me alone.

"We'll be back soon," Dad said. And they left. What did he mean by *soon*? How much time did I have?

The house breathed in the silence. They almost never left me alone, and I'll never know why they did it then.

Dad must have thought that after he beat me up and put me in the hospital, I'd never disobey him again. He must have thought that I was broken, that I was helpless, that he had total control over me. The one thing he had to have been sure I wouldn't do was see Becca again. And the truth was, I hadn't been planning to. My right shoulder ached from my months-old injury. The bruises on my face were gone, but I still saw them every time I looked in the mirror. There was no way I'd risk that happening again, or him doing the same thing to her.

But as I stood there alone that night in our living room listening to the house breathing, the plan I'd thought of came back to me. It probably wouldn't work, but it was a chance. There was something I could do with these precious minutes. I wasted a few of them thinking about it, standing still, afraid to move. I imagined Dad coming back and stopping me. I imagined waking up in the morning and going through the next day and the next and the next without anything changing. I imagined my eighteenth birthday, here in this house.

And I sprang into motion.

I ran out the front door. It was the first time I'd been out that door alone in probably years.

I landed on Becca's porch, breathing heavily, and knocked hard. Becca's stepmom answered the door. She had never met me before. I'd seen her in the yard or getting into her car. She must have seen me through the window. But this was the first time we'd ever spoken.

"Hi, is Becca home?" I asked. I wiped sweat from my forehead.

"Sure. Lisa, right?" She was about my height, with short brown hair. She was wearing a mid-length skirt and a nice sweater, like she'd just come home from work.

"Yeah." I went inside. Everything was flipped around. Their house was a lot like ours, but I always came in the back way. My head spun as if everything was upside down too.

"Becca, Lisa from next door is here to see you."

Becca came out from her room. She was wearing leggings and a baggy T-shirt. Her hair was in a ponytail. Her eyes opened wide. "Hi!" She waved me back, and I followed her to her room, feeling her stepmom's confused eyes on me. Becca was my best friend, but nobody knew that but us. I never knew if I was hers. How could I be, when she had this whole life?

"You came in the front door! Did something happen? Why haven't you come over in like four months? Are you okay? I wanted to go over there but I didn't know if it would be bad, so I just tried to catch you in the window. I saw you, but you never looked over here."

"Yes, something happened," I said. It was as if I was stepping back from my body, watching myself talk to her. It had to be like this, like I wasn't the one doing it. I was only watching. There was nothing I could do. If I didn't really do it, then he couldn't blame me.

"Well? What?" She sat down on her bed and stared at me.

I couldn't tell her. There was too much. I didn't have time to explain anything. Dad said he'd be back *soon*.

"Can I use your phone?" I asked.

She reached into her backpack and fumbled for it.

I saw her alarm clock in my peripheral vision, its red numbers blasting into the room. How long was soon?

Eons later, she found the phone, unlocked it, and handed it to me. My whole body turned cold. I shivered. I tried to take a deep breath.

"Lisa, maybe you should sit down."

My finger hovered over the keypad. I typed.

9-1-1.

"9-1-1, what is your emergency?"

"I have information about a missing person. Her name is Alyssa DeAndreis, and she disappeared from Eugene, Oregon, nine years ago." I gave them the address where we lived now.

"How do you know this girl?" the operator asked.

"I just do. She needs help." I hung up the phone.

"Is that you?" Becca whispered.

"I have to go," I said. The clock blasted its numbers at me. I turned from Becca's bedroom and ran. My body went first, and my spirit ran after. Desperate to stop me, maybe. But it was too late. I'd done it. I'd set everything in motion. There was no going back.

But even though I called 9-1-1, I didn't know if they'd come for me. I didn't know if the police would care. I knew Mom was still looking, but she was far away in Eugene. Dad had been paranoid for years, but they'd never found me. I'd been in the hospital, and no one found me.

And when they *did* come, they didn't put him in jail and keep him there.

There were two people in the world who were alive and cared about me: Carlo and Miss Sheila. And neither of them could protect me from Dad.

I didn't believe there was a way out, and I still don't believe it.

30

Eugene

now

So if I didn't believe they'd help me, why did I ask the law to find me?

Because more than one thing can be true.

Because the Earth is six thousand years old and 4.5 billion.

Because people are living on the moon, but you can't see them.

Because sometimes you have to believe in things that are impossible. Because I can't stop myself from being willful. Because he couldn't beat it all out of me. Because I didn't want to die. Because I didn't want to stay in that house.

Because I didn't know what else to do.

But there isn't a way home from here. I still belong to someone else. I can go for a walk at night, but I have to come back. I can fall into sin with Tree, but he can't save me.

I'm inside the dark house. Everyone else is asleep. I go to the bathroom and wash my face. I wipe my lips with a soapy washcloth, trying to get the dirt and grime of Tree off me. I gargle with mouthwash.

What came over me? Not what, who: the contrary girl, the willful girl, the girl who wants to disobey. The girl who saw Becca and that boy on the couch. The girl who felt things she shouldn't have felt and wanted things she shouldn't want. The girl who wanted to be like Becca.

Tree is the path to being like Becca, not the path home.

Becca's life isn't my life.

I can't live on the moon.

I need to take that girl's willfulness and her strength and turn them toward God's purpose, toward having the courage to fulfill my Trial. To do what has to be done without questioning. To obey my brother.

I pace around the house, quietly, in my socks. Up and down the halls, around and around the living room.

My bruises are healed now. I am strong. It was all leading up to the final test. I have to look past God's flawed messenger, Dad, and find the truth of the Word. Once the devil is out of my life, I'll be free to go home. With whoever I want. Carlo and I can go to Zebulun together. The law may have Dad for what he did against it, which was take me from Mom. But the law won't have me.

Four people dead in three states and others sick. That means no one will suspect anything. Randomness is my cover for American law. And also for Mr. Brandon's rules. But God knows I'm only doing what He asks.

I pace and pace and pace, and I recite passages from the Word that I know by heart, all the lines about adultery and obeying one's father and how God assigns his Trials and the rewards for completing them. For nine years I've read and read and read and recited and rewritten these words, all so that now, when I have no papers in front of me, I'll know them.

It's 5:00 a.m. when I enter my bedroom, open the closet, and pull out my duffel bag. I reach into the pocket and pull out the drawstring bag, and I walk quietly back down the hall to the kitchen. I open the refrigerator and reach into the far back. I push aside the three cans of pop and pull out a container of yogurt. It's one of the ones Tree bought. The one I retrieved from the trash can as soon as he walked away. The one I stuffed into the back of the refrigerator, behind three pop cans, as soon as I got home yesterday.

God helps those who help themselves. I had to make sure we had yogurt, and it's a good thing too, because Barron threw the rest out, and he also took out the trash bag. God knows what shape those containers are in. This is a different brand, the store brand.

God ensured that Mom would have a habit of eating in the middle of the night. We've all seen her bowls in the sink, her spoons, her forks, her plates with crumbs.

I slide open the foil, take a spoon, and dish the yogurt out into the sink. I run the water until it's all gone down the drain. I set the used spoon in the sink and throw the container in the brand-new trash bag.

Then I set about making breakfast. I get out all the ingredients for pancakes. I find a new package of bacon. I dig through the immense fruit drawer and cut up apples, nectarines, strawberries. I make sure everything's almost ready, and then I take out the milk. I pour a glass for each of us and set them on the table. I hand out the pancakes. I add the bacon to the plates. I dish up the cut fruit. I open the drawstring bag and pull out a screw-top container that once contained some fancy brand of lip balm, that once belonged to some lady walking down the street in Seattle. I tip the contents into Mom's milk. I use a butter knife to stir it around, so it's distributed evenly and Mom won't taste it. Dairy products are great for masking the taste.

I walk down the hall and knock on Mom and Barron's door. "I made breakfast!" I call. I knock on Liam's door. "Breakfast! Pancakes and bacon!"

As everyone pads out of their rooms, I wash the dishes I've used: the bowls, the pan, the butter knife.

"This smells amazing!" Barron says. His hair is sticking up on his head, which highlights his receding hairline. He's wearing a white bathrobe that's pilling all over. Mom is wearing her blue bathrobe and bunny slippers. Her hair is flat and needs to be washed. Liam is jumping around, already full of energy.

"Can I help?" he asks.

"Oh, no, it's all ready. You just enjoy."

"You didn't have to do this," Mom says.

"I know that, Mom. You know I'm starting school in a couple weeks. I'll probably never have the energy again."

"Promise?" She raises an eyebrow at me.

"Be careful what you wish for," Barron says. "I could get used to this." He sits at his usual spot at the table.

I dry my hands.

Liam stands between my plate and Mom's. He plucks a strip of bacon from Mom's plate and picks up the glass of milk.

"Liam, that stuff's Mom's," I say. "Put her milk down and drink yours."

He sets the milk down again. It sloshes, a little bit flowing over the side.

"Sorry!"

"No worries." My vision blurs. I walk over to my seat. I feel like I'm floating. It's like my feet don't touch the ground.

Mom sits and picks up the strip of bacon that Liam dropped. She takes a bite. "You really cooked this perfectly," Mom says. "I always seem to burn it."

"Thanks," I say. "Second time's the charm." I take a bite. I don't tell her that I didn't have a lot of bacon to practice on in Port Angeles, that I couldn't just open up the refrigerator door and pull out whatever food I wanted.

Barron takes a sip of his milk.

I take a sip of mine. It tastes bland, like store-bought milk does.

Mom takes a sip of hers.

I pour syrup on my pancakes. I cut a large piece and drop it into my mouth. It's delicious. I take another sip of milk.

Mom takes a bite of pancake. "Maybe I *should* be careful what I wish for," Mom says. "It's not bad waking up to breakfast."

"Don't forget to eat some of your fruit," I say to Liam.

"That's what Mom's supposed to say," Liam says.

Mom laughs.

"Lucky you, Liam," Barron says. "Two moms to tell you what to do!"

"You should really eat some fruit, too, you know," Mom says, taking another sip of milk.

Liam pops a strawberry into his mouth and chews.

I can't see anything. It's like a curtain has dropped over my eyes. My head begins to pound.

Suddenly I'm back in that basement in Zebulun, hiding with Dad. I'm trying not to speak, trying not to breathe. I'm thinking that if I'm quiet and good and sweet, then Mom will come and be with us.

I'm in that moment when I realized she wasn't coming.

I hear voices. Liam's voice. He's not much older than I was, and he's about to lose his mom. Liam is the product of sin, but he's too young to have sinned himself. He's innocent. I could take him with me. But the law would never let me do that.

I'm in the basement, in the dark.

I reach out blindly for the milk. Instead, I hit Mom's arm.

"Alyssa, are you all right?"

I feel around the table. My hand connects with the glass. It sloshes, but nothing comes out. She's drank some already. I pull it toward me, tip it into my lap. The cool liquid hits the front of my blouse.

My eyes clear. They're all staring at me.

"You spilled it," Liam says.

I stand up. Milk drips down my chest. I stumble past Mom toward the kitchen counter. My head pounds. My heart beats. My hands move toward my phone. I'm back in Becca's room taking her phone from her. I'm opening up the phone app. I'm staring down at the wrong thing and the right thing and the way out, and knowing there's no way out, not really. But I can't do this. I can't complete the Trial. I can't obey my father and brother. I give up.

I dial the numbers: 9-1-1.

"9-1-1, what is your emergency?"

"I give up," I say.

"What? I didn't catch that."

"Poison."

"Did someone ingest poison?"

"Yes. Please come. Yogurt."

"No one ate yogurt," Mom says.

"You did!" I yell. "You drank it. The milk."

Mom squints. She looks at Barron, then back at me. Her eyes widen. Her jaw drops. She knows exactly what I'm talking about. She knows Dad. She understands.

"We're sending an ambulance." The operator asks to confirm the address.

"Yes. Please. She was poisoned. I poisoned her."

Barron and Liam and Mom all stare at me.

Mom comes toward me, and I brace myself for the blow. But that's not how Mom is. She never hit anyone. She pulls me into her arms.

I burst into tears. "I couldn't do it, I couldn't do it," I repeat.

"I know. I'll be fine. I didn't drink that much. I'll be fine." She suddenly releases me and turns to the sink. She gags and throws up into the basin.

Barron looks like he's going to throw up too. "Was it in ours? In Liam's?" he shouts.

"No! No, I would never . . ." But I don't know what I'd never do. I don't know if there's anything. What if Dad had told me to poison all of them? Would I have done it? I don't know. Even now, I can't say. I didn't choose to call 9-1-1, I just had to. My body dragged me over to the phone. Maybe I couldn't have poisoned them. But I don't know.

The sirens burst into my ears. The ambulance peels into the driveway. Barron rushes to open the door, and two women in uniform charge into the house.

Mom walks over to them. "I just threw up," she says. "I drank maybe half a glass of poisoned milk."

The next thing I hear is a police car.

This time they're not coming to save me.

31

now

I tell the police everything. I tell them that Dad and Carlo and I came up with a plan that if I ever got taken back, Carlo would poison yogurt in stores in three states, and then after several people had died, I would poison Mom and make it look like she ate the yogurt, and then it would look like it was random. I tell them about how Mom got up and snacked late at night and how everyone would believe she ate the yogurt.

Mom is sitting right next to me when I tell them, and so is a lawyer she and Barron hired.

The cops ask questions, and I answer. Until there's one question I can't.

"Alyssa," the police officer says, leaning forward. "Why did you agree to participate?" Her eyes are kind. Their whole attitude, these two police officers, both women, is of shocked disbelief.

I shake my head.

"We're just trying to understand what was going on in your mind. You said you called the Port Angeles police to report your whereabouts. Did you call because you wanted the chance to poison your mother?"

"No!" I turn to her. "Mom, I didn't. I swear. I called because . . ." I turn back to the police. "I had to get out of there. But . . . " My voice dries up. I don't know. I don't understand myself. But when the police came to get me, I took the poison. I packed it up and brought it with me. I did it.

"I know exactly why," Mom says. "Art abused her, beat her, locked her in the house, and brainwashed her into thinking she had to do it. I'm sure there was hellfire and banishment and being called dead all threatened."

I say nothing. All that is true. But that isn't it. Not all of it. It wasn't just about the punishment I'd get if I didn't do it, it was also about going home. It was about seeing Miss Sheila again and being her granddaughter and getting married and having a whole life. It was about what I wanted too. But mainly it was what Dad wanted because he hated Mom, because he thought he owned me, because he couldn't stand for me to get away. He would have killed me. Or he wouldn't have. I don't know. But he wanted to kill her, and that proves she wasn't already dead. He just wanted to kill her, and that was why he planned everything. And I didn't see it, and I feel so stupid. He lied to me, and I know that now. Miss Sheila lied, too, but she didn't know. She believed that Mom was dead, and Dad didn't.

"If you want to charge her with this, we'll fight it every step of the way," Mom says. "This child is not responsible for what that man and that cult did to her."

Mom's lawyer, a short man in a tan suit, leans forward. "I think that was a pretty good proffer. I'm renewing my offer for Alyssa's testimony in exchange for immunity."

The police officer nods. "We'll take that to the prosecutor. I think it's a likely outcome."

The lawyer leans back. He told us he thought they'd take it. It all sounded so simple when he explained it to us. All I have to do is testify against my father and brother and send them to jail for the rest of their lives, and then I can go free and live my life.

Mom heaves a huge sigh of relief.

Bile rises in my throat. I know it's what I have to do. I know murdering people is wrong. I know I deserve to go to jail, too, and this is my only chance to save myself. I think about those people who died. If I'd called 9-1-1 sooner, they'd be alive. It never occurred to me to do that, any more than it occurred to me that I could have a phone or talk to a boy or go to school. I could never have turned Carlo in, no matter what he did. I can't understand how he could do this any more than I understand how I could. He's a good, loving person who saved my life. And he's a murderer. Both things are true.

"I don't want Carlo to go to jail," I say.

Everyone looks at each other. No one looks directly at me.

"He's a good person." I look down at my lap.

"Alyssa." Mom takes my hand. "He went to all those grocery stores and put poison in yogurt. He's killed six people so far and made a dozen more sick. Random, innocent people."

"That was Dad," I say. "Maybe he didn't poison the yogurt himself, but he ordered it. He had control over everything."

"And he'll pay for what he did too." She pats my hand.

"Can I see Miss Sheila?" I ask. "I want to see her."

"I have to advise you not to do that," the lawyer says.

"I'm so sorry, honey," Mom says. "But I know the Word. Sheila isn't going to be able to talk to you. You'll be dead just like I am after you testify."

I let the tears roll down my face. I've lost everything and failed everyone. There's no going home again. There's only trying not to keep doing the wrong thing. If I'd killed Mom, I never would have gone home either. I know that now. I know that I can never have the life Miss Sheila promised me. I have to have this life, whatever it is, as long as they let me.

"Mom, I'm sorry. I'm so sorry. I'm so glad I didn't kill you." I put my face in my hands and cry.

Mom puts her arm around me. "I know. I'm glad too."

When I open my eyes, everyone has found some other direction to look in. One of the police officers has left the room and the other one is looking down at her laptop, seemingly engrossed in the screen. Mom's lawyer shifts awkwardly in his seat.

"I bet I'm the weirdest client you've ever had," I say, sniffing and wiping my eyes with my sleeve.

"Weirdest," he says, "but definitely not the worst."

I laugh a little bit. Mom laughs a little bit. Her arm is still around me. I'm taken back to when I was little, when we'd sit on the couch together and watch TV, and she'd put her arm around me like this. I thought about that a lot, especially in Zebulun, when even though I knew it wouldn't happen, I still imagined her walking down the street toward me, imagined her alive again, and back with Dad, and making the family Miss Sheila said we were supposed to have.

The police officer who had left comes back in. "The DA has agreed to immunity," she says to the lawyer. "He'll send you the paperwork."

"Great." The lawyer stands and shakes the officer's hand.

Mom and I both stand too. I wonder if I should shake the officer's hand, but I don't.

"Thank you," Mom says.

"I wish you all the best," the officer says to me.

The other officer is still looking at her computer.

"You too," I say, and I head for the door. I walk out of the police station with my mom and the lawyer. I'm wearing my long skirt today, and my hair is in a bun. And next week, I'm supposed to start my sophomore year in American high school. All I have to do is turn against my father and brother, and I'll be free.

32

now

The next time I see Dad, I'm walking down the aisle of the courtroom. I'm still wearing clothes appropriate for a woman of the Word. I want him and Carlo to see that. I want them to see that I haven't abandoned everything that matters. I'm following American law, and I'm admitting that what I did was wrong. I still don't know if it was wrong by the tenets of the Word. But it was wrong absolutely. My body knew it was wrong when it forced me to stop Mom from drinking the milk. Something deep inside me wouldn't let me physically do it.

On that, there's only one truth. Murder is wrong, even if the person you're trying to kill is already dead. And I don't believe Mom is dead. A part of me always knew it wasn't true in the same way that two plus two equals four is true. But the part of me that did believe helped me survive, so I have to be glad for it. I have to thank my faith for protecting me when no one else would.

But I have to remember that I know the truth now, that the Word gave Dad power he didn't deserve, and that like Jesus, he's just a man and not a god.

I sit on the witness stand, and I look at Dad, who's sitting at the defense table. Carlo isn't here today because his trial will be separate. His lawyer is going to claim he was coerced by Dad, but according to my lawyer, that won't get him off, because coercion isn't a defense to murder. Even if somebody puts a gun to your head, you can't murder somebody and get away with it. Carlo was the one who put the poison in the yogurt. But I'm here to tell these twelve men and women that he did it because Dad told him to.

Dad glares at me.

I look away and try to breathe.

I raise my right hand, and I answer the questions. I tell the jury about how he beat up Mom while she was pregnant, and how he told me to climb out the window, and how he taught me about the Word, and how we lived on the streets, and how we got to Port Angeles, and how he made me stay in the house, and how he beat me and put me in the hospital. His lawyer tries to stop me from saying all of it, but the judge lets me say it because it's necessary for the jurors to understand what happened and why.

I look at Dad while I testify.

He glares at me. When I talk about how he beat me, he tries to speak, but his lawyer shushes him. He leans back in his chair and folds his arms. The expression on his face says that I'm lying. But there are medical records, and we have them. It's all relevant, the judge says, because it's part of how he coerced me.

We get to the part where I put the poison in the milk, and I have to stop talking. Mom sits in the back of the courtroom nodding at me, so I wipe my tears away and keep going. I tell them how I stopped and how I called 9-1-1 for a second time.

"Why did you call 9-1-1?" the prosecutor asks.

"Because I couldn't kill my mom," I say. "Because she wasn't already dead like Dad said she was. Because he convinced me that it didn't matter because she was dead, but it wasn't true. Because none of what you told me was true." I don't feel the entire gravity of the truth until I say it. It hits me as if the whole ceiling just fell in. Mom wasn't dead my whole life. She was right there in Eugene, alive. Saying she was dead didn't make it true. Dad *wanted* her dead, and he tried to make me do it. He thought I'd just do whatever he said because all those photocopied books said I was supposed to. Because Miss Sheila and Mr. Doug, who treated me like their granddaughter, said I was supposed to obey him. "You beat her up, and you beat me up, and you didn't have the right to do that, and you didn't have the right to kill her," I say. "I called 9-1-1 because I wanted it to stop, because I wanted you to be punished, because I didn't want to live in fear of you anymore."

The defense counsel asks me questions. He tries to convince me that Dad never told me to poison Mom and the whole thing was my idea. But I don't waver from my story. I won't let him brainwash me.

"You never had any communication with your father after you left Port Angeles," the lawyer says.

"No, I talked to Carlo, and he told me to go ahead with the plan."

"You never heard the conversation between your father and Carlo."

"No, but I heard him making the whole plan. I heard him tell Carlo that he'd have to be the one to poison the yogurt. And he told me to poison Mom, the night before I called 9-1-1 to get away from him."

And on and on for a long time like that.

Until finally it's over. Until the jury comes back and finds him guilty, until the judge sentences him to life in prison without the possibility of parole.

It's only then, when the trial is over, when my case has been on the news, when a sketch of me testifying has been posted on every website, that I have the courage to make the call I've been wanting to make since the day I arrived back in Eugene.

"It will be all right," Mom says. "From everything you've told me, I think she's the kind of person who'll understand." She gives me a hug and leaves me alone in my bedroom. As the door clicks shut, I stare at myself in the full-length mirror. I'm wearing a long skirt, but it's an American kind of skirt, something that wouldn't look weird in a high school hallway. My hair is in a ponytail down my back. I'm not the person she knew, and I wonder who she is now. But I can't put it off any longer, or I won't do it.

I press the screen.

Ring. Ring. Ring. I'm calling from a number she doesn't know. Maybe she won't answer.

"Hello?"

I can't say anything for a second.

"Hello? Who is this?"

"Becca, it's Lisa."

There's a silence. Either she can't say anything, or she's hung up.

"I'm sorry. I'm so sorry," I blurt. "I didn't mean to lie to you. I didn't think I was lying. I couldn't tell you. I . . . " I trail off. I don't even know where to start with everything I need to tell her.

"Lisa! I can't believe it! I saw you on the news. *I'm* sorry! I never knew how bad it was. I should have done something to help you. I—"

"My mom's not dead. The Word says she is, but she isn't, and I knew that. I know it's not the same. I'm so—"

"It's okay, I know that."

I can't think of what to say. I want to start at the beginning, but where is that?

"I read about the Word and Zebulun and how they banish people and say they're dead and cut people off from their families. I wish I would have known so I could tell you it's not true. So you could have gotten away earlier. I should have guessed what was going on, with the stuff you said you couldn't do. I should have called the police myself."

"No, you couldn't," I say. "You couldn't. I had to do it."

"You shouldn't have had to. Someone should have helped you. I should have helped you."

"I've wanted to call you all this time," I say. "But I didn't know if you could forgive me."

"Forgive you? You didn't do anything. I wanted to call you, but I didn't know if I could because there was the trial, and I didn't know if you'd want to talk to me."

"*Me*, not want to talk to *you*?" I try to laugh, but I realize I'm crying, and she is too. I was so afraid she'd be angry that I don't know what to do now. I just want to be her friend again. "So, how have you been?" I ask.

Becca laughs, and I hear the sound of a nose blowing. "I'm learning how to play tennis," she says. "There's a team at school that I'm going out for." She pauses. "Isaac and I broke up, but we're still friends. I met someone else." She goes on and tells me about her new boyfriend. She halts and pauses, as if she's not sure what she should tell me. I cling to my phone and listen, just taking in her voice and the fact that she's talking to me at all. When she's done talking, I tell her about Tree and about my mom and Barron and Liam. I tell her about American school and what it's like to walk down the street all by myself.

Finally, I can tell her the truth.

After I'm done with my story, there's another long silence. There's so much more to say.

"So, should I call you Lisa or Alyssa?" she asks.

"Lisa." There's no hesitation. I've been tiptoeing around this with my mom, but the truth is that I've been Lisa since I was seven years old, and Lisa feels like me. "My dad made me change it, but it's been so long. I like it better."

"You get to decide," Becca says.

"Yeah, I do." Nobody else has said that to me. I should have known she'd be the one. I should have known she'd understand, and now I can't imagine how I was so afraid to call her.

We promise to talk again soon, and when we eventually hang up, I look at myself in the mirror again, and something has changed. This skirt, this top, this hair, this face—they all seem to belong to me, Lisa. I'm the person who lives here in America with my mom and also the person who lived in that house in Port Angeles, who was friends with Becca. My image seems to waver in front of me. I fit and then I don't and then I do again.

"He's never getting out of prison," I say to the mirror.

"He's never getting out," I say again.

I look myself in the eyes. "Never."

It's over for him but not for me.

33

now

It's January, and I've been in high school for a year and a half. Tree and I sit at a picnic table in the park. We're within sight of the merry-go-round, but it's not dark out now. It's the middle of the day, and the sun is shining. We're both wearing puff coats, and we can see our breath. I'm wearing jeans, and my hair is tucked inside my coat. I still have it long down my back, but I did get a trim. A lot of the top part is blonde now. I'm trying to fit into this universe as best I can, even though it's still weird. I still don't feel like I really belong.

Tree is in college now, but he's at the University of Oregon, so we're still together. We're the two weird homeschooled kids, trying to find our way in a normal life.

I look down at my phone and smile.

"What happened?" Tree asks. He pops an almond in his mouth. We sometimes hang out in the park and have a picnic, but we never eat yogurt. We don't even talk about yogurt. We pretend that yogurt never existed.

"That was my friend Jean," I say. "The one from the Word. She made it to her aunt Rachel's house in Portland."

"That cult-rescue group helped her?"

"Yep."

"Phew."

"Yeah. She was terrified of getting stuck with a bunch of kids, but she was also afraid of the outside world. You know, all the dead people. She used to have these nightmares about her aunt. But I told her she'd be okay once she gets used to it. Like I am."

Tree and I both laugh. Whether I'm okay is an open question. But I'm existing in the world. I'm going to school. I'm in a relationship. I'm even getting along with my mom, although I still infuriate her sometimes. I still spout off sayings from the Gospel of the Citizens of the Word and insist on cooking dinner when she thinks I should be lying around. But I think she believes that I don't believe it anymore. I don't think that women are supposed to serve men or deserve to be punished for disobeying. I don't think the world is six thousand years old, and I don't think it's likely to end any time soon. If anyone told me to do something that was wrong, I would say no.

I've learned that it's my right to say no and my right to say yes. It's my right to walk around outside alone, to talk to men, to wear whatever clothes I want, and to go to real school. It's no one's right to lock me up inside a house or to hit me or to tell me how to live my life.

I understand that Carlo was part of everything Dad did to me, and that it would be bad for me to see him. I haven't seen him since the night the cops came for me, because he ended up pleading guilty, so I didn't have to testify. It's not that I don't love him anymore, it's that right now, I can't handle it. I plan to visit him some day, but for now, I just write him letters. I tell him that I love him and that he saved me, and that he'll always be my brother, but I can't see him. He tells me that he loves me, too, and he understands. He says he wants me to be happy, and I believe him. He got life with the possibility of parole, so I don't know if he'll ever get out of prison or not. But I believe he's truly sorry for what he did. He says he doesn't write to Dad, and I hope that's true, but of course, I don't know. They had a bond that I thought would never be broken. What I do know is that I won't be writing to Dad. Dad is gone from my life forever.

Apparently Miss Sheila is gone forever too. Mom was right about me being dead. I wrote to her, and she never answered. But I know she loves me. I still hold out hope that someday, she'll realize that a lot of what she taught me wasn't true, that the part that was true, about women holding on to their own selves inside, is the most important thing of all. I still wear the necklace she gave me all the time. But I'm not going to hold on to any hope that I can go back. Now I want to focus on the future. I want to be with people who want the best for me and know I'm alive, and today, after all the virtual hangouts, I'm finally going to see Becca in person.

I look toward the sidewalk, where she said she'd be coming from. I crane my neck.

"I'm expecting some kind of goddess after all this buildup," Tree says.

"She pretty much saved my life," I say. And there she is. I immediately recognize her by her long red hair, which flows out from beneath her winter hat. I stand up and wave.

She waves back, and we both start to run. In the middle of the grassy park, we fall into each other's arms.

I pull back and look at her. "I can't believe you're actually here!"

"Lisa! You look great!" Becca says. Her wide smile fills her face. "Your hair is so blonde!"

"You look great too! I can't believe I'm seeing you outside your house. There are so many things we can do now!" My grin is almost breaking my face.

"Introductions!" Tree says.

"Right. Becca, this is my boyfriend, Tree. Tree, my best friend, Becca."

"Pleased to make your acquaintance," Tree says, bowing.

"Um, you as well." Becca bows awkwardly.

"Shall I escort you ladies to my chariot?" Tree sticks out both his elbows, and we each take a side. We head for Tree's 2010 Honda Accord. I'm about to ride with my best friend in a car with a boy. The whole world is in front of me.

Notes

The book Lisa takes out from the library in chapter 14 is *The Aviary* by Kathleen O'Dell, Alfred A. Knopf, 2011.

The quote Lisa writes in her notebook in chapter 16 is from *A Universe from Nothing: Why There Is Something Rather Than Nothing* by Lawrence M. Krauss, Simon & Shuster, 2012, p. xii.

Acknowledgments

Thank you to my brilliant editor, Lauren Knowles, and the entire team at Page Street Publishing for shepherding this book into the world with care and patience, including Rosie Stewart, Lizzy Mason, Lauren Cepero, and Kumari Pacheco. Thank you to amazing cover artist Evangeline Gallagher and Page Street designer Emma Hardy for creating a cover that so perfectly captures Lisa's story. To my agent, Jennifer Azantian, who took a call on this offer the day after she brought home her newborn and never missed a beat. Thank you to Wesley Chu for introducing us. To my beta readers, Madelyn Rosenberg, Kristen Lippert-Martin, and Lenore Appelhans Eisenhour for their insightful comments and unwavering support. Also to Angele McQuade and others in the DC YA community who have supported me with their friendship and comradery since 2015. Those who sacrifice goats together get their books published! To friends and family who have cheered me on since I made the ill-advised decision to quit my job and go off to NYC to get my MFA in writing for children, especially Wendy Fuller, Brent Stricker, Martha Greaney aka Mom, and John Thompson aka Dad. Finally, to my boyfriend, Can Ertoğan, for believing I'm normal despite much evidence to the contrary. All of you have made this book possible.

About the Author

Mary G. Thompson was raised in Cottage Grove and Eugene, Oregon. She is the author of the contemporary thriller *Amy Chelsea Stacie Dee*, which was a winner of the 2017 Westchester Fiction Award and a finalist for the 2018-2019 Missouri Gateway award, and other novels for children and young adults. She practiced law for seven years, including five years in the US Navy, and is now a law librarian in Washington, DC. She received her BA from Boston University, her JD from the University of Oregon School of Law, and her MFA in Writing for Children from The New School.